THE FROWN OF FORTUNE

A Luke Tremayne Adventure

THE FROWN OF FORTUNE

A French Affair 1653

GEOFF QUAIFE

 www.trafford.com

North America & international
toll-free: 1 888 232 4444 (USA & Canada)
fax: 812 355 4082

THE LUKE TREMAYNE
ADVENTURES

(in chronological order of the events portrayed)

1648-49   *The Irish Fiasco: Stolen Silver in Seventeenth Century Ireland*
(Trafford, 2008)

1650   *Chesapeake Chaos: Malevolence and Betrayal in Colonial
Maryland*
(Trafford, 2009)

1651   *The Black Thistle: A Scottish Conspiracy 1651*
(Trafford, 2010)

1652   *The Angelic Assassin: Criminals and Conspirators London 1652*
(Trafford, 2011)

1653   *The Frown of Fortune: A French Affair 1653*
(Trafford,)

1654-55   *The Spanish Relation: Murder in Cromwellian England*
(Trafford, 2007)

Forthcoming

1656   *The Dark Corners: Malice and Fanaticism Wales 1656*
(Trafford, *2014*)

LEADING CHARACTERS

Cromwell's Men

Luke Tremayne (Colonel)	Cromwell's special agent
Harry Lloyd (Captain)	Luke's deputy
Andrew Ford	Luke's senior sergeant

Royalist Exiles

(At the Court of Charles II and his mother, Queen Henriette
Marie, in the Chateau de St. Germain, near Paris)

Lucy Harman (Lady)	Lady-in-waiting to Queen Henriette
Catherine Beaumont (Lady)	Lady-in-waiting to Queen Henriette
Elizabeth Mortimer (Mistress)	Lady-in-waiting to Queen Henriette
Mary Gresham (Lady)	Lady-in-waiting to Queen Henriette
Jane Torrington (Lady)	Lady-in-waiting to Queen Henriette
Nicholas, Lord Ashcroft	Charles II's Head of Security
Simon, Lord Stokey	Soldier, Courtier and Diplomat

Inhabitants and Friends of the Chateau des Anges (near Rouen)

Henri St. Michel	Marquis des Anges
Antoinette St. Michel	Henri's first wife
Charlotte St. Michel	Henri's second wife
Emile St. Michel	Henri's half brother
Alain St. Michel	Son of Henri and Antoinette
Josette St. Michel	Henri's half sister
Odette Bonnet	Henri's "cousin"
Pascal De Foix	Tutor to Henri's children
Louis Morel	Henri's chaplain
Mathieu Gillot	Henri's steward, a lawyer
Philippe, Vicomte Rousset	Henri's friend, French aristocrat

Others

Evangeliste (Mother)	Abbess of the Abbey des Anges
Mary (Sister)	Prioress of the abbey
Georges Livet	Canadian adventurer
Marcel, Comte de Guarin	Confidant of Mazarin and commander of his musketeers
James, Lord Harman	Lucy's father, Catholic peer
Lucinda, Lady Harman	Lucy's mother
Guillaume Heritier	Lieutenant, French marines

Real Historical Personages

Henriette Marie (Queen)	Mother of Charles
Charles II	Exiled king of England
Sir Edward Hyde	Charles's chief minister
Oliver Cromwell	Commander of English Republican army, later Lord Protector
Cardinal Mazarin	Recently restored chief minister of France

HISTORICAL PROLOGUE

FOLLOWING HIS DEFEAT AT WORCESTER in September 1651, Charles II, after many adventures, escaped to France where his Royalist government in exile struggled to survive. It had no money, and the European powers showed little interest in supporting a lost cause.

Initially, Charles relied on the generosity of his mother whose independent court was absorbed into her son's and relocated in the fortress chateau of St Germain—just outside of Paris. Charles had a simple objective—obtain money and win support. The republican government of England and its leading general, Oliver Cromwell, were determined to prevent both. Part of their campaign was to infiltrate the royal court with their secret agents.

1

The Welsh Border, Late 1645

THE FOUR-HUNDRED-YEAR-OLD STAINED GLASS WINDOW in vibrant blue and silver illustrating the life of Mary, Mother of God, lay shattered in a thousand pieces. The beautiful screens in luminous yellow and orange depicting a rising sun were smashed—and burning brightly. The fire was threatening to engulf the whole of the chapel.

The family pew, hacked into pieces, fuelled the growing conflagration. The liturgical linen, heavily embroidered with gold and silver thread, had been ripped from the altar and trampled into a floor covered with the excrement of horse and human. The white linen purifactor used to wipe the chalice clean was covered in human faeces.

Completely missing were the gold and silver vessels—the chalice, patens, ciboria and the magnificent and priceless monstrance. Three pure golden candlesticks had also disappeared. The statues of the saints that had dominated the side altar were in fragments, and the holy relic, a drop of our Lord's blood, had been desecrated. The vial containing it had been filled with urine and then shattered.

The sacrilege was rivalled only by the inhumanity. The priest had been drawn and quartered, and the dismembered parts nailed above the chapel entrance. A dozen worshippers, all servants of the family, had been taken into the churchyard and shot. Their bodies were mutilated and hacked into pieces.

Simon, Lord Stokey, one of England's senior Catholic peers was sickened by what he saw. He wept for his faithful servants. Simon, a major general in the army of Charles I had surrendered this ancestral home to the army of Parliament three months earlier. The troops that then occupied the manor respected his person and property and the religious beliefs of the household. Simon, assured that his estate would be protected, had been in London assisting the king in his futile negotiations with the recalcitrant Parliament.

When units of the national army, which initially occupied the estate, withdrew, local military authority fell into the hands of nondescript gentry who barely controlled a militia composed of religious radicals and conscripted riffraff. A wandering patrol of these irregular, ill disciplined troops had come across the chapel deep in the woods of Stokey Court. They found it occupied and a Papist priest conducting the abominable Mass. Murder, mayhem, looting, and arson took over.

The atrocity had taken place only a couple of hours before Simon's return. He fell on his knees as the chapel burned to the ground. He gave thanks that his family had been sent for safety to London months earlier, just before the original assault on Stokey Court. Simon was unmarried, but his heir, his younger brother and family, and his aged mother normally lived on the family estate. If they had been at home, they would have attended this regular Mass.

As he prayed, he felt the presence of the Archangel Gabriel. A series of visions flashed before him. A pragmatic soldier and able diplomat, he put these hallucinations down to the shock of what he had seen.

In the quiet of his study several days later, he had second thoughts. God had sent him a message. What had happened in his family chapel was a harbinger of what lay ahead should England fail to agree on its form of government and religion. An ever-powerful military force of extreme Protestants, controlled by tinkers and tailors, would not tolerate the existence of Catholic compatriots or the privileges of the nobility.

He took his concerns to the two leading Catholic peers, Henry Howard, Earl of Arundel, and Henry Somerset, the Marquess of

Worcester. He explained that God had warned him that the fabric of Catholic worship must be preserved. Its liturgical vessels and aids, vestments, icons, and holy relics should be collected from every Catholic household in England and taken abroad for safety. The two peers, alarmed by what had happened at Stokey Court, agreed and sent couriers across England asking that households, which wished to contribute to this rescue scheme, should send their ecclesiastical treasures to a designated manor house.

Three Months Later

Six Catholic peers and a priest gathered at the nominated house to complete the project. Their assembly rendered each one of them liable to arrest and possible death. The peers had accepted the responsibility to prepare their people for the dangerous times that lay ahead and to protect the fabric of their faith.

The senior earl present noted, 'Few of those expected tonight have arrived. Some of the absentees are dead, imprisoned, or have escaped to the continent. Others have not been able to avoid the parliamentary patrols that are everywhere. This is the last area in which the king's army has some presence, but its days are numbered.

Arundel and Worcester asked our Catholic community to gather their liturgical vessels, holy relics, icons and paintings, and ecclesiastical robes and fittings and deposit them here for safekeeping. Unfortunately, our coreligionists are independent, have little contact with each other, and are divided as to the nature of their faith. Their response to the offer has been disappointing. Nevertheless, the ecclesiastical treasure accumulated in the cellar of this house has filled several large caskets, which we must get out of England as soon as possible.'

The priest spoke, 'I will escort the caskets across the channel, claiming that they contain the bodies of good German Protestants who had died in the service of Parliament.'

The Earl was not impressed. 'Reverend Father, as a Jesuit, your very existence invites the death penalty. The agents of the government are most alert to the presence of your order. Your every movement is watched. That is why this meeting must be short. You or any one of us could have been followed.'

One peer questioned the need to move the objects out of England. Most of them had vast estates with hidden passages, cellars, and outbuildings. The treasures would never be found if hidden on his lands. Another agreed and suggested that they should select by lot which of them would hide the religious treasures.

The earl thought for some time and declared, 'The treasure will be hidden, and no one except the selected guardian will know its location. The guardian will decide whether it will be safer abroad or at home.'

The earl went to a side table where a chessboard had been set up ready for a game. He picked up five black pawns and one white one. 'My lords, draw a pawn from my hat, but do not reveal the colour you select! We will all immediately leave the building. The person who has the white pawn will return as soon as he is in a position to remove the treasure safely.'

Before the pawns were drawn from the hat, James, Lord Harman spoke. 'My lords, I have received representation from many of my neighbours and tenants that the Parliamentarians will confiscate much of our property because we fought for the king. We will not be able to stop the plunder of our lands, but we can prevent the plunder of our moveable wealth.

I propose that we assist our fellow Catholics to hide their silver and gold coins and plate and their expensive jewellery in the same manner as we are doing for the religious treasures. It must be done immediately before the parliamentary government begins an audit of our personal wealth.'

The Earl shook his head and replied, 'To hold such accumulated wealth would be a very sacred trust—and a great temptation. I would not trust my personal wealth to the care of any of you. Mine will be well hidden from the investigators.

Nevertheless, if people are anxious enough to want their wealth removed from the grasp of the greedy and pernicious Parliament, then we have a duty to help. Let such a collection begin. There will be no need for another meeting. The person who draws the white pawn in a few minutes will return in six weeks and collect any caskets containing earthly treasure and hide them wherever he thinks fit.'

Simon, Lord Stokey, who had raised the issue of the protection of the religious treasure in the first place protested. 'My lord, it would be more equitable if the caskets were entrusted to a different person. Let us have another meeting and another draw at the appropriate time!' The earl disagreed and was supported by three other noblemen.

Stokey was unhappy.

The six peers selected a pawn from a hat and concealed its colour from each other. Stokey prayed that Lord Harman had not drawn the white pawn. There were rumours that he was close to several Parliamentary colonels. As Simon left, he could do little but deplore his contemporary world—a world turned upside down. Once well away from the meeting place, Simon looked at his pawn. It was black.

Paris, Late 1652

The sobbing and sighing annoyed the man who had just removed his mask. He waited in an antechamber while his lover continued to torment and torture a wimp of a girl with a hot poker, semi strangulation, and the threat of removing her fingernails. The girl, pale and frightened, nevertheless seemed unaware of her ordeal. She prayed continually and only rarely directly answered the questions of her tormenter.

She was constantly asked where the treasure was hidden, and her answer was always the same. 'The treasure, through the intervention of the Virgin Mary and the ministrations of Mother Church, resides in my soul.'

The torturer, convinced that these ravings were a deliberate evasion, did not comprehend the girl's spiritual confession. To the tormenter, the victim knew exactly where an immense treasure of gold and silver was hidden—and she would reveal it. It would just take time.

The woman left the girl and returned to the antechamber. The unmasked man was troubled. He had more religious sensibilities than his partner and now doubted that the stricken girl knew anything about a treasure of gold and silver. He upbraided his female companion. 'Maybe you have misunderstood her comments concerning treasure. Perhaps there is no material booty? All along, this sad creature has been referring to her spiritual graces.'

'Then what do I do now? You are safe behind your mask but the wench knows me and could report me to the authorities,' asked the frustrated and anxious woman.

'Don't worry! This girl is on the edge of madness. No one will believe her wild stories induced by lack of food and sleep and her grotesque self-flagellation. Any pain you have tried to apply was a gentle caress compared to what she regularly does to herself. I have seen many a man whipped to an inch of his life whose back remained in better condition than that of this girl. As soon as her condition is noticed, she will be forcibly removed for her own protection to a closed convent where her ravings will be ignored.'

The woman was not convinced. 'Do not leave yet! I will question the girl one last time.' The man reluctantly agreed and helped himself to another drink while his lover attempted to force a confession from the victim.

After a few minutes, he realised that the girl had stopped sobbing and praying. He burst into the room. His lover with a satisfied grin on her face announced, 'She is dead. Get rid of the body!'

Her companion was furious, 'You fool! Whatever you just did incriminates me as well. Leave at once! I will arrange for the body to be returned to her apartment at St. Germain. You are an imbecile.'

The man may have been less critical of his partner if he had known that the dead girl was the daughter of the Catholic peer who years earlier had drawn the white pawn.

2

St Germain, Late 1652

SIR EDWARD HYDE, CHARLES'S CORPULENT chief minister, was worried. He summoned Nicholas, Lord Ashcroft who doubled as commander of the King's bodyguard and as head of internal security. 'My lord, every move that His Majesty makes is known to our English opponents—in the case of letters, the contents are known in London before the epistles are received at their lawful destination. Our own agents have intercepted correspondence between General Cromwell and an unknown spy here at St. Germain. Evidence suggests that it is someone close to the Queen Mother. Have you discovered the culprit?'

'Her Majesty will not cooperate. She is still bitter about the absorption of her semi autonomous court into that of His Majesty, especially as the new court depends on her generous pension as a princess of France. She refused to allow me to interview any of the five women I suspect.' Hyde sighed, 'And she will continue to be obstructive. She hopes that my failure to unearth this traitor will force her son to replace me with one of her cronies. Are there none of our people among her ladies-in-waiting?'

'The queen has handpicked them all, with one exception. The spy is one of the five younger ladies-in-waiting who are not French and, who in various ways, have links to our parliamentary opponents. A sixth young Englishwoman, Lady Mary Gresham is the only one favourable to our cause, and she was forced on the queen very recently by her son.'

Next day, Lady Mary readily acceded to Sir Edward's request that she watch her fellow English-born younger companions to the Queen and report anything suspicious. Two days after this arrangement was made, Sir Edward was horrified to hear that one of these young ladies, and one of Lord Ashcroft's suspects, Lady Lucy Harman, had died in suspicious circumstances.

Ashcroft was initially delighted. He believed that Harman was the spy who had killed herself when she realised that she was under surveillance. Hyde was much more pessimistic. 'No, my lord! The real spy murdered Lady Lucy because she was about to reveal incriminating evidence to Lady Mary or yourself. We must be doubly vigilant.'

Cromwell's Apartment, London

Cromwell decided to send his most successful agent Lieutenant Colonel Luke Tremayne and Tremayne's deputy, Captain Harry Lloyd, to the Royal Court. He summoned them for a briefing. 'Tremayne, are you known to many Royalists at Charles Stuart's court in Paris?'

Luke's reply was sensible and cautious. 'I do not know who resides at the lad's court, but, in ten years of mutual conflict, I would most likely have come across someone who now resides there and who would recognise me. After my Scottish adventure, I am personally well known to young Charles.'

Cromwell systematically tapped his desk. 'I feared as much. How's your brother?'

Luke was apprehensive. His older brother was politically neutral and had devoted all his energies to assisting their ailing father administer the family Cornish estates. What could Cromwell want of his quiet and retiring sibling? 'My brother is quite well.'

'Good! Then you will go France as your Royalist brother with information to ingratiate yourself into the king's court. As you do not speak French, Lloyd, who does, will accompany you.'

Luke responded angrily, 'My brother is not a Royalist.' Cromwell raised his hands in a calming gesture, 'I know. Your brother never stirred from your family estates, and outside of his local area is unknown. Nevertheless, you will grow your hair long and cultivate a cavalier moustache and a broad bushy beard. That will distinguish you from your Roundhead brother, Luke.'

'Why is it so urgent that I join the Stuart court in exile?' 'We have few agents at the court—all unknown to each other and none in a position to garner worthwhile information. Now, one of them has been murdered, another is in danger of being uncovered, and a third is a double agent.'

Luke could not contain his many concerns. 'This is ridiculous, General. Our Royalist enemies are not fools. They will suspect any new arrival, especially a military man.'

Cromwell responded, 'They will not suspect a man who will uncover for them a major republican agent. You are to incriminate the spy whom I no longer trust. That should bring you credibility.'

Harry, who had initially felt intimidated in the general's presence, also had doubts. 'My lord general, this will never work. The very arrival of a Tremayne at the king's court will raise questions, and Lord Ashcroft, the commander of his bodyguard, whom I know, will be suspicious from the start.'

'Captain Lloyd, I must have Tremayne at the court as soon as possible. Do you have a better plan?'

'Yes! Fifteen years ago, Luke fought with the Dutch army and speaks the language. Charles Stuart is desperately seeking Dutch help. The Dutch are divided into numerous political entities, each doing its own thing. Luke can arrive at the Stuart Court as a Dutch military officer anxious to help the king.'

'An interesting idea, Harry, but I would still be recognized, especially by the King.' 'Not if you were disguised.' 'You forget one feature that I cannot hide—my bright blue eyes.'

Cromwell smiled. 'I like your ideas, Lloyd. The two of you go away and bring me a detailed plan in the morning!'

'No!' replied Luke forcefully. 'Too complex! Charles Stuart is a perceptive young man. He will recognize me despite any disguise. Keep it simple. Send me to the Royal Court as your secret emissary. Charles harbours a hope that the army will turn in his favour. My presence at his court with a direct link to you as commander of the armed forces of the Commonwealth could exploit that hope—especially as his situation currently appears hopeless. Only he need know of my role as a direct conduit to the English army. To the rest of his court, I will be Luke Tremayne, a senior cavalry officer who has defected to the King.'

Harry was sceptical. 'Will Charles Stuart risk having an active agent of his mortal enemy as part of his court?' Cromwell held up his hand to stop the discussion. He paced up and down the apartment at an ever-increasing speed.

After a considerable time, he spoke quickly but quietly. 'I will write a vague letter nominating you as my agent should Stuart wish to contact me regarding his and England's future. As a sweetener, you will give him the name of one of our spies, but not before you have satisfied yourself as to this agent's guilt.'

'But if this agent has betrayed us to Charles, what is the point?' asked Luke. 'This person's loyalty is not to Charles Stuart who, at the moment, counts for nothing in the world of espionage. Discover the real paymaster of this devious agent!'

It was Luke's turn to remain silent for some time. Eventually, he said, 'Let me be clear on the mission. It is to discover for whom one of our alleged agents is working and remove the traitor, flush out the murderer of another of our agents, and prevent a third from being unmasked by the Royalists?'

Cromwell nodded, and as he motioned the two soldiers to leave, he half whispered, 'All of our agents at St. Germain are women.' Cromwell turned his back on his departing officers to conceal his knowing smile, acknowledging his favourite spy's womanizing reputation.

Three Days Later

As the Dutch fleet blockaded the Straits of Dover, Luke and Harry sailed from Portsmouth on an armed Portuguese merchantman, the *Virgem do Porto* bound for Le Havre. On reaching Le Havre, they would follow the Seine to Rouen and then on to Paris.

On the *Virgem do Porto,* only travellers willing to pay an exorbitant fare were given temporary use of cabins normally used by the ship's officers. Most passengers were located on deck sitting on bales of sheepskins or other appropriate cargo. If the weather turned unfavourable, they would be herded below into the crowded sleeping quarters of the motley and unpredictable crew.

Luke was surprised that a large number of his fellow passengers were Irish mercenaries on their way to serve the Portuguese king in his conflict with Spain. Luke had never approved of the English government's policy of licensing the recruitment of English, Scottish, and Irish troops to serve the Catholic kings of Spain, Portugal, and France. He suspected that most of these recruits were defeated Royalists who were keeping themselves ready to return to England at the right time to overturn the republican government.

Luke felt uneasy. A soldier kept staring at him and then moved out of sight only to return with a distinguished looking gentleman, who was probably his commanding officer. The soldier pointed in Luke's direction, and the officer overtly perused the target of the soldier's interest. Luke caught his eye, and the officer immediately turned away and disappeared behind a pile of cargo.

Harry, who had been dozing on a soft pile of sheepskins was awakened and immediately told of Luke's disconcerting experience. Harry was not impressed. 'Why worry? You have spent much time in Ireland. It is not surprising that you are recognized by somebody.'

Luke was unhappy. 'It is still unfortunate. The least number of people who know about our journey, the better. They will speculate. What was Colonel Tremayne, Cromwell's trusted servant, doing on a Portuguese ship bound for Lisbon via Le Havre?'

The shouting of the ship's master stopped the conversation. Bearing down on the *Virgem do Porto* was a small frigate, flying the colours of the king of Scotland, Charles Stuart. Luke commented, 'A Royalist privateer. As Portugal is an ally of our republic, its ships are prime targets for these licensed pirates.'

The commander of the Irish recruits approached the master of the vessel, and after a brief discussion came straight to Luke. 'Colonel Tremayne, I am Captain Dennis O'Brien. I recently served the English government under General Monck in Northern Ireland and met you once at Dublin Castle. I now command a regiment of Irish troops drawn from all sides in the recent conflict that have enlisted to serve the king of Portugal. I have just offered the services of my men to the master of the ship to repel this privateer. I hope you will join us, although the master claims he is so well armed that the pirate will not get close enough to board.'

The master's confidence was well placed. The privateer was surprised that the merchantman had two rows of cannon and shocked that the Portuguese gunners partly disabled it in a preemptive cannonade. The sight of soldiers on deck ready to repel boarders further discouraged the Royalists.

Luke had hoped to talk further with O'Brien, but as the privateer faded into the distance, the Irishman disappeared. Luke and Harry resumed their seats on the sheepskins, and dozed until the general hubbub among the sailors indicated that they were entering the harbour of Le Havre, the Atlantic base of the French navy.

3

LUKE AND HARRY DISEMBARKED AND as they made their way to the nearest inn, they noticed O'Brien on the quay in deep conversation with a French naval officer. Again, Luke was apprehensive. 'Why is O'Brien talking to a French officer? He had no need to disembark. He is probably reporting that senior Cromwellian soldiers are entering France surreptitiously.'

'Luke, you have been a bit jittery all day. O'Brien is more likely telling the French officer that a company of Irish troops are aboard and that they are headed to Lisbon and should not concern the French authorities.' After a few glasses of wine, a large cheese, and chunks of freshly baked bread, a fraught Luke and a tired Harry retired early.

Next morning, over breakfast, Harry asked the other patrons of the inn the best way to get to Paris. They suggested two options—board a small coastal ship taking advantage of the tidal surge as far as Rouen, and then take a slower horse drawn barge on to Paris, or obtain horses and ride the full distance.

While Luke considered the situation, a square set man, balding, and with a muscular physique approached Harry. After a prolonged negotiation with the man, Harry presented him to Luke, 'This is Jacques Blanc, coxswain on a coaster, *La Chouette*. It sails for Rouen within the hour. He suspects we are in a hurry but demands a considerable sum for himself and his captain. If you are still worried about O'Brien's discussion with the French authorities, we can leave immediately with Blanc.' Luke did not hesitate and passed over a number of silver coins to the coxswain. The two Englishmen followed him out of the tavern.

It was a wise decision. *La Chouette* had just left the quay when Luke noticed the naval captain that had been spoken to by O'Brien running along the riverfront gesticulating to the master of the coaster to stop. Following the naval captain was a platoon of marines. Luke's worst fears were confirmed. The French authorities were after him.

Luke wanted to know if horsemen could reach Rouen before *La Chouette.* The reply was disconcerting. Harry translated Blanc's answer, '*La Chouette* would reach Rouen hours before any single horsemen but as Le Havre is a naval base, the government has a system for the fast delivery of information and orders. Horses are located a few miles apart and ridden at a gallop between stations reducing the time to one fifth that of the casual rider. Yes, the navy can get information to Rouen ahead of our arrival.'

Luke groaned and asked, 'Find out from Blanc where we can alight before Rouen and not immediately be discovered!'

Harry returned for more coins to pay the greedy but informative Blanc and later summarized the sailor's information. 'Just before Rouen, there is a large loop in the river that encompasses a low plateau, which includes the forest of Roumare. This forest contains the odd chateau and a number of small hamlets, but large areas are uninhabited except for deer, boar, and squirrel. It is an oak and beech woodland in which, with a little skill, you could hide for years. That's the good news.'

Luke winced as Harry continued, 'The bad news is that *La Chouette* cannot stop. The tidal surge is too strong. However, *La Chouette* will sail along the edge of the forest as it rounds the southern extremity of the loop. We will have to jump and swim for it. Fortunately, the tide will push us towards the river bank at that point.'

'Then jump we will,' pontificated Luke. Harry was silent for a while and then spluttered, 'Luke, this is ridiculous. Disembark at Rouen, visit the local authorities and show them your letter from Cromwell to Charles Stuart, and seek their assistance to reach the young would-be king.'

'No, Harry, that letter could have both of us killed. To most Frenchmen, it does not matter whether you are Royalist or Parliamentarian; you are English. Would you trust a foreigner wandering around Normandy with credentials implying a relationship with Cromwell, whom the French government suspects wants to invade France, and with Charles Stuart, who is seen as a parasite on the French Crown and leading it into paths it does not wish to follow? No. I will destroy the letter and claim we are English soldiers who have deserted the Parliament and wish to serve Charles Stuart or, even more acceptable to the locals, to join a British regiment within the French army.' With that, he produced the letter, tore it into several pieces, and threw them into the Seine.

A very agitated Jacques Blanc approached them. He took Luke and Harry to the stern of vessel and, during a straight stretch of the meandering river, pointed out a French naval frigate rapidly gaining on them. Even though he did not understand a word of French, Luke was in no doubt as to Blanc's orders to Harry. At the very first bend that temporarily obscured the view from the French frigate, they were to jump.

Harry explained further, 'This will not be ideal, but the river does front the forest of Roumare at this spot, but we will have to hide in the reeds until the frigate sweeps past. Doing this with the surging tide will not be easy, and it will be pure luck that there are reed beds where we hit the riverbank. Blanc does not think we will have time to scramble up the embankment before the frigate looms into view.'

Luke was somewhat touched that a group of sailors led by Blanc gathered around them as *La Chouette* rounded the next bend. Then, without warning, the sailors picked up the two Englishmen and threw them overboard. Luke, taken completely by surprise by his sudden ejection from *La Chouette*, hit the fast-flowing water completely unprepared.

Although he had no memory of it, his head hit a rock only inches below the waterline. He was dragged under and swept for some distance before he could orientate himself and move towards the shore. There were no reeds, and he was crushed against some rotting pylons that had once supported a small jetty. They were sufficiently large enough to hide his head as the naval frigate sped past. After it disappeared, Luke stood up. He clambered up the embankment onto a broad pathway that edged the river. He followed it into the safety of the forest.

This muddy path revealed footprints and wheel tracks. It was not an uninhabited part of the forest. He would have to be careful. He picked up a piece of broken glass that he placed in his pocket.

Hearing several voices coming along the path, Luke moved deeper into the surrounding woodlands until he found a clearing. Here, he removed most of his wet clothing and draped the various items over the undergrowth. He sat against a fallen tree and soaked up the warming sun.

Soon, the sun would disappear. The weather was turning for the worst. Luke gathered some dry wood and grass, and, using the piece of broken glass to concentrate the sun's rays, he lit a fire. This assisted in the drying of his clothes and protected him from the encroaching cold as nightfall descended.

He was hungry. By the noises that punctuated the evening air, the forest was alive with animals. Luke kept his fire ablaze to keep this wild life at a distance. In the morning, he would look for food.

Instead, the food came to him. Despite his efforts to the contrary, he fell asleep, and, during the night, his fire burnt out. When he awoke, wild pigs were rooting around the edge of the embers, sniffing at the burnt soil, leaves, and grass.

Half asleep, he made a grab for the nearest piglet that had no trouble in avoiding him. Unaware that the squeals of the youngster had aroused its male parent, Luke turned his back on the boar. He moved as quietly as he could towards another piglet, which he tried to catch by throwing his cape over the animal. He was so intent on being the successful predator he did not hear the thundering trotters of the boar hurtling towards him.

He suddenly felt the excruciating pain of a knifelike incision into the back of his upper left leg and the sensation of being hurled through the air. By the time he realised what had happened, the boar had turned and was pawing the ground ready for a second charge. Luke's sword lay yards away on the other side of the embers. He had his dagger, but as he tried to rise to defend himself, he almost passed out from the pain. Blood ran profusely down his leg.

Boars cannot climb trees but the nearest oak was four or five yards away. Any painful movement towards its safety might incite the boar to commence his run. The boar didn't need any incentive; it charged. Luke struggled forlornly towards the tree but slipped in his own blood and passed out.

When he came to, he was lying under the body of the boar. A distinguished looking huntsman towered over him. The hunter's servants dragged the boar from Luke, and one attended to his horrendous wound. The hunter gave orders, and several of his men disappeared. They reappeared sometime later with a stretcher on to which Luke, who was passing in and out of consciousness, was carefully placed.

When Luke awoke, he was lying in a large four-poster bed in a magnificent chamber. The pale blue doors were decorated with silver angels. Was he a prisoner in a Papist convent? Present in the room were three female servants who had been attending to his wound; the pain from which was still intense.

On his wakening, one of them left the room and soon returned with a tall bearded man whose demeanour and dress indicated high status and an equally well-dressed gentlewoman who immediately addressed Luke in English. 'Kind sir, I am Charlotte, Marquise des Anges. This is my husband, Henri, the Marquis des Anges, and you are in the hunting lodge of our Chateau des Anges. From your ramblings as you slept, we realise you are English and, from your clothes, a military gentleman. What is an English officer doing in our forest?'

'My lady I will answer your questions, but, first, inform your husband of my sincere thanks. One of his men saved my life.' Luke and the Marquis saluted each other, and Luke began his story—and then stopped with a blank expression dominating his face.

He was silent for some time as the realization of his incapacity dawned on him. 'I can't remember anything before I scrambled up the embankment.' The Marquise repeated the story to her husband who then spoke at length to her. He was clearly unimpressed.

They left the room, and, shortly after, the three nursing servants were replaced by three armed liveried guards who stationed themselves at the door and the two windows. Luke's status had changed from patient to prisoner.

4

TWO DAYS LATER, THE MARQUISE returned—and explained. 'My husband is the magistrate for the rural areas to the west of Rouen. That city's magistrates informed him that they had received news from Le Havre that two English spies, known associates of General Cromwell, had entered France and were heading for Rouen.

Naval authorities believe they are here to spy out the land prior to an expected invasion by Cromwell on behalf of French Protestants and also to contact French rebels around Bordeaux with the aim of reenforcing them with English troops. Either way, they are a threat to the security of the French Crown. You are one of those agents. Henri doubts that you have really lost your memory, although the massive bruise and swelling on your head supports your story.'

'What is to happen to me? Am I to be summarily executed as a spy? And if I am one of the spies you mention, where is my companion?'

'Calm yourself! For the moment, you will stay here. Your wound is serious. Henri will wait until you recover before he decides your fate. A woman from one of the hamlets on the estate will be here shortly to dress your wound with healing herbs. I have no faith in the physicians of Rouen, and Henri wishes to conceal your presence from all outsiders. Nothing is known regarding your companion.'

Luke was devastated. He did not know who he was, or why he was in France.

A week into his stay, at the Chateau des Anges, he received his first answers. The Marquise told him, 'My husband visited the magistrates in Rouen yesterday and sought further information about the identity and fate of the two English spies spotted in Le Havre. Officially, neither has been found. However, the decapitated body of a man who may be one of them was washed ashore along the Seine twenty miles downstream from here. The original informant knew the identity of only one of the men. He was Lieutenant Colonel Luke Tremayne, a close associate of General Cromwell. He had one unmistakable feature that could help identify him—sparkling bright blue eyes.'

The Marquise looked intently at Luke and smiled warmly. She held out her hand and remarked, 'As have you. Welcome, Colonel, to our chateau.'

Luke kissed the outstretched hand. Tears ran down his cheeks. 'Thank you, my lady. You cannot understand the dreadful feeling of not knowing who you are or why you are here. At least now, with your help, I can start to fill in some of the gaps. I hope the decapitated body was not my companion.' Luke continued, 'My lady, you speak perfect English. How did this come about?'

'Tremayne, your brain must have been affected by the knock. I speak perfect English because I am English. For five years, I served Queen Henriette Marie as a lady-in-waiting. When she came to France in the forties to raise funds and ammunition for her husband, I came with her. It was just after the death of my first husband. While in France, I met Henri; and after a year, I married him and settled here.'

'And yet another question—now that you know my identity, will you report me to the authorities?'

'That is for Henri to decide. He hopes you will regain your memory so that you can be questioned as to your mission in France. If he believes you are here as an enemy of France, you will be executed. If your reason for being in France has nothing to do with the security of France, he will send you back to England. Until then, and certainly until you recover the use of your leg, you will stay here, and your presence and identity will not be divulged to anyone outside of the chateau.'

'I am grateful for your assistance Lady Charlotte, but how am I to fill in my days here?' 'You speak no French. Our children's elderly tutor lives on the estate. A daily French lesson will eat up the days and possibly help you to recall whatever your mission in France might be.' Luke was not convinced, but after a week of boring convalescence, he acquiesced.

Pascal de Foix was a delightful old man with a sense of humour and a strong liking for the cheaper wines of Bordeaux. He also impressed Luke as a former soldier who had fought for the French Protestants in 1629 in their unsuccessful defence of La Rochelle against the forces of King Louis XIII and Cardinal Richelieu. Pascal had been told that his new pupil was a senior associate of the extreme Protestant, General Oliver Cromwell. This created an immediate empathy.

Luke asked undiplomatically, 'Monsieur de Foix, are you still a Protestant?'

The old man smiled. 'Yes. It is a pity that you have lost your memory. My people who still live at La Rochelle have heard rumours that General Cromwell is about to invade France to restore the freedoms we Protestants enjoyed in the reign of the king's grandfather.

Do you think your mission was to assess the military strength of the French Protestants and the feasibility of English help? This is certainly the time to strike. The king is a minor and under the sway of a very unpopular Italian, Cardinal Mazarin, who has just returned from exile.

Government is a compromise between the Queen Mother who sides with Mazarin and leading nobles who have deserted the revolt to rally behind the young King in the name of French unity. The revolt of the nobles and cities, the Fronde, is almost suppressed, and lingers on only in the region of Bordeaux with some assistance from Spain—and maybe forthcoming help from the English.'

'I hope that that is not my mission. If it is, your master will have me executed immediately. I have no idea why I am here. It is a strange and horrifying feeling not to know who you are, except for a meaningless name. What do I believe? Am I an escaped murderer, a Jesuit priest in disguise, or a Puritan assassin?

As well as teaching me French, you must give me lessons in current politics. I am supposed to be an associate of General Cromwell. Who is he? Lady Charlotte mentioned a civil war in England. Who fought whom? At the moment, I am an empty shell. I know nothing except my name.'

Luke and Pascal became close friends. The tutor insisted that, in the mornings, Luke continue his French lessons. In the afternoons, which Luke enjoyed immensely, Pascal recounted the events of the world over the previous decade. Luke was amazed that civil war and revolution had engulfed most of Western Europe. He peppered Pascal with questions.

St Germain, Early January 1653

Cromwell sent a coded message to a female agent at the Stuart Court informing her that he was sending her assistance in the person of Colonel Luke Tremayne. The agent was unhappy to receive the coded message at the time she did. She feared her every movement was being watched by one of the other women courtiers and that her invaluable codebook would be discovered. She could not communicate without it as the code allotted to her was completely random. It conformed to no pattern nor system.

She kept it hidden in one of the outlying chapels in the grounds of St. Germain. She was returning from the chapel after decoding Cromwell's missive when Lady Mary Gresham, a favourite of the King, confronted her.

Lady Mary was wrapped in a royal blue cape and wearing a large brimmed hat to deflect the flakes of snow that had begun to fall. She engaged Cromwell's agent in light-hearted banter, which, to the agitated listener, was interpreted as sinister probing.

'My dear, what are you doing out in this weather and visiting that small church. I am surprised that an English Protestant should seek the comfort of that chapel in particular. It is the place of worship for a most extreme group of Catholic worshippers that give their allegiance to the Pope, rather than to the French king. Even Her Majesty shuns that particular form of Papism.'

The agent admitted her ignorance of the chapel's devotees and explained that she was interested in its stained glass window, which was very similar to that in her parish church, which had been destroyed during the recent civil strife.

A week later, she was forced to retrieve her codebook once again. An urgent message had arrived from Cromwell. She at least remembered by heart his coded signature. She headed for the chapel but stopped in her tracks. The chapel was alight with candles and full of worshippers.

She waited several hours before returning. It was dark, and she was scared. Her taper was struggling against the falling snow, as her attempts to shield it were proving difficult. She entered the now-deserted chapel, found her codebook, and painfully deciphered the message.

She could almost feel Cromwell's wrath as she decoded the missive. He was furious. He had not heard from Tremayne. The agent penned a simple coded four-word answer. 'He has not arrived.'

She returned her codebook to its hiding place and folded her reply into one of her many petticoats. She would give it to the courier as soon as possible. She now shared Cromwell's concern. Colonel Tremayne and Captain Lloyd should have arrived at least a week ago. Where were they?

After Harry hit the water, he received a glancing blow from a large log, around which he managed to cling. As the frigate rounded the bend, he put his head under water without releasing his grip. After the ship passed, he was at the mercy of the log, which was too large to be influenced by Harry's attempt to propel it towards the shore. Fortunately, after some twenty minutes, the log drifted close enough to the riverbank for Harry to release his grip and swim towards dry land. Clambering up the steep embankment, he realised that he was still on the edge of the forest, but he could see, upriver, the outskirts of Rouen.

Harry was miles away from where he and Luke entered the water. In the vastness of the forest, it would be impossible to find each other, assuming that the colonel had survived the river. He decided to continue to Paris and carry out Luke's mission.

He had walked for over an hour along a well-worn path when he heard, ahead of him, a string of curses in French. He advanced slowly and saw a villager bent over a trap he had prepared for rabbits. An inedible squirrel had activated it, much to the annoyance of the poacher.

Harry crept up behind him and slit his throat. The poacher felt no pain. Harry dragged the body into the undergrowth. He stripped the corpse of its clothes and dressed it in his own. He clothed himself in the woodsman's habit.

He then took his sword and decapitated the body. He buried the head, and moved back to the river, dragging the headless body on his army greatcoat. He threw the torso and greatcoat into the Seine, and, noticing that the tide had turned, hoped it would be carried back towards Le Havre.

Now, in the persona of a French peasant, Harry walked jauntily along the riverside path into the centre of Rouen. There, he found a number of horse-drawn barges ready to be hauled up river. He found one that required a man to assist with the horses. Thus began the slow journey to Paris.

5

TWELVE MILES TO THE WEST of the city was the towering fortress palace, the Chateau of St. Germain. At the entrance to the chateau, Harry was accosted by an armed patrol commanded by a young ensign. The young soldier was surprised when Harry responded to his challenge in English. He was incensed when Harry haughtily demanded to see the king.

He struck Harry a stunning blow with his clenched fist. 'You churlish jackanape! Our king does not receive scum.' A shaken Harry responded lamely, 'I am Captain Lloyd come to serve the King—and with information to his advantage.' The soldiers ignored his plea and dragged him to an outbuilding of the Chateau. Harry heard a large wooden bar pulled across the door. His head ached, and he bled profusely from mouth and nose.

Some hours later, the door was opened and a plate of unpalatable stew placed on the floor. Harry appealed to his gaoler, 'If you will not take me to the king, may I speak to the commander of the guard?'

The man did not reply, but half an hour later, the door was reopened, and Harry was escorted across a courtyard into a wing of the chateau. He was taken into a chamber furnished with a very large desk, behind which sat a man whom Harry immediately recognised.

Lord Ashcroft was equally surprised. 'God's blood! If it is not young Harry Lloyd! Your Puritan family was the bane of my existence as the king's lord lieutenant before the war. What is a Parliamentarian extremist doing in the vicinity of the Royal Court? My young ensign thinks you are an assassin.'

'My lord, you know full well that Puritans of my ilk would assassinate no one, but I can see why you would find unbelievable my story that I am here to offer my services to the king. The king is expecting me. Please inform him that Colonel Luke Tremayne's deputy wishes an audience with him!'

Ashcroft was bemused. 'Puritans of your ilk would assassinate no one! Your murder of the late king negates such meaningless blather. But let me see whether young Charles really does expect you. I will inform him of your arrival.'

Ashcroft left the room. Sometime later, he returned and signalled Harry to follow him. On reaching an inner courtyard, Harry saw an athletic young man standing in the middle of the cobbled square. Ashcroft motioned for him to join the king who addressed him immediately, 'Captain Lloyd, I received a request from General Cromwell that Colonel Tremayne be stationed at my court as a go-between between myself and the English army, which I understand is increasingly critical of the English republican government. Where is Tremayne?'

'Sir, I do not know. There is a strong possibility that he is dead—drowned.' Harry related to Charles the details of his journey as they slowly crisscrossed the cobbled courtyard well out of hearing of any of the king's men. Eventually, Harry asked, 'What happens now?'

The king was silent for some time. He placed his arm around Harry's shoulder and said, 'I accept General Cromwell's suggestion, but you will act in place of Tremayne. To maintain your cover as a recruit to my cause, you will be Lord Ashcroft's deputy as part of my personal bodyguard. Ashcroft will be the only other person informed of your real role. You will thereby earn your keep in this impoverished court.

Your experience with Tremayne will enable you to assist Ashcroft's investigation into a few problems that we have. Recently, my mother's youngest lady-in-waiting, Lucy Harman, was murdered. I want to know by whom and why. Was her death part of a conspiracy that might endanger my person, or was it a private matter with no political implications?' With that, he signalled for Ashcroft to join them and informed the commander of the situation.

Back in his chambers, Lord Ashcroft was surprisingly pleasant. 'Welcome to St. Germain! I trust you have personal means to maintain your status here. The king has no money, and his mother helps only her favourites. There are several empty apartments in the outbuildings of the chateau. While you are on duty, you can share this room and the guardhouse.'

Harry was then taken to the guardhouse, which contained the men who were not currently on duty. Ashcroft introduced Harry as their new deputy commander. Harry saw the ensign who had struck him and congratulated the now-nervous soldier on his earlier effective detention of a suspect. He expected more of the same. The man beamed. It was a politic beginning.

Harry settled into a small apartment in one of the outbuildings of the extensive Chateau of St. Germain only recently vacated by the French Court when it returned to the Louvre. He was anxious to begin his mission, but he could not contact Cromwell as he had no codebook. Any overt correspondence would easily be intercepted.

This dilemma ended three nights later when there was a knock on his door. On the doorstep was a tall gentlewoman with a cape wrapped around her and a curving hat that covered much of her face. She whispered, 'You are a friend of Colonel Tremayne?' Harry nodded and invited the lady to join him for supper.

The tall sinewy redhead introduced herself as Lady Catherine Beaumont and explained that General Cromwell was furious that he had not heard from Tremayne. Harry explained the situation. She replied, 'I will get a message to the general immediately.'

Harry advised, 'Please inform him that the king has accepted me in place of Luke, and I seek his endorsement of my actions. Second, can I copy your code book so that I can contact the general directly?'

Cate Beaumont was not impressed, 'Not without the general's express authority. Until he grants it, I will come here whenever you need to communicate. You are an attractive young man, Captain

Lloyd. The court will soon surmise that you and I are lovers. It will provide a perfect cover, and conform to the culture of this pernicious and godless court.'

'I am surprised, Lady Catherine. I assumed that the court of Queen Henriette Marie was upright and exceedingly moral.' 'As far as the Queen Mother and her intimate circle are concerned, it is; but since the young King has taken up residence, his friends have attracted several profligates whose sole purpose is to deflower as many women as they can.'

Harry awkwardly asked, 'Have you been a victim of such unwarranted attention?' 'No, but it is an ever-present concern. That is why any rumour that you and I are lovers will afford me some protection.'

Harry blushed and changed the topic, 'My lady, I do not know how much General Cromwell has told you of our mission. Part of it is to uncover the murderer of one of your number and a fellow agent—a task that I have also been given by the king—reveal another as a triple agent, and prevent the third, presumably yourself, from being unmasked.'

'I know very little. My role is simply to send coded messages containing any information that I consider would be useful to the English army about events at the Royal Court. It is usually secondhand as the king rarely keeps his mother informed, and she is determined that none of the younger English women will corrupt her son.

It used to be impossible for us to fraternize with the close male associates of the king. We were banned from the sections of the chateau allocated to Charles, his council, and what is laughingly called a court. In recent months, these prohibitions have been ignored.'

'Who are the English ladies closest to the Queen Mother?' 'There are only three Englishwomen in the inner circle, the Dowager Duchess of Hakebourne and the Countess of Stokerton, both very old; and, recently, a younger woman imposed by the king—Lady Mary Gresham. The two aristocrats served the Queen in England for decades and are devoted to her. The only intrigues they engage in are to protect the Queen Mother at all costs.

Lady Mary is a favourite of the king, and maybe, to ensure that she does not become a closer favourite, the Queen Mother accepted

Mary into her inner group. Mary's intimate role enables the king to keep an eye on his mother and for Queen Henriette Marie to monitor any liaison between Charles and Mary. Mary is also close to Lord Ashcroft.

With the death of Lucy, and, excluding myself, there remain only two other women close enough to the political action to be possible agents—Elizabeth Mortimer and Jane Torrington. No one else is in a position to obtain information that would warrant the risk to themselves or their alleged paymasters, although I would be surprised if any of them are paid. I serve General Cromwell not for financial reward but because of what the Royalists did to my late husband. I have no particular antagonism towards the young king.'

'Tell me about Lucy Harman!' 'She was very young, still in her teens. Her appeal to Queen Henriette was that, of all the English-born women, she was the most devoted Papist. That is why I am astonished that she should spy for a Puritan extremist and regicide in the person of Oliver Cromwell.'

'What about her family?' 'Her father is a leading Catholic peer. There are rumours that he contributes to the Parliamentary cause in the hope of improving the conditions for English Catholics. These overtures have been rejected by the fervent Protestants controlling Parliament, but the military are more tolerant and latterly Harman, anticipating an army coup, is suspected of doing a deal with Cromwell.'

'How do you know this?' asked an impressed Harry. 'When Lord Ashcroft investigated Lucy's murder, one of the questions he asked us all related to her loyalty to the king, given her father's alleged behaviour in delivering Catholic support to Cromwell.'

'Perhaps she was murdered as a suspected enemy agent. But if her death was not politically motivated, what other reasons could there have been? What about her personal life?' 'She was closely watched and protected by Queen Henriette from the male predators gathered around the king, although it was unnecessary. Her overt distain for men and her excessive Catholic morality isolated her from the world of flirtation and seduction and led the rest of us to call her *the Nun*.'

'Could she have been raped and then murdered to conceal the act?' 'I don't know. None of us were told the circumstances and nature of her death. Lord Ashcroft can tell you more.'

Harry suddenly remembered the need to get a message to Cromwell. He outlined what he wanted to say, and Catherine took cryptic notes that she would later encode and dispatch. After they had finished, Lady Catherine moved from the table to a comfortable lounge. Within minutes, she was asleep. Harry let her doze.

When she awoke in the early hours of the morning, he escorted her to her apartment at the other end of the chateau. A guard on duty recognized his new deputy commander and winked as Harry and Catherine passed by. The rumours would spread. Harry felt good. Cate Beaumont was not only a valuable agent, but also a strikingly beautiful woman.

6

LUKE BUILT UP HIS STRENGTH by long walks alone or with Pascal through the manicured gardens and lawns of the estate, but he could not face any excursion into the surrounding forest. Luke mentioned to Pascal during one of these walks that he wished there was a way to repay his hosts for their kindness. Pascal commented that he might soon have such an opportunity. Some days later, Lady Charlotte invited Luke, who was now walking with just the trace of a limp, to join her and Henri for supper.

Although the main meal was eaten mid afternoon, supper served late in the evening was not a meagre affair. Luke had not previously entered the main part of the chateau. The great hall oozed opulence and power. Henri, Marquis des Anges was very rich.

Supper reflected wealth and elegance. No wooden trenches and utensils for this household. As befitting their title, plates, goblets, candelabras, knives, and spoons were of silver. A large table had places set at each end and several along the side. The liveried retainer leading Luke to his place moved through this great hall into a small antechamber. It was even more opulent.

The inner room had a smaller table, and Henri and Charlotte were already seated—and all the utensils and plate were gold. This was an intimate dinner for three. An array of hors d'oeuvres was placed in front of Luke.

The first, in the shape of a sausage, was delicious. Charlotte explained that it was a ballotine of pheasant. The birds' legs had been deboned and the space filled with a seasoned stuffing and chopped meats. The second was deep-sea oysters, which Henri had obtained fresh from St. Malo and, the third, lobster meat in aspic.

Luke had only commenced the lobster when a pompous servant led three underlings into the room. Each carried a tureen of soup—a beef and onion spiced with paprika and garlic and sprinkled with lemon juice and gold leaf, bisque of shellfish with a mushroom infusion, and, the third, a pumpkin soup that no English gentlemen could stomach. Luke's instinctive reaction forced him to remember that pumpkins were cattle food and not fit for human consumption. Useless information, but it was a beginning for an otherwise empty mind.

Next came the main courses with a range of hare stew, mutton in garlic jus, roast beef with carrots and horseradish, and a wild salmon. This was quickly followed by a green salad with violet and borage flowers, hard-boiled eggs, a mushroom soufflé, and an iced cheese. Throughout these many multidished courses, a servant continued to fill Luke's golden goblet with a red wine that Henri claimed was the best that Bordeaux could produce.

Suddenly, Henri clapped his hands. Luke expected the arrival of another series of dishes. Instead, every servant left the room, and Henri instructed the last to exit to leave the doors open, presumably to prevent eavesdroppers hiding behind them.

Henri took several sheets of paper from inside his doublet. He turned to Luke. 'Charlotte and I wished you to dine with us tonight for three reasons: to enjoy your company, to inform you a little more about your past, and, given that, to seek your assistance.'

Luke was mellow, but any information about his past had him excited and eager. Henri continued, 'I enquire about you everywhere I go. Last week, in Le Havre, I met a friend who surprisingly knows you very well. Less than a year ago, you and he were engaged in some clandestine operation that affected the security of both England and France.

He is Claude, Comte de Sauvel, who would have returned here in person to see you, but he had just received orders to sail his squadron of warships south to blockade the mouth of the Garonne.

The government hopes the display of naval power will extinguish the remaining embers of the revolt against our king and his mother.'

Henri canvassed the detail that Sauvel had related to him and concluded, 'Therefore, Luke, you are definitely a close associate of General Cromwell and have been employed by him to solve several difficult cases, including many murders. Sauvel says you are an experienced and effective inquisitor.'

Luke inwardly beamed at both the laudatory remarks and the satisfaction of knowing more about himself. He had no memory of the Comte de Sauvel, but the new information filled in more of the vacant spaces in his mind. He was so taken with this additional information that he fell silent.

Eventually, Henri took several sips from his goblet and said, 'De Foix tells me that you wished to repay us for our hospitality. The evidence from Claude de Sauvel gives me confidence that you may be able to help Charlotte and myself in a very important regard.'

'My lord, your man, Mathieu Gillot, saved my life. Anything I can do will be small recompense.' 'If you are successful, you will save two lives in return for your own—hardly small compensation. Put simply, I could be arrested for treason at any moment and executed, and Charlotte has already survived two attempts to murder her.'

'Sacre bleu!' exclaimed Luke. The marquis and his wife smiled at Luke's use of his newly learnt tongue. But he quickly reverted to English asking, 'Do you know who is trying to destroy you both?'

'Yes,' replied Henri, 'It is my son by my first wife—Alain St. Michel.'

Charlotte took up the account. 'When Alain was fourteen, his mother died in shocking circumstances. These have never been fully investigated. The tragedy unhinged the boy, who accused his father of the murder, and then went on an irrational rampage through one of the hamlets in the forest. He decapitated seven or eight women villagers before Gillot's men stopped him.

Alain swore that he would avenge his mother and assume his place as the rightful Marquis des Anges. The local magistrates, prompted by Henri, declared him insane and had him incarcerated in an old fortress prison near Toulouse. That was ten years past.'

Henri interrupted, 'Several months ago we heard that Alain had escaped and, in the current political turmoil, apparently convinced several key figures in the government that he had been wrongly imprisoned and that I had done it to hide my murder of his mother. It is not a coincidence that, since his escape, there have been two attempts on Charlotte's life. In Alain's mind nobody but his mother is the legitimate Marquise des Anges.'

'And from the same time', interposed Charlotte, 'local authorities have begun to question Henri regarding his loyalty during the recent troubles and more recently about the death of his first wife. Alain must have convinced someone in authority that Henri is both a traitor and murderer.'

'How specifically can I help?' asked Luke.

'You must prove that I did not murder my first wife and that, politically, I have remained loyal to the King and am neither a Protestant nor a Frondeur. In the short-term, and to achieve these aims, you must find Alain and those who are being influenced by his poisonous ideas. As important, you must uncover who in this Chateau is carrying out his orders and has attempted to murder Charlotte.'

'Whom in this Chateau do you suspect?' asked Luke intuitively.

'None of the servants! Alain's murder of the villagers and his abuse of servants since he was a child won him no supporters among the lower orders. Quite the reverse, some have openly threatened to kill him should he ever return. Alain is very disturbed in this regard. He equates servants with animals, both provided for his pleasure to torture and abuse at will.'

'If the servants are beyond suspicion, are members of your family responsible?' 'I think not, but I cannot be certain. I let you recover in the hunting lodge and kept you isolated from my household as I did not trust them to conceal your presence and identity. Now that Claude de Sauvel has confirmed your identity and indicated your special abilities, you may make the hunting lodge your permanent home, but I expect you to dine regularly with the household, whom you can hear at this moment carousing in the great hall. I want you to assess their loyalty.'

'Who graces your lordship's table?' asked Luke. Charlotte answered, 'Our twin children, Marie and Paul, Henri's youngest half sister, Josette, and Odette Bonnet, the sister of Henri's first wife, although the others are not aware of this relationship. They have been told that Odette is a distant cousin. Outside of the family are Henri's longtime but intermittent friend, Philippe Rousset and our senior servants, the chaplain, Father Louis Morel, the steward, lawyer Mathieu Gillot, and your friend and tutor, Pascal de Foix.'

'Apart from the children, any one of them could be Alain's agent, although I think the women are innocent,' concluded Charlotte. 'That's not completely fair my dear. I trust them all—until Luke proves the contrary. The person I know I can rely on is my friend Philippe, Vicomte Rousset, who currently commands a company of musketeers in the Royal garrison stationed at Rouen.

He lives here when not on duty. He has renewed our friendship after nearly a decade's absence, a hiatus due to his unfortunate support for the late rebellion. His estates are in the south of France. It is not politically wise for him to associate there with his former allies who opposed the queen and cardinal.

He will be back here in a few days. As a fellow soldier, he would be a worthy partner in your investigation, and I know it is not in his interests for any misfortune to befall me.'

Henri clapped his hands, and servants brought in plates of fruit and edible sugar animals. After biting off the head of a chubby confectionery rabbit, Luke responded quietly, 'My lord, I would be honoured to assist you in these times of trouble. My French is not good enough to effectively conduct the intensive interviews that will be necessary. In the absence of Vicomte Rousset, may I use Pascal de Foix as my secretary assistant in this endeavour? That does not mean he is removed from the list of suspects.'

Henri nodded approval. He rose and, followed by Charlotte, left the room. A servant indicated to Luke that the meal was finished and led him through the great hall to the entrance. At the same time, Pascal joined him, and the two men walked back together to the hunting lodge.

Pascal asked, 'Will you help the marquis? I hoped I had convinced him that you would be ideal for the task, but it was the news from the Comte de Sauvel that confirmed your suitability.'

'I said yes, but my French is not yet of a standard that I could conduct probing interviews. I have asked the marquis that you should be my assistant in this enterprise. Will you accept?'

Pascal was delighted. 'Yes. Over the years, I have done my own bit of sleuthing, especially into the death of Henri's first wife and the unspeakable behaviour of the monstrous Alain St. Michel. I have taken meals with this somewhat dysfunctional household for decades and can give you my views on all of them.'

'We'll commence our work in the morning. As of tomorrow, I will join you at dinner and supper and add my assessment to yours.' Luke had his first unbroken sleep since his arrival at the Chateau des Anges.

7

PASCAL WAS EAGER TO BRIEF Luke on the inhabitants of the chateau or rather to unburden himself of years of accumulated gossip. Luke faced a torrent of random opinion and possible misinformation, which he eventually tried to focus by commenting, 'The problems seem to start with Henri's first wife. Tell me about her!'

To Luke's astonishment the question stopped the voluble and gushing Pascal in his tracks. He sat mute for several minutes. Tears began to flow down his cheeks. He finally regained his composure.

'Antoinette was a beautiful woman, both in appearance and character. She was adored, if not loved, by all who knew her. From her marriage to her death, she was a warm outgoing woman who was the centre of Rouen and Parisian society. Sadly, she was too trusting and a little naïve in her relationships with men; and her world was limited to the artificial creations of royal courts, aristocratic estates, and bourgeois salons.'

Luke belatedly realised that Pascal's view of Antoinette was highly coloured by his obvious affection, if not more, for the late marquise. He quietly asked, 'How did she die?' 'Which account do you want to hear—the legal findings of the magistrates or the truth?' 'Give me the official account first!'

'The fully clothed marquise tripped while walking through the woods and, while presumably unconscious, was fatally savaged by a wild boar. Mathieu Gillot, the man who saved you, found the body.' 'And you do not believe this report?'

'We all know otherwise. Gillot found the body in this hunting lodge. Antoinette was dressed only in a flimsy chemise, and her body riddled with stab wounds. All sorts of rumours circulated regarding the incident, and Henri asked for a conspiracy of silence and, with the agreement of his fellow magistrates, concocted a story for the investigating officer, who was also well paid to ignore the obvious facts. The justification for these falsehoods was to save the reputation of the beloved Antoinette. We all agreed to support the official version—except for young Alain.'

Pascal continued, 'He was shattered by his mother's death and went berserk, accused his father of murder, and rampaged through the hamlets decapitating several women. The same magistrates who went along with the concocted story of Antoinette's death quickly agreed with Henri that his son was mentally unstable and should be immediately confined to a prison in southern France.'

'Why was she murdered?' 'The motive lies hidden within her multitudinous affairs. Antoinette was a striking beauty and a precocious lover. She did not hesitate to take the initiative in her lovemaking, yet she still made men feel important. After the birth of an heir, Henri accepted his wife's liaisons. In the last five years of her life, Antoinette had half a dozen lovers, and almost every male in this chateau, at one time or another, fell victim to her charms.

One of these lovers, not willing to accept the conventions of the society within which these affairs were conducted, perhaps in a fit of rage, murdered her ladyship. The only other possibility is to believe Alain that Henri had finally tired of his wife's indiscretions and ordered her execution.'

Luke chuckled, 'You make my task appear easy. Antoinette was murdered either on the orders of her husband or by a discarded lover. Who was she sleeping with at the time of her death?'

Pascal hesitated, 'Rousset, a regular visitor in those days, Gillot, the penny-pinching lawyer, and myself all knew her ladyship intimately in this period. There were others in Rouen and Paris that we were vaguely aware of—and then there was Emile.'

'Emile, that is a name I have not heard!'

'Emile is Henri's half brother, who was certainly too close to Antoinette. His sudden departure for Canada some twenty-five years ago was related to this over familiarity with his sister-in-law. He may have returned secretly fifteen years later, killed his lost love, and disappeared back to Canada, but it is an improbable explanation.'

Luke had become aware that Pascal was increasingly uncomfortable with questions concerning Lady Antoinette. He directly confronted his tutor. 'Old man, you would prefer it if I did not investigate the death of the late marquise?'

Pascal, with tears cascading down his cheeks, answered, 'Yes. What good can come of your enquiry? Rather than investigate the death of the first marquise, Antoinette, you should concentrate on the alleged attempts to murder the second, Lady Charlotte.'

'But the Marquis explicitly asked me to prove that he did not murder his first wife.'

'It is a waste of time. After ten years, no evidence can be produced to prove the issue one way or another. It is a futile task. Knowing the marquis, he does not want an exhaustive enquiry. He just wants sufficient evidence to allay the suspicions of the authorities who will soon lose interest, unless continually fired up by an outside force.

That should be the direction of your enquiry. Who is trying to undermine Henri's credibility with the authorities and who, if anybody, is trying to murder Charlotte? And those answers will be found within the chateau rather than elsewhere. Forget about Antoinette!'

That evening, Luke joined the household for supper. It was a small group. There were five men, including himself, and two women. He sat next to Pascal who introduced him to the rest of the diners. The three remaining men were Louis Morel, priest, Mathieu Gillot who, whatever his titles, was manager of the Chateau, the estate, and the forests, and Philippe Rousset, who had arrived unexpectedly, soldier and aristocratic friend of the Marquis. The two women were Henri's half sister, Josette St. Michel, and his first wife's sister, Odette Bonnet.

Luke was at his diplomatic best, provoking and listening to a torrent of small talk, and answering questions about his own position. Henri had informed them that he had employed Luke to investigate the attempts on the life of his current wife and the scurrilous attack on himself as the murderer of his first wife.

It was a pleasant evening, and all parties seemed to enjoy each other's company. They warmly welcomed Luke to their small circle. Luke picked up seductive vibes from Odette Bonnet and a feeling of camaraderie from Philippe.

Mathieu Gillot did not mention how he found Luke injured in the forest, and Luke thought it proper not to raise the issue until they were alone. The circumstances of Luke's arrival at the chateau should, for now, remain a secret from his dining companions. During this pleasant evening, Luke indicated that he would talk to them individually over the next few days as part of his investigation.

His French lessons continued the next morning; at the conclusion of which, Luke asked Pascal whether he suspected any of the household in the attempts to murder Charlotte and to denigrate Henri. Pascal's reply surprised him, 'Has there been any real attempts to murder the marquise? Henri has given few details, and Charlotte, none at all. Start your questioning with the marquise! Your weakness in French will not be a disadvantage. You can probe your countrywoman in her own tongue.'

Luke sensed an element of dislike creeping into Pascal's comments about Charlotte. Had the discussion of the first marquise the day before created nostalgia that was reacting against the image of Antoinette's successor?

In the afternoon, Charlotte, Marquise des Anges, formally received Luke. Given her dress, Luke guessed incorrectly that this was not to be the intimate chat that he had hoped for. Charlotte was emphasizing the difference in their status.

An expensive, bejewelled dark green coif embroidered with gold thread covered most of her black hair, which just reached her shoulders. Her bodice was of a similar green, with the slashed sleeves revealing a golden underlining. Her collar was very wide and made of lace that appeared to include threads of gold; as did her lengthy cuffs. Her skirt in matching green was open at the front revealing a golden under skirt. Her opulence was emphasized by an enormous brooch, which covered her left breast with five of the biggest diamonds Luke had ever seen.

As if to compete with the sparkle of her brooch, Charlotte's large brown eyes seemed to twinkle, and her long and thin face tapering to a pointy chin exuded a happy expression. As a patient, Luke had experienced a warm and outgoing Charlotte. Would the change in his status affect their relationship?

Luke's fears were not realised. Charlotte eased any potential tension by proclaiming warmly, 'Luke, I hope you are not going to apply your renowned investigative techniques on me. Sauvel told Henri that you are ruthless. The Spanish Inquisition would be proud of you. What do you wish to know?'

Luke was ruthless. 'Forgive me your ladyship, but have there actually been any attempts on your life?' Charlotte was taken off guard by the question and more than a little disconcerted. Luke continued, 'I ask because no one except you and your husband seem to know anything about these attempts. Is this a game you are playing for the benefit of the household?'

Charlotte in faltering soft tones finally replied, 'There have been two attempts, but as I cannot prove for certain the incidents were attempts to kill me, Henri insisted I not go into details.'

'If I am to help, you must go into details. Maybe someone in the household is not out to kill you but simply to frighten you and irritate your husband. Having had one wife murdered, to lose another in a similar fashion would not help Henri's credibility.'

'Strange that you should say that! The first attempt was almost identical to Antoinette's official demise. I was in the woods lying on a grassy verge with several of my maids when a wild boar, probably herded in our direction, charged our party. At that point, I would have gone along with your view that someone was out to frighten me, but as we hurriedly fled the forest, I sensed danger. Luckily, at a crucial moment, I tripped over a log, and an arrow sped over my head. If I hadn't tripped, I would be dead.'

'How did Henri react when you told him?'

'He swore at length and immediately decided that the attempt to kill me was part of a plot to destroy him. The second attempt occurred just before you arrived. Initially, Henri thought you were the would-be assassin and that your alleged loss of memory was a clever way of getting close to me so that you could try again. If the Comte de Sauvel had not vouched for you, you would be dead. Someone tried to push me over the battlements of the northwest tower of the chateau.'

Luke looked at Charlotte with the face of a schoolmaster confronted by a mendacious child. It provoked an angry response. 'You disbelieve me before you have heard the facts!' 'Do you blame me? If someone tried to push you over the battlements, where is the evidence?' asked Luke in an inquisitorial tone reeking of menace.

Charlotte was unsettled by this hardheaded and hardhearted approach from someone she had increasingly treated as a friend. She remained silent for some time and after wiping a tear from her cheek, eventually replied in a soft and quavering voice, 'Let me explain. On clear nights, I climb the northwest tower to view the stars through one of the new complicated lenses that Father Louis brought with him from Italy. He and Pascal regularly watch the heavens.

On the night of the attack, I met Louis at the bottom of the tower steps. He was on his way to fetch Pascal so that he might come and view an interesting celestial formation. I climbed the stairs, and, on reaching the roof, I bent over the telescope to make some adjustments. Eventually, everything came into focus, and I watched the heavens for five minutes or more. Then I felt strong hands around my neck that tightened so quickly, I could not utter a sound. Just before I passed out, I heard Father Louis singing as he climbed the stairs, and I think he called my name.'

8

LUKE SOFTENED HIS APPROACH. 'DID you see your attacker? Did he say anything? Did he smell unusual? Were there any clues that might help identify him?'

'No, but the incident is a mystery. When Father Louis reached the roof of the tower, he saw nobody. Eventually, he noticed some clothes placed precariously across the parapet. I was that bundle of clothes. Someone had lifted me onto the wall with the intent of pushing me off. But there was no one on the roof, and Father Louis did not pass anybody on the stairs.

I explained to my husband in the presence of Father Louis what had happened. Henri was sceptical until he saw my throat and neck. The bruises inflicted by my attacker were pronounced. Because of the mysterious disappearance of my attacker, Henri asked Father Louis and me not to mention it until a plausible explanation could be devised.'

Luke was alerted. This reaction to a crisis seemed characteristic of the marquis—a conspiracy of silence followed by a lie.

Next morning, Luke went to the tower. He climbed the circular staircase that was only wide enough for one person at a time. If Father Louis was to be believed, no one left the roof by the stairs. Luke moved out onto the wall. Neither could the attacker have descended the outside of the wall, unless he had a ladder or grappling gear. The mortar covered the complete gap between the stones, providing no indentations into which a person could safely place his foot. Nor were there vines of any type on the wall that might aid a descent.

Luke was perplexed. His mind wandered. He idly watched the stable boys deposit a load of straw and horse manure outside the stable doors, which were adjacent to the foot of the tower. Lost in reverie, he did not immediately notice how high and wide the pile of stable waste had become.

He was jolted back to reality by the voice of Pascal. 'How goes your investigation of her ladyship's alleged attack?'

'You doubting Thomas! I am inclined to believe her story.'

'Rubbish! It can only be true if she was attacked by Father Louis—there was no one else in the tower at the time,' Pascal riposted with obvious delight.

Luke scrambled onto the thick wall and stood upright peering at the growing pile of manured straw that lay below. 'If I was not recovering from a leg injury, I would show you how Lady Charlotte's assailant escaped before Louis arrived. Any able-bodied person could jump off the tower into a huge pile of stable waste and escape injury.'

Luke made as if to jump and convinced himself that it was the explanation and asked half jokingly, 'Did anybody come to the table that evening smelling of horse manure?'

'Lady Charlotte's adventure took place after supper, so the household did not gather as a group until after noon the following day,' Pascal replied.

Luke left to find Father Louis. He discovered the priest on his knees in front of the altar in the estate's tiny chapel. Luke knew from his discussions with Pascal and Charlotte that Louis was born into an aristocratic family in southeast France, close to the Italian border. He became a hardworking parish priest and after a trip to Rome, joined one of the new pious moralistic confraternities of clergy dedicated to the reformation of the priesthood. His family knew Philippe Rousset who recommended Louis to Henri following the death of the marquis's elderly chaplain.

Father Louis had curly dark brown hair that did not reach his shoulders. His tall stature and inordinately long arms and legs highlighted his moonlike face. He had an olive complexion and seemed to wear a permanently serene expression, which bordered on astonishment. He was dressed as the more frugal clergy in a black coat moderated by a very narrow, white lace collar. Luke irreverently pictured him as a black spider.

When he replied to Luke's questioning, he did so with a slight stutter. Father Louis completely confirmed Charlotte's account. He had returned to the tower and, calling to Charlotte, received no answer. On reaching the roof, he took some time to realise that the discarded clothing on the parapet was her unconscious body draped in the most precarious position on the edge of the wall. Louis confirmed the frightful bruises around her neck. He was most relieved when Luke suggested that there could have been a man on the roof who had escaped by jumping into a large pile of stable waste.

Luke then asked, 'Who might wish to kill Charlotte?' Louis became inexplicably agitated. 'I cannot betray the confessional.' 'Don't play games with me, priest! As chaplain, you are privy to a lot of information that is not derived from the confessional. I repeat, who might wish to harm Lady Charlotte?'

Louis began to sweat and his initial attempts to reply were curtailed by an involuntary stammer. Eventually, he regained his composure and admitted, 'Some members of the household do not respect or like Lady Charlotte. I only arrived three years ago, and the established senior servants, especially Pascal, constantly compared the staid English widow unfavourably with the charismatic first marquise.

When Philippe returned here, he initially expressed a similar view. However, in the past month or so, Mathieu and Philippe seem to have modified their attitudes, although Pascal is still openly contemptuous. He is convinced that the claims of a murderous assault on Lady Charlotte are false, despite my description of the bruises around her ladyship's neck. He sees the allegation as an attempt by her to gain sympathy and place herself on the same pedestal enjoyed by Lady Antoinette. Did your revelations regarding the pile of straw finally convince him that Lady Charlotte and I were telling the truth?'

'Hopefully, but why does Pascal feel so strongly that he would wish to discredit Lady Charlotte?' 'I do not wish to speak ill of the dead, but, from what I have gleaned over the years, Lady Antoinette was a wanton woman and, so far had the Marquis moved away from God's house that he accepted her notorious behaviour. There were rumours, at the time, that she had taken her son's tutor as a lover. That tutor was Pascal de Foix.'

'I know that, but I do not see the connection. Just because Pascal was a lover of the late marquise, why should that lead him to denigrate her successor?' Louis was quiet for some time. He concluded, 'In his eyes, she is not a worthy successor to Lady Antoinette, and, while he would quite openly discredit her, he has no reason to wish her dead.'

'Then how do you explain the attack?' 'Charlotte is not the primary target. Whoever is trying to kill her is doing it to punish his lordship. The deranged Alain is the most likely culprit. I visited him once when I was a parish priest in southeastern France. He is a very disturbed, violent, and dangerous character. He has much greater reason than Pascal or other members of the household to attack the woman who replaced his mother and an overwhelming reason to punish his father by depriving Henri of his latest love.'

'What about Philippe and Mathieu?' 'Philippe who fought with my uncle in the recent rebellion and who obtained this position for me, speaks very tenderly of Lady Antoinette. But, anything I say about him, you will probably discount. However, Mathieu and Lady Charlotte have become much closer in very recent times.'

Luke was slightly annoyed, 'Are you suggesting that the current marquise is adopting the same attitude towards men as her predecessor? Does Henri continue to be the cuckold?'

'I have said enough,' replied Louis who fell to his knees and prayed aloud, rudely ignoring Luke's attempts to continue the interrogation. Luke reluctantly left the chapel furious with the clerical snub.

The Chateau des Anges was not the harmonious household that he had first believed. He must next confront the man who had harboured and then employed him. Henri's role appeared critical.

Luke retired to the hunting lodge and pondered the answers given by the moralistic but gossipy priest. The only achievement of his investigation so far was the plausible proposition that Charlotte had indeed been attacked and that her assailant had jumped from the tower onto soft stable waste.

Luke poured himself a glass of Bordeaux red. There was a loud knock on the door. Pascal entered, smiling like the proverbial cream-swallowing cat. 'How was your discussion with the nefarious priest? He, no doubt, filled your head with numerous suspects while claiming the moral high ground for himself and his patron, Philippe.'

'He certainly knows more than he is revealing and is ready to fall back on the confidentiality of the confessional to keep his secrets, but, fortunately, his gossipy nature provided some useful facts. He suggested that the attacks on Charlotte were a means of punishing Henri for his treatment of his first wife.'

Pascal was dismissive. 'Ignore the wild ravings of a dangerous priest, who, if he had his way, would introduce a Spanish style inquisition into France and try the rest of us as heretics! Do not trust him. Since he arrived a few years ago, the atmosphere of the chateau is less pleasant. People are tense, and Henri has receded into his shell.

And Philippe, now that he is back on the scene after a decade's absence, also wants to throw his weight around. Despite their denials, he and Mathieu suddenly wish to cultivate Lady Charlotte's favour.'

'I am glad of your visit, but I suspect you have come to tell me something important.' 'Yes, and you will not like it. Stop your investigation of the alleged attacks on Lady Charlotte. There was no such attack. Your explanation of the assailant jumping off the tower into the pile of horse manure seemed plausible. I had one of the stable boys do it this afternoon with no ill effects. It became part of a game with the stable boys trying to outdo each other with their leaping.

Mathieu, who was passing by, ordered the boys back to work and sought from me an explanation of what was happening. He, too, was quite impressed by your logical explanation of the would-be killer's escape. He asked me when the attempt had taken place. He was silent for some time and then uttered several oaths. Then he pronounced your explanation invalid.'

'What do you mean, invalid?' 'For a week or so, either side of the alleged assault, the stables near the tower were under repair and all the horses there were removed to another location. There were no horses; therefore, no manured straw in the stables and no pile of it placed under the tower. If anybody jumped from the tower that evening, his lifeless body would have been found on the hard cobblestones below. Either Lady Charlotte was never attacked, or the assailant was the only other person in the tower—Father Louis.'

9

Luke now assumed that Henri and Charlotte, with Father Louis's connivance, had created this fiction. But why was he asked to investigate a nonevent? Was it a test by Henri to assess Luke's investigative abilities for a much more serious task? Or was it a clever ploy to discover how much an outsider could discover about any deeply hidden secrets concerning the Chateau des Anges? Or, more simply, was it a way to keep him occupied? None of these possibilities pleased him. After a few minutes of contemplation and indecision, he reluctantly decided to continue his investigation despite these doubts as to its purpose. He would talk to Philippe.

From the beginning, Philippe oozed resentment against Mathieu. His answer to every question was to deflect the blame or responsibility on to Mathieu, whom he refused to recognise except as Gillot. The steward had too much influence over both the marquis and his wife. The attack on Charlotte was staged to bring much-needed glory to Gillot. Philippe alleged that Charlotte pretended to be attacked, and Gillot was to arrive and rescue the damsel in distress. Morel's unexpected presence in the tower prevented the heroic deed.

'Why would Mathieu plan such a charade with or without the Marquise's compliance?' asked a cynical Luke. Philippe's vitriol continued, 'Henri is starting to believe the accusations that I have levelled against this trumped-up lawyer. The staged rescue of Lady Charlotte would regain Henri's trust for this pathetic bourgeois.'

Luke changed the direction of the discussion. 'You recommended Father Louis for the position of chaplain?'

'Colonel, you know my ancestry. I am one of the many illegitimate sons of the great Prince of Condé. When I became of age, the prince bestowed on me numerous estates in the southeast from which I take many titles. Long established aristocratic dynasties hold many of these estates as my tenants. One such family is the Morels. My father asked me to keep an eye on young Louis and ensure that he had a proper education. He became a priest and did an excellent job in the parishes of my estates—until he went to Rome.'

'What happened in Rome?' asked Luke. 'The experience turned his mind. The easygoing parish priest changed into a moralistic monster, obsessed like your English Puritans with a desire to reform the behaviour and purify the thoughts of all his parishioners, including mine.

Rural life does not need to be distracted by such obsessions. My tenants approached me to remove this troublesome priest who interfered constantly in the relationship between man and wife, even preaching that beating one's wife was against God's Word.

The death of Henri's chaplain provided a ready answer to my prayers. Father Louis can do little harm on this estate and could, as chaplain, also to the Abbey des Anges, direct his obsessions to the equally puritanical nuns in the Abbey.'

Luke muttered, 'A fanatic is never harmless. Some of the servants believe he is the person who attacked Lady Charlotte.'

'Rubbish! Louis is a moralistic prig and obsessed with personal reformation, but he is no assailant. Have you seen the man? He is a thin beanpole with no strength in his spindly arms or legs. As a child, he was a sickly lad. That is why he was directed into the church and not the army. Even Charlotte would have been able to fight him off.'

'So what happened on the roof of the tower?'

'Charlotte half choked herself to leave marks around her neck, clambered on to the parapet with half her clothes draping over the edge, and feigned unconsciousness waiting for Gillot to come and despatch the nonexistent attacker. When Morel arrived instead she used him to confirm to all that someone had tried to murder her. Do you have a better explanation?'

Luke had to agree with Philippe that Louis would have had great physical difficulty in attacking Charlotte. He lacked strength. Sadly, Pascal was right. If Louis did not attack Charlotte, then there was no attack. The Marquis and Marquise des Anges were playing games with him. He would seek an appointment with Charlotte for the following day. In the interim, he would, nevertheless, complete his questioning of Philippe.

'I understand you knew the first Marquise, the Lady Antoinette?'

'Yes. Undoubtedly, you would have heard that, like many males at the time, I had an affair with her. Unlike her affairs with other men, ours was not complicated by love or romance. You're a soldier, Tremayne. You understand the role of these casual liaisons for a soldier at war. All of the time that I knew Antoinette, I was fighting the Austrians and the Spaniards. Antoinette enjoyed my brief visits home from the front. She was bored by foppish courtiers and contrived love affairs. I gave her a real man.'

'How did you reconcile this with your friendship with Henri?'

'Henri, once he had sired an heir, lost interest in women. He preferred that a friend such as myself satisfy his wife, rather than the aristocratic and bourgeois riffraff who were attracted by Antoinette's charm.'

'Did she ever name the lovers who created problems?'

'She denied that she had any problems with the lovers drawn from Rouen or Paris society. She certainly regretted her involvement with men associated with the Chateau des Anges. Her affair with Pascal de Foix was over before I knew her, and he became and remained a very close and loyal but obsessive friend. She had problems with a lawyer, a tall young man who took the relationship too seriously.'

'Don't tell me it was Mathieu Gillot.' 'Precisely! Gillot probably murdered her after she threw him over for the latest man in her life. Gillot controls the forests and its inhabitants. He could have easily arranged for the wild boar to be herded into the right place and goaded into a fury. He could have enticed Antoinette to the hunting lodge, where you are currently living, by pretending her latest lover was waiting for her and then forced her into the woods where she was killed.'

'Come, Philippe, your tale does not ring true. If you were close to Henri and held these views, why did you not convince him of their validity at the time or inform the authorities yourself?'

'I told Henri that Gillot was the prime suspect and that the magistrates should investigate his role. But it is not in the makeup of the high aristocratic families such as the St. Michels to refer family matters outside the family circle. I am absolutely amazed that he asked you, an outsider in so many ways, to probe these sensitive matters.

Henri told me that Gillot had an alibi, although he did not tell me the details. The matter was to be dropped, and the official version of events was to be publicly supported by all associated with the Chateau des Anges.'

'If Gillot is guilty, why have you done nothing in the last ten years to bring him to justice or at least destroy his influence over Henri?'

'I only resumed my regular acquaintance with the Chateau des Anges three months ago, although I wrote to Henri several times a year. I spent most of the forties on the frontiers of France, fighting Spain and for the last five years on my southern estates, inciting Frondeur and Huguenot activity.

As Pascal has probably told you, I initially joined the revolt of the nobles, led by my half brother, the current Prince of Condé, against Cardinal Mazarin and Ann, the Queen Regent. I commanded many of the lesser nobles of southern France in this attempt to destroy the influence of the Italian cardinal.'

'Why did you change sides so dramatically and reconcile yourself with Queen Ann and the hated Mazarin in recent months?'

'When our leading general, Marshal Turenne, changed sides and began to rally the senior nobles around the symbol of the young King Louis XIV, the revolt of the Fronde was dead. Only my obstinate half brother holds out and has now foolishly offered his services to the king of Spain.

I am no fool. Any ambitious nobleman would make peace with a government heading for unconditional victory. This I did, and, because of my Bourbon blood, the Queen asked me to carry out several delicate missions to heal the wounds of the civil war. A personal vendetta against an upstart lawyer did not have a high priority. I did not visit the Chateau des Anges from the death of Lady Antoinette until my appointment to the Rouen garrison three months ago.

Since my return, I hoped that Louis might use his role as chaplain to uncover evidence against Gillot, which I might use to discredit him. Unfortunately, our high-minded priest claims the confidentiality of the confessional and refuses to indict Gillot of any crime. Instead, my protégé, Father Louis, has little time for me. He upbraids my whoring, heavy drinking, and, generally, my military lifestyle. A priest with religion is a dangerous animal.'

'Will you now be a regular guest here?' asked Luke concerned for the harmony of the household. 'No. Apart from my routine garrison duties, I can be called on at any time to undertake a mission for Queen Anne or for young Louis himself. I will not be here long enough to undermine Gillot's standing with the marquis and the marquise. You should take up that role!'

Luke ignored the suggestion and continued his interrogation, 'Ten years ago, did you ever entertain the thought that Henri himself had ordered his wife's murder? Cuckolded husbands, no matter how outwardly accepting of the situation, must harbour resentment or even hatred towards the men who create their humiliating situation?'

'Ah, Colonel, you reveal the prejudices of an Englishman—and of a lesser gentleman. The French higher aristocracy do not hold the same moral objection to such behaviour as your countrymen. As far as Henri was concerned, Antoinette had done her duty in bearing him a son and heir. Her role in his life was finished.

It is surprising they continued to live together at the same location for another fourteen years. Most aristocrats would have sent a wayward wife to another of their estates—as far away as possible. Henri's problem was that he quite enjoyed his wife's company and the social circle she gathered around her. If he was deranged by his wife's activities, why wait over a decade to do something about it? No, Henri was not responsible for Antoinette's death.'

'Think again, Philippe. In reality, Antoinette had not fulfilled her duty. Alain, given his mental abnormalities, could never assume the position of marquis. Henri desperately needed a new heir. And if

Antoinette was too old, then he needed a new and younger wife. The marquis had a very pressing reason to kill Antoinette.'

Philippe looked genuinely shocked at the suggestion and eventually retorted, 'I cannot agree.'

Luke changed the subject, 'As soldier to soldier, is Charlotte following in the footsteps of her predecessor?'

'What do you mean—as a potential murder victim or as an adulteress?' 'Both.'

'Charlotte has never been popular within the household. She would be lonely. Maybe Gillot took advantage of the situation and tried to become her lover. Although Charlotte is a Catholic, she exhibits some of the moral austerity and convictions of your English Puritan. Gillot may be very interested, but he would meet strong resistance.'

A big smile spread across Philippe's face as he gleefully announced, 'I have solved both your problems. Charlotte was attacked by Gillot, for the same reason that he murdered Lady Antoinette so long ago—rejection by the object of his lust.'

'Enough, Philippe, you are not taking this seriously. With one breath, you assert that Gillot has aided Charlotte in her charade, and, in the next, you allege that he is the would-be murderer.' Philippe simply smiled and walked away. He was very pleased with himself.

10

MATHIEU MET LUKE AT THE hunting lodge arriving with quivers of arrows and two English-type longbows. 'I thought we might do a bit of hunting as we walked and talked.' Luke knew little of archery. Warfare had long dispensed with bowmen in favour of musketeers. Archery only survived as a hunting option for the upper classes.

Luke would not to be diverted from his inquisitorial mission. He took his bow and arrows without comment and asked, 'Your enemies describe you as a menial gamekeeper, a merciless bailiff enforcing discipline and exacting fines and rents or a conniving and corrupt lawyer looking after yourself at the expense of the marquis and marquise. Your supporters praise you as an efficient and loyal manager of the St. Michel estates. How do you see yourself?'

'I can name from that catalogue of characteristics to who you have been talking. Unlike you English, we French simply pile responsibilities and titles on top of each other. I am all of the things you list without the negative accretions added by my opponents.

In England, you would call me steward. I am responsible for the financial and legal well-being of the marquis and marquise and for the administration of Henri's judicial responsibilities on several estates. My enjoyment of the minor role of head gamekeeper was a special perquisite I sought from Henri's father when he first appointed me as the family's lawyer. I enjoy the outdoors life and physical activity. It keeps me in touch with the peasants who inhabit the forest hamlets which in turn keeps me sane in what, from time to time, can be a very dysfunctional environment.'

'Such as now?' queried Luke.

'You are very perceptive for an Englishman.'

'No, just persistent,' replied a serious Luke. 'And I have had plenty of time on my hands while I recovered. Thank you for saving my life. I was very lucky that you arrived when you did.'

'No luck involved, Colonel. One of my men followed you from the moment you entered the forest. Unfortunately, the other intruder, much further north, was not found.'

'Do you know anything of my partner?' asked a hopeful Luke.

'My men have examined the area and questioned the neighbouring hamlets. For some reason your friend and a local peasant came into conflict. One of them died, and the other decapitated the body, buried the head, and threw the torso into the Seine. He then left the area. Your partner and a peasant are missing—one is dead.'

Mathieu pointed to some dry leaves under a large oak tree. Luke removed his cloak, placed it on the ground, and sat with his back against the tree. Mathieu settled on a fallen trunk of what had been a gigantic beech. Luke asked with some intensity, 'Who is trying to kill Charlotte?'

Mathieu smiled, 'You have not asked the logical first question, which Pascal has undoubtedly raised. Is anybody trying to kill Charlotte? To which I would answer, I do not know.'

Luke quickly responded, 'You too have doubts about the story that the marquis has advanced? Why would he lie and then ask me to investigate it? Does he think I am an idiot?'

Mathieu smiled again, 'Charlotte certainly had severe abrasions around the neck, but I suspect they were caused in embarrassing circumstances that Henri wishes to cover up by his fiction.' 'Such as?' 'Ever since I have known Henri, he has stumbled from one cover-up to another. His attempt to cover up the circumstance of Lady Antoinette's death was a major mistake and has now returned to haunt him. His inclusion of that disaster in your brief surprised me.'

Luke would not be side tracked, 'I'll come to the case of Lady Antoinette later, but, first, in what other ways could Charlotte receive extensive bruising around her neck?'

'Don't be naive! There are two possibilities that his lordship would want to conceal. Despite his relaxed demeanour, Henri has a fierce temper when pushed too far. He could have inflicted those bruises on Charlotte during some domestic squabble—and these do occur.'

'So Henri has a temper?'

'He is very slow to anger, but, on few occasions, he has completely lost it. These episodes are rare, but when they happen, they are frightening.'

'Strange, no one else has raised this issue. It could be crucial to both investigations. What is the other explanation?' Mathieu rose from the beech trunk and sat beside Luke. He was silent for some time in which he annoyingly flicked at the leaves with a long stick. Eventually, he half whispered in a faltering voice, 'Charlotte may have attempted to hang herself.'

Luke was taken aback. He had not considered such a possibility. It was now his turn to be silent. He then asked the obvious question, 'Is Charlotte depressed enough to take her own life?'

'As an Englishwoman and a replacement for Antoinette, Charlotte has not been well received by the household. She is subject to continual ridicule by Father Louis, Pascal, and Philippe—all out of Henri's hearing but evident to their victim. Sadly, Henri is not the understanding person that Charlotte needs in such a situation.'

'But you are?' asked Luke provocatively.

'You have been listening to the innuendos of the evil three I have just named. Yes, I have become closer to Charlotte, which has sent the devilish trio into fits of jealousy and outbursts of petty spite. I am sure that Father Louis and Viscount Rousset are trying to inveigle her ladyship into some inappropriate action, which they could then report to his lordship. Maybe the bruises around Charlotte's neck were the result of such inappropriate behaviour; after which, Henri has chosen to stand by his wife, rather than believe the lies of that treacherous triumvirate.'

Luke was surprised at the bitterness of Mathieu's attitude to the other senior members of the household. He moved on to the second part of his interrogation. 'Tell me all you know regarding the death of Lady Antoinette!'

'I have held my peace for ten years, but if the authorities are out to denigrate Henri and accuse him of murder, then the crazy cover-up of a boar attack must be swept away, although it will be difficult after all this time for you or the authorities to find any concrete evidence on the matter.'

'What really happened? At the time of her death, was there not considerable antagonism between Antoinette and yourself?'

'Yes, she hated me intensely. She did everything to obtain my dismissal, including spreading a false story that I had an affair with her.'

'Why did she hate you?'

'She was on a continual spending spree, demanding more and more money. As steward, I allocated a generous amount each year for her whims. When I refused to give her more, she attempted to seduce me, which I rejected. I offended her in the two areas she considered the basis of her life—her ability to seduce men and the unlimited funds she needed to dazzle Parisian salons and the Royal Court.'

'What happened on the day of her death?'

'I was at the far end of the forest. Around midday, I was surprised to be found by a servant who gave me a letter. It was from Antoinette wishing to improve our relations. At sunset, she would visit the hunting lodge where I then lived. I saw this as yet another trick by her to tempt or bribe me into releasing more funds for her enjoyment. I deliberately delayed my arrival. She could wait for me. I therefore arrived home half an hour after sunset.'

Luke was transfixed. Mathieu continued, 'I entered the lodge and found Antoinette clothed only in a chiffon chemise. She was stretched on her back in the middle of my bed. Her body and the bed were covered in blood, which congealed around multiple stab wounds. Some attempt had been made to clean up both the body and its surroundings.

I called for my servants. No one came. I later discovered that they had received an order, purporting to come from me, to gather at sunset at the servant's entrance to the chateau. I sent no such letter.

Antoinette was dead, the victim of multiple stab wounds. The wounds indicated that she was the victim of a frenzied attack. My first thought was to run to the chateau and inform Henri. I had second thoughts and decided to clean away the remaining blood, and, at least, give her some dignity. Then I saw it. Clasped in her closed hand was a crumpled letter.'

'Did it explain the situation?' asked a fascinated Luke.

'It completely altered my perception of this catastrophic event and sent warning bells through my brain. The letter, purporting to have come from me, invited her ladyship to the lodge just before sunset and suggested that we might use the occasion to settle our differences. Whoever murdered Antoinette was trying to pin the crime on me.

I cleaned the body and my blood-splattered room. I dressed her ladyship and carried her into the forest. I laid her beside a tree. I then went to find Henri.'

'How did he react?'

'He was surprisingly calm. I explained what I had done, and he appeared grateful. I have never thought that he murdered his wayward wife. In fact, he gave me information that suggested a conspiracy to involve Antoinette, Henri, and myself.

He, too, had received a letter suggesting that if he visited the hunting lodge at sunset he might discover something to his advantage. He forgot—an endearing characteristic of the marquis. He was temporarily overcome with guilt believing that if he had gone to the hunting lodge, he may have prevented the tragedy. Does this clarify the position?'

'The opposite. It complicates everything. Your story could be the perfect cover for your own involvement in the murder. You get rid of your servants for the night, kill Antoinette, and then rearrange the situation to protect your interests. Did you keep the letters?'

'No, but I did examine and compare them. They were all in the same hand and taken from material that Pascal kept in his schoolroom. The writing was not his, but I suspect he recognised the source. He visibly flinched when I showed it to him. Someone in the household or someone Pascal had taught was responsible. My enquiries ended when Henri decreed the official account of the boar attack and forbade any further comment or investigation.'

'What then is your explanation of Antoinette's murder, especially in the current circumstances when Henri wants the issue revisited, and some unknown person is inciting the authorities to intervene and question Henri as the possible murderer?'

'I know five facts. Antoinette was murdered. It was a crime of passion—there was no need to inflict fourteen stab wounds on a body that ceased to breathe after the first two penetrated her heart. Henri did not kill her. I did not kill her. It was part of a conspiracy to destroy Antoinette, possibly Henri and myself. Find the person who passionately hated all three of us, and you will have your murderer.'

Luke liked Mathieu, but could he be believed? Was his last comment an attempt to direct Luke's investigation toward Pascal and Philippe?

The two men simultaneously felt that there had been enough talk. Both rose, picked up their bows, and each removed an arrow from his quiver. Mathieu pointed towards a narrow path that led deep into the woods. Luke followed him hoping to confront a deer or rabbit.

Suddenly, he began to shake. Panic set in. He felt completely defenceless against an illusionary rampaging boar. Bad memories overwhelmed him. Mathieu assessed the situation immediately, and the two men returned quickly to the chateau where the steward administered a large brandy to a shivering Luke, who took some time to recover his composure.

11

TWO OTHER MEMBERS OF THE household had known Antoinette—Josette St. Michel and Odette Bonnet. According to Pascal, Josette had married a much-older man and, on her wedding night, had an adulterous affair. This led to the immediate annulment of the marriage.

Her father dispatched the then twenty-three-year-old to the family abbey on the northern edge of the estate. Fortunately, when her half brother, Henri, succeeded to the marquisate, he offered her accommodation at the Chateau des Anges. He gave her use of a wing of the extensive complex where she created a separate establishment but took supper with the larger household two or three times a week.

Luke sought a meeting with Lady Josette who invited him to dine in her apartment the following noon. Luke had not been to this part of the chateau. He was astonished at its opulence. Either Henri (and the usually frugal Mathieu) had been exceedingly generous or Josette had additional sources of income. In comparison, Henri and Charlotte lived in a relatively unadorned section of the rambling building. Josette's servants even wore a livery quite distinct from those of the marquis.

Ushered into the entrance hall, Luke was immediately joined by his hostess. She was a striking beauty and looked ten years younger than her chronological age, which Luke accurately estimated as in the early forties.

She had bright blue eyes that rivalled Luke's, separated by a long straight nose and small tight lips. Her face tapered to a pointed chin. Her appearance was dominated by her excessively long and tightly curled strawberry blond hair, which was partly controlled by an excess of ribbons. The ribbons were of deep azure blue, which blended into the similar hue of her bodice and skirt.

Her bodice was low cut, revealing almost half of her more-than-ample breasts. Her skirt was partially open at the front displaying the lighter blue of her silken underskirt. This was a very attractive woman who had set out to impress her English inquisitor.

Her personality proved equally attractive. Over a splendid meal, Josette revealed an outgoing, warm, amiable, and affectionate personality that concealed a resourceful self-reliance. She was a show-off and began to use her charms to confuse Luke. Any chance of a clinical analytical interrogation was sidetracked by Josette's flirtatiousness and diverting ploys.

Eventually, the combination of fine wine and pleasant company relaxed both parties. It was Josette who brought this pleasant interlude to an end. 'I am sorry for my frivolous approach. It is not often that I have an attractive man to myself. Please ask me what you will—and I promise to be serious.'

'Henri has asked me to look into the murder of his first wife and the attempts on the life of his second. Do you have any comments to make on either problem?'

'Luke, you are no fool. Doesn't it surprise you that my brother asked a stranger and a foreigner whom he hardly knows to uncover a family skeleton—a skeleton he has spent most of his life trying to keep buried. Why suddenly resurrect a painful incident ten years after the event, especially given the stratagems he adopted to conceal the truth from the authorities at the time?'

'You do not accept your brother's desire to clear his name before the authorities reinvestigate the case?'

'Your question assumes a premise I do not accept. Where is the evidence that the authorities are about to reopen the case? And what authorities are involved? Henri dominates the local magistrates, and Queen Anne has always been a friend. Look closer to home! This unsubstantiated fear has been introduced into my brother's mind by Philippe—a devious bastard aristocrat, who has now lied his way into the confidence of Ann, Queen Mother of France, as he had earlier into the camp of her archenemies, the great nobles of the Fronde.

I have never understood my brother's relationship with Philippe, Viscount Rousset. My brother has no worries regarding Antoinette's murder. I have absolute proof that he is innocent.'

'And what is that proof, my lady?'

'When my brother's life is really threatened, I will tell all. At the moment, I remain silent. I owe my brother a lot. Without his intervention, I would be rotting away in a Spanish convent. He persuaded father instead to banish me across the forest to our then-relaxed Benedictine abbey, which the family has supported for centuries; and when father died, Henri has been exceedingly generous in allowing me use of a large part of the chateau. I will defend him to the end. Nevertheless, I will help you isolate the malevolent forces within the chateau that I believe are undermining him. The attempts on Charlotte are part of a campaign to destroy Henri.'

'So, you believe Charlotte was attacked?'

'I saw the bruises around her throat.'

Luke took a deep breath. 'Thank you, Josette. I will return to Charlotte later. Were you close to Antoinette?' Luke was taken aback. The carefree relaxed attitude of Josette disappeared. Tears welled up and ran down her face. When she spoke, her words were muffled, and her exposition was constantly interrupted as she incessantly blew her nose and wiped her eyes.

'Antoinette and I were the closest of friends for seven or eight years. From the time I arrived here at the end of 1635 until her death, we were always together. She spent more time with me than with Henri or any of her alleged string of lovers. We were the centre of Rouen and Parisian society. They were marvellous times.'

'You were each other confidantes?'

'We were as sisters and knew more about each other than anybody else.'

'In the months before her death, did anything occur that alarmed Antoinette or give any hint that her life might be in danger?'

'She was constantly annoyed by and with the men of the household. She detested Philippe. He could not accept that she had put an end to their relationship. She felt suffocated by Pascal's devoted service, which she saw quite rightly as a sublimated form of an overwrought obsession with her. And she and I loathed Mathieu's curtailment of our expenses. He did, and still does, believe in that bourgeois heresy that money is to be saved. He has never understood that being an aristocrat obliges you to spend.'

'He could not have been too mean. Your apartment must have cost a fortune to renovate and to maintain.'

Colour had returned to Josette's cheeks, and her eyes sparkled as she recalled her days with Antoinette. 'Antoinette and I had other sources of income that were poured into this wing of the chateau.'

'Without wishing to cause you offence, did you offer Antoinette rooms in your apartment to entertain her lovers?'

'Yes, my apartment was an oasis in the desert, cut off from the surrounding world and whose secrets were closely guarded by my personally selected servants.'

'Josette, you aided and abetted Antoinette in adulterous affairs that made your own brother a cuckold countless times over. How could you do that to Henri?'

'Ah, you are an English Puritan. Antoinette had given Henri a son and heir. There needed to be no more to their relationship. Most men in Henri's position sent their wives away to a distant estate and never saw them again. Henri wanted Antoinette close by—and her use of my apartment prevented it becoming a stifling relationship for both parties.'

'Just before her death were there any strange developments?'

'Yes, there was a growing problem. About a year before her death, she returned from a month or two in Paris and appeared very troubled. She told me that she had seen, at a distance, at the Palais Royal, a figure from her past. She appeared quite shaken. A month or two later, she thought she had seen him again in the market square of Rouen.'

'Do you know who it was?'

'No, but a far more serious and pressing development was the growing obsession of her son Alain. He began to follow her everywhere and seemed embittered towards any men that she attracted. Pascal de Foix had to imprison the boy in the schoolroom many a day to allow Antoinette to lead a normal life. In the end, my servants were given orders to prevent him entering my apartment.'

'Did either of these developments contribute to her death?'

Josette avoided a direct response. 'Antoinette led a dangerous life. She had affairs with many important people, including Princes of the Blood, leading generals, and even churchmen. She expected something in return, and most of her lovers showered her with gifts, many continuing their generosity long after the affair had ended. There was a pecuniary streak to Antoinette. At times when Gillot had cut off our funds, she would not hesitate to seek support from a former lover, who by this time may not have welcomed the request.'

'Antoinette, Marquise des Anges, blackmailed her former lovers?'

Josette just smiled as Luke continued, 'Then any one of these former lovers could have arranged her murder?' 'It is possible.' 'What about Alain? Could he have murdered his mother?' Josette appeared uncomfortable but decided to come clean. 'Alain was not right in the head. His growing obsession with his mother was a dangerous development, and if he had found her in bed with one of her lovers, he could have stabbed her to death in a blind frenzy.'

Josette's tone suddenly became confidential and she whispered, 'Henri believes Alain is the murderer. He covered up the circumstances of the death to protect his son. The boy's subsequent rampage through the hamlet gives weight to this theory. And, yes, the current attempts on Charlotte may be inspired by Alain, who has escaped from detention and for these past months, cannot be found.'

'Would any members of the household assist Alain in this campaign against my countrywoman?' 'No, Odette Bonnet, whom Henri says is our cousin for her own protection, only arrived here last year but has become Charlotte's friend. The males unfairly compare the current marquise unfavourably with her predecessor, although, recently, I have sensed tension between Philippe and Mathieu regarding her.'

'Are they having an affair with Charlotte?'

Josette giggled and looked seductively at Luke. 'She would not know how to conduct an affair—she is English. Mathieu seems genuinely sympathetic about her situation, but Pascal refuses to believe that she was attacked. Father Louis would be my suspect. He lived in the south of France most of his life a short distance away from where Alain was confined. They may have met and become friends. Louis was in the tower when Charlotte was attacked and is stronger than he looks. And he was appointed after Philippe wrote Henri a series of pleading letters.'

'Yes, it had to be Morel or nobody because he was the only one in the tower,' confessed Luke reluctantly.

Josette looked incredulously at him, and then a warm smile broke out as she realised she could impress Luke and give him a vital piece of information.

'Not so, Luke; it could have been anybody. The tower has a hidden staircase. When we were children, our grandfather showed us many secrets of the chateau—concealed passages in the main buildings and a second staircase in the tower. You can leave the tower using the open staircase or down a ladder concealed within the stonework.

The staircase compartment is a perfect circle. If you look at the tower from the outside, it is oval shaped. The difference hides a ladder by which you can ascend and descend without using the open staircase. Sadly, Colonel, this makes your task even harder. Anybody may have strangled Charlotte and escaped down the ladder as Father Louis climbed up the stairs.'

12

LUKE ENJOYED JOSETTE'S COMPANY BUT could hardly wait to follow up her information regarding the tower. Josette sensed his change of interest and offered to show him the tower's secret entrance. She gave him a taper from her dining hall so that he could light his way down the concealed ladder.

Josette found a small sculptured head of an angel in a niche near the top of the tower stairs. She twisted the statue and a stone at its base moved slightly. Luke pushed heavily against the loosened masonry. Gradually, the block slid inward, leaving a narrow slit into the darkness of the hidden part of the tower.

With the aid of the taper he could see there was a small platform on the other side. To fit through the narrow slit he had to remove his weapons and outer clothing. Once inside, he accidentally touched the door through which he had come—it shut fast.

He was now imprisoned. He looked around for the ladder that Josette had described, but there was no ladder. A sudden dread overcame him. Did his accidental knock force the door shut permanently? Could Josette reopen it? Could he escape?

These fears quickly evaporated. After examining the platform and the walls, Luke saw a series of steel rings for the hands and sculptured indents into the wall for the feet. Luke carefully and slowly made his way down the wall.

Eventually, he reached the bottom. Panic set in again. How would he get out? As he searched, something gleamed in the taper light. There, lying on the stone cobbles, was a silver button. It was not covered with dust. It had not been there long.

The only protruding item that might help release a hidden exit was the last iron ring of his descent. He found that it could be turned clockwise, and part of the wall moved inward. Luke pulled it further into the secret compartment. This created enough room for him to squeeze out—but not into the enclosed stairwell. He was in the garden.

Shrubs, many that were decidedly prickly, surrounded the base of the tower and concealed the hidden door. On one of the thorn bushes, he saw a torn piece of what he thought was fabric. Later Mathieu identified it as bear fur, an identification that was laughed at by Louis, Philippe, and Pascal.

Luke was jubilant. Charlotte had been attacked, and the assailant had escaped down the secret ladder, avoiding Father Louis as he climbed the stairs. He now had an irrefutable clue to the person's identity, a silver button, which was probably forced from a doublet as its owner tried to squeeze through the narrow exit.

Luke hoped to keep his discovery of an alternative way of ascending the tower a secret but Josette told Charlotte who summoned him the next day. 'Colonel, I hear that with Josette's assistance you have discovered a secret way of escaping the tower, which was undoubtedly the avenue taken by my attacker.'

'Yes, my lady! This removes any doubt that you were attacked. And it frees Morel from suspicion.' Luke did not mention the button but revealed that the hidden ladder had been recently used. There was little dust on some of the iron rings, and footprints were evident on the dusty floor.

Charlotte asked for an update of his investigations into the attacks on her and the murder of her predecessor. Luke replied truthfully. 'With the latest evidence, I will soon know who attacked you. As regards Antoinette, those of the household who knew her have given me conflicting opinions, but a consensus is beginning to emerge. The role of Philippe and Mathieu in both assaults interests me. They have tried to implicate each other. You have known both for some years. Who would you believe?'

'Mathieu. He has always treated me well. My demands on the estate's finances are so small compared with my predecessor that I immediately impressed him as a serious economic mistress of the Chateau des Anges. I have heard that he bullied and terrified Antoinette over her spendthrift ways, but I have never been subject to any reprimands. Indeed, over the last month or so, he has become a friend and confidant.'

'Nothing more?'

'Colonel, you forget yourself. Such a question is impertinent.'

'My lady, forgive my insensitivity, but I am sure much of the malaise that surrounds the chateau is related to the personal relationships of Antoinette and now yourself. If you were too friendly with Mathieu, that might be a motive for your husband or other jealous males to have you assaulted.'

'I can assure you, Colonel, that Mathieu Gillot and I are not, nor ever had been, lovers. One reason I found Mathieu good company was that before your arrival, he was the only member of the household, apart from the pedant de Foix, who spoke English.'

'What about Philippe?'

'I have known of him since my marriage, but I never met him until a few months ago, when he began to revisit the chateau. His life is dominated by his birth. Everybody has to know that he is an illegitimate son of a Prince of the Blood. He lives off and plays on this Bourbon heredity. He has used it to inveigle himself into highest society and to escape punishment for his treason to the Crown during the current revolt. In all, his role at Chateau des Anges and his relationship with Henri remains a mystery.

I do not know why Philippe inflicts himself on us, but Henri will not hear a word against him. Philippe's one open attribute is his dislike of Mathieu, which he does not hide from anyone. He would do anything to destroy Mathieu, including harming me.'

'You suspect Philippe?'

'I have no proof but he has a motive and he is physically a very powerful man.'

Something caught Luke's eye. The late afternoon sun picked up several silver buttons very similar to the one that he found in the tower. He noted, 'The sun is reflecting off the buttons of your bodice. What is the motif that they bear?'

'They are pure silver, and, in my case, as the marquise, each is etched with three angels. Henri, as the marquis has four; the heir, who is now young Paul, has two. The rest of the senior household wear silver buttons with one angel etched into them while the liveried servants have plain silver buttons.'

Luke was tempted to produce the button he had found and immediately count the number of angels it contained, but he resisted the temptation and asked, 'Do Philippe or Mathieu wear such buttons?'

'Mathieu, as steward of the estate, does, but Philippe would have no cause to wear our angelic buttons; and, on official occasions, his doublets include golden buttons befitting his princely pedigree; but, normally, he wears the common uniform of the garrison at Rouen—the gold and black livery of special units of the line.'

'Charlotte, I have talked to all the senior members of the household except for Odette Bonnet. Tell me about her!' 'Odette, has become a good friend. This is surprising as she is Antoinette's youngest sister. Henri gave her sanctuary here but pretends to the outside world she is a distant cousin. Her husband of over twenty years was a Protestant and a leader in the recent revolt against the young king and the Queen Mother. These rebels, with the help of Spain, controlled much of southern France and have only, in the last few months, been evicted from most of that area.

The Comte de Bonnet was defeated on the battlefield and, having been declared a traitor, was summarily executed. His estates were confiscated and his crops and buildings, razed to the ground. His children have disappeared.

Fortunately, his wife Odette was in Paris at the time of the tragedy. She came straight here. She hopes, in vain, I fear, that her children, three teenage sons, were spirited away to Spain or Italy by one of the family servants. I asked Philippe, given his vast possessions in the south of France and his one-time leadership of the rebels in the region, to help me locate the Bonnet boys. I don't think he has done anything.'

Luke was about to leave when Odette entered the room. She apologised for the intrusion and before he could respond, Charlotte announced, 'No, your arrival is well timed. Colonel Tremayne was about to seek you out and ask you a few questions regarding your sister. I must speak to the housekeeper regarding some unsatisfactory servants.'

Without further ado Charlotte left the room, and Odette sat on the richly padded sofa that the marquise had just vacated.

'Madame, can you comment on your sister's relationship with her husband? Did she write you letters, keeping you up to date with her life?' Luke was unprepared for the answer. 'Colonel, my sister was an obsessive writer of letters. She wrote to me weekly from the time of her marriage to that of her death because for most of that period, we were at the opposite ends of France.'

'So she wrote to you in the period leading up to her death?'

'Yes.'

'Did she seem worried?'

'Very much so! The letters were longer and were permeated by some unknown dread.'

'I suppose those letters were destroyed when your estates were razed.'

Odette's face beamed, as if she had just had a great victory. 'No, Colonel! I kept the letters of the last year of Antoinette's life and secured them in my brother's castle until quite recently. I brought them here with me as I thought Henri may wish to have them.'

Odette rose and whispered to Luke, 'I must leave now. Visit me tomorrow, and I will answer your questions in a more relaxed atmosphere.' Luke and Odette left the room together and went their separate ways.

Luke hurried back to the hunting lodge. The servants had already lit the candles. He entered his bedroom and removed the silver button from the pocket of his doublet. He was so excited that the button flicked from his hand and rolled across the floor. Luke casually fell on his knees expecting to find the button within seconds. It was nowhere to be found. Luke placed two candles on the floor beside him and, once again, carefully explored every inch of the surface.

Frustration set in. To be so close to indentifying Charlotte's assailant and, through carelessness, lose the only piece of solid evidence he had found was unforgivable. His only option was to wait until morning when he could search with the benefit of daylight. He would prepare for bed. He removed his boots and slipped his feet into a pair of ornate slippers.

His foot soon confronted a small stone like object in one of the slippers. A big smile transformed Luke's face. The stone was indeed the silver button that had bounced into his footwear.

He looked at the button carefully, not believing what he saw. Etched into the button were four small angels. This button had once been part of the clothing of Henri St. Michel, Marquis des Anges. Luke was shaken by the realisation of the implications of this discovery.

He poured himself a massive goblet of French brandy. Had Henri tried to murder his second wife, or had he only attempted to frighten her? If anyone in the chateau knew about the secret ladder, it would be someone who, as a child, was shown it by his father or grandfather. If his sister knew about it, it is probable that Henri did also. After several more brandies and thousands of random thoughts, a disconcerted Luke fell asleep in his chair.

13

CHARLES STUART QUICKLY ABSORBED THE court of his mother, Henriette Marie, into his own. Her attempt to isolate her ladies-in-waiting from the bevy of predatory males that had gathered around the young king failed completely.

The integration of these courts aided Harry's investigation. He mixed socially with the male courtiers, and his sudden conversion to gambling, worried his Puritan conscience but won him many new friends. His position as deputy to Ashcroft gave him some status, and his often-noticed private conversations with Charles created an air of mystery about his real identity.

A cut above the rest of his new acquaintances and a man who quickly became a close friend was a Catholic peer—Simon, Lord Stokey. Stokey had been a courtier since childhood. He was a pageboy to Queen Henriette Marie from 1627 to 1637.

In 1638, as a twenty-year-old, he inherited his title and became one of the queen's closest confidants. When the civil war broke out, the queen influenced her husband to appoint him the youngest major general in the Royalist army. He was defeated in the field in 1645, and the conditions of his surrender forbade him from taking up arms against the parliament.

The Queen sent him to Ireland and, later, as envoy to Spain and the Italian states to raise money for the Royalist cause. He lost faith in Charles I and followed Henriette into exile. When Charles II arrived in France and combined his court with that of Henriette, Simon, who admired the young monarch, transferred his basic loyalty to the new king and rather undiplomatically ignored the Queen Mother. Charles immediately put this experienced fundraiser and diplomat to work.

Harry invited Simon to his apartment for drinks and came quickly to the point. 'Simon, the king has asked me to look into the murder of Lucy Harman. You were close to the Queen Mother and her ladies for some years. Tell me about this unfortunate young girl!'

'Lucy was a naïve child, completely unsuited to court life. She knew nothing of the world. She spent her whole life in Spanish and French convents to which her father sent her during our civil conflict. I knew her quite well as I could speak both French and Spanish with her. Hardly anyone at this court can speak more than their English regional dialect as you have probably noticed.'

'Can you give me details of her death and the original investigation?'

'Yes, when I first transferred my allegiance from his mother, Charles gave me the position you now hold, as deputy to Lord Ashcroft. The body was found in her apartment with a single stab wound to the heart administered by a hatpin through her back, but there was no blood or any sign of a struggle.

Weeks later, a stable boy claimed he saw, on the night before the body was found, a group of four or five hooded men carry something into Lucy's apartment. He assumed it was a heavy piece of furniture. Further attempts to question the lad proved fruitless. He simply disappeared, probably murdered. Lord Ashcroft's investigation was stymied. There were no witnesses to either foul deed.'

'Lucy was killed elsewhere and her body brought home by a group of men. That is very strange. Why bring the body home? Why not drop it in the Seine? Was it mutilated?'

'No, apart from her scarred back, the result of self flagellation that she had learnt in those frightful Spanish convents, her body revealed nothing unusual except the tiny hatpin wound which was well hidden by her macerated back. It was badly infected. The poor child was in constant pain, which she relished as a sign of her piety and virtue.'

'Had she been raped?'

'No, the doctor that examined the body had no problem in affirming she had never known a man.'

'If she wasn't murdered to hide a sexual assault, why would anyone kill a naïve Christian child? Did you or Ashcroft have any theories?'

'Only the broadest of generalities! She must have seen something or somebody or knew unfavourable information about somebody. The only possible motive would have been to keep her quiet.'

'But what sort of deadly information could this religious isolate possibly discover?'

'My own guess is that she saw someone of importance visiting one of her fellow ladies-in-waiting that could have been devastating to both parties. Such activity, reported to Queen Henriette Marie, would have led to immediate dismissal of the woman concerned.

The single stab wound suggests that a woman may have been the murderer. She may have believed that by stabbing Lucy through the back, the scars and scabs of her self-flagellation would have concealed the entry wound. The body may have been returned to her apartment in the belief that any casual inspection of the corpse would have assumed that she had died from natural causes. She was a sick child.'

'Some think that Lucy Harman was an English republican spy?'

'Ridiculous; this innocent young girl knew nothing of politics—and she was a fanatical Catholic. Why would she support the atheistic extreme Protestants of the English Parliament?'

Harry decided he could confide in Simon, but he would slightly alter the facts to hide his sources. 'The king's spies in England have long been worried that Lord Harman, Lucy's father, and a leading Catholic was negotiating, not with the Parliament but with General Cromwell. He seeks to obtain a better deal for English Papists should the army come to power.

Young Lucy, as any devout Catholic daughter, would obey her father without question. She may not have realised what she was doing, and, in letters home to her father, she could have inadvertently passed on matters of interest to Cromwell and the army.'

Simon was quiet for a time and replied, 'I have been blind. You could well be right. I know Lord Harman very well and have suspected his loyalty for some time. Years ago, when the religious and secular treasures of English Catholics were gathered, I was unhappy that Harman was selected as their guardian. I am about to return to England for a family funeral and will enquire further into any possible connection between Lord Harman's political activities and the murder of his daughter. But I doubt that even Harman would have knowingly involved his own unwell daughter in such sordid events.'

Harry was thoughtful. The lack of any sexual abuse and the girl's strong moral character removed the most obvious motive for murder. Nevertheless, Lucy's attitude to men may have irritated or threatened the more lascivious lifestyle of her fellow ladies-in-waiting. Did any of them display hostility towards Lucy?

Next morning, he visited Catherine Beaumont and outlined everything he knew about Lucy's murder. He asked Cate whether she could add anything more to the information she had given him earlier. She was delighted to see Harry and called on her servants to bring refreshments.

'I am sorry Harry. I have not been able to glean much information from the other ladies. I suspect they have been encouraged not to talk to me. Perhaps my naming as an agent of General Cromwell is imminent. But two things might interest you—Mistress Elizabeth Mortimer was very evasive when I mentioned Lucy and the virtuous Lady Mary Gresham knows more than she pretended. Question both of them!'

Harry nodded as he devoured his favourite marzipan animals. Cate rose and retreated to her bedroom. Harry was confused. Was this a signal to which he should respond? He had almost overcome his Puritan sensibilities and was about to follow the vivacious Cate into her boudoir when she reappeared carrying a sheet of paper.

'Harry, I received a coded message from England earlier today and had not quite finished transcribing it when you arrived. There are specific instructions for you. I will read them out once, and then burn the paper as ordered.

Cromwell has dismissed Parliament and replaced it with an assembly of religious notables. You are to inform Charles Stuart that this is only a temporary measure to appease certain radical elements, but the final constitutional settlement of England will contain a monarchical element. You must convince Charles that, in the end, the army will be on his side.

You are to have your own codebook, but your messages home will be fiction, providing the Royal Court with what Cromwell wants them to read. Your code has been deliberately leaked to Lord Ashcroft. This will help cement your place at court. You will ignore all apparent instructions sent directly to you. Genuine instructions and information will come as in the past through me.'

Before Harry could read the coded message for himself, Cate consigned the paper to the fire and watched intently until it had been totally consumed. Harry was annoyed. He resented having to take orders through Cate, and he was unhappy that his newly created direct contact to Oliver Cromwell was to be nothing more than a clever piece of propaganda to keep Charles Stuart on side.

On the other hand, Harry was strongly attracted to Cate. He grabbed a number of smaller marzipans in preparation for his departure. Cate had other ideas. She kissed him passionately, took his hand, and led him into her bedroom.

Hours later he arrived back at the guardhouse where Simon awaited him in a highly agitated state. 'What is it Simon? You look very upset.'

'I am devastated. I have just returned with the king from a visit to the French Court. We expected to be received by Queen Anne who has always been sympathetic to Charles's request for money. Instead, we were sent like beggars across the courtyard to the Palais Royal and cooled our heels for hours before a lackey admitted us into the presence of Cardinal Mazarin.

Mazarin has recently returned from exile and is now clearly the real ruler of France. He had all sorts of excuses regarding his failure to offer a regular pension to our king. France already provided his mother with considerable sums, which Mazarin argued should be enough to cover all English exiles at the English Court. In addition,

France provided spacious accommodation in the Chateau St. Germain. Given recent troubles, the French king's treasury had very little to distribute.'

'Probably a reasonable approach,' said an unthinking Harry.

Simon could not stop his diatribe, which amounted to a string of insults against Frenchmen, Italians, cardinals, and other lesser mortals who did not treat Charles Stuart, rightful king of England, Scotland, and Ireland with respect.

'Harry, Mazarin won't help Charles because he wants to do a deal with the English Republic. We may all have to leave France.' Harry found himself surprisingly sympathetic, 'Where will we go? Most of Europe either recognizes the English Republic or will do nothing to provoke its rampaging military.'

Simon was crestfallen. 'To be blunt, no one wants us. The frown of fortune is directed totally in our direction. We can only pray that our luck will change and European governments recognise the potential danger to all of them of an English republic, especially one under the control of the army and the megalomaniac regicide, Oliver Cromwell.'

'How does Charles intend to respond?'

'The King and Lord Ashcroft will leave court in a few days. They will visit the United Provinces, the independent northern Netherlands, in the hope of raising funds.'

'You will get nothing out of the wealthy burghers of Amsterdam. They are pouring their wealth into building up an impressive armed merchant navy, which is currently more than a match for the English Republic. You might be more fortunate in dealing with the House of Orange that provides military leadership for the United Provinces, and their head is, except in name, king of the Dutch Republic.'

'I am well aware of the politics of the region. The king is hoping that his sister, who is one of the guardians of her son, the current head of the House of Orange, will help him.' 'I hate to disappoint you Simon, but Mary Stuart has little real power since her husband died and is probably as penniless as her brother.'

Simon sighed. He would leave for England in the morning to attend the funeral of his nephew. Harry put his arms around the distraught peer and led him to a small private cellar that adjoined his reception room. They were soon consuming fine French wine. Harry drank in moderation, but the overwrought Simon drank himself unconscious.

14

Apartment of Cardinal Mazarin, Palais Royal, Paris

THE CARDINAL HAD JUST RETAKEN control of the government
of France after several years of turmoil and exile. The uprising
against the centralising power of the monarchy by a chaotic coterie
of high nobles had been put down, and the young boy king, Louis
XIV, and his chief minister had the growing support of a nation tired
of instability. Most of the former rebels, having made their peace
with Mazarin, were now leading French armies against the traditional
enemy, Spain, well away from the centres of power.

Mazarin summoned a lesser luminary of this coterie of
irresponsible aristocracy—Philippe Rousset, an illegitimate son of the
late Prince of Conde´. Mazarin welcomed the noble officer who was
surprisingly dressed in the lowly gold and black livery of an officer of
frontline musketeers.

Mazarin put his visitor at ease. 'Captain, I never had the
opportunity to thank you for saving my life and perhaps that of the
King, when a rebel mob attacked us as we fled from Paris. I understand
that since you left the side of your half brother, the present Prince
of Conde´, you have been of great assistance to Queen Anne and
her son. I am surprised that these good deeds so far have not been
rewarded and that you waste away as a company commander of our
garrison troops in Rouen.'

'My exile to Rouen has been at my own request. I have good friends near Rouen and spend much of my time on their estate. It is close enough to Paris for me to continue my social relationships in this city.'

Mazarin smiled. 'It is one of those relationships that suggested you to me for a major mission on behalf of King Louis. I am about to offer you two positions that could influence the course of our relations with a foreign power.

A few days ago, the English army overthrew the government of the Parliament and installed an assembly of religious fanatics to replace it. Real power resides with General Cromwell and the formidable army and navy under his control. Much to our disadvantage, our enemies, especially Spain, are on good relations with this new military power.'

'How can an infantry captain play a decisive role in such high politics?'

'Not much, but a high ranking aristocrat, a cousin of both our King and the Queen Mother of England and who has friends at the English Court, can.'

Philippe was wary given the Cardinal's reputation as a flatterer and manipulator and asked, 'How can an agent of whatever rank, stationed at the English Court in France, develop better relations with the English army led by Cromwell who is in London?'

'The exiled king of England is currently protected by the French government, and we have provided accommodation for his court in the Chateau of St. Germain. This generosity is a stumbling block should I negotiate with General Cromwell. Cromwell has secret agents at the court. I want you to identify them as they will be useful contacts through which to commence secret negotiations.'

'How can I ingratiate myself into a court of second-rate Englishmen when my only entree is as an acquaintance of one of Queen Henriette's ladies-in-waiting?' sneered the pompous aristocrat.

'I will give you two new roles of relatively high standing. You will be King Louis's personal representative at the English Court. Your second role will prove much even more interesting. The English have taken upon themselves to investigate crimes, which were probably committed on French territory. The soldiers associated with the

English Court appear to throw their weight around in the areas surrounding the Chateau St. Germain. You and a company of your musketeers from Rouen will be transferred to St. Germain to control the perimeters of the Chateau and execute sole authority outside its boundary. The English can do what they like within the estate, but I will not have them usurping French sovereignty in any way.'

'But you want me to infringe that of the English by questioning the women of the English Court about Cromwellian spies.'

'My dear Rousset, introduce yourself not to Charles Stuart but to his mother, a princess of France, who has no time for the discipline imposed by Lord Ashcroft and his recently arrived deputy. Work through the exiled English Queen!

Take up your military post immediately but leave the diplomatic role for a week. I have so discouraged young Charles that he is about to leave Paris to seek aid from the Dutch. On his departure, his mother will assume control of the English Court.'

With a dismissive wave of the hand, the Cardinal ended the interview, and Rousset rose to leave. As he reached the door, Mazarin halted his departure.

'Captain, I almost forgot. I have read an old report from naval intelligence at Le Havre that two of Cromwell's leading agents entered France through that port and subsequently disappeared in the Rouen region. You meet socially with the nobles and magistrates of that area, have you heard any rumours about the whereabouts of these spies?'

Rousset was about to deliver what would have been a major coup in his relationship with the crafty Mazarin. Yes, he knew the location of Cromwell's most able agent. Tremayne was employed by a close friend, the Marquis des Anges, and lived on the very estate where he also had quarters. They dined together regularly.

No, he would hold back. This was information which he could reveal at a much more propitious time. It would also give him time to talk to Tremayne and perhaps gain some advantage over the Englishman. He replied, 'No, Your Eminence, the local magistrates believe that both men have drowned. One body was found downstream near Le Havre.'

Rousset left the Cardinal's chambers with a wide grin across his face. Not only would he be able to continue his affair with a woman at the English Court, but he could advance a project that had stalled with the death of Lucy Harman. He could now monitor what the amateur English sleuths had discovered on the matter.

Above all, he was delighted to be a trusted agent of Cardinal Mazarin and in a position to assist the young king's favourite. He could climb the social and political ladder at the French Court and, eventually, exercise the power that befitted his Bourbon blood. He had failed to achieve this by opposing the monarchy. He would now succeed by supporting the king and cardinal.

Later that afternoon, the Cardinal received one of his agents—a woman who had regularly reported to the French government material she had gleaned at the English court in exile. Mazarin praised her achievements. 'In my absence you provided the king's government with valuable information regarding the situation in England through your dual roles as an agent for the King of England and for the English Parliament. You play a very dangerous game. Are you still above suspicion?'

'Until recently, the answer was, yes. My parliamentary masters in London have been very satisfied with the information I sent them, and the king of England is grateful for any information he receives.'

'You said "until recently." What has changed?'

'In the first place, my English masters have just been overthrown by General Cromwell. I have no contact with the General, and there are rumours that Cromwell has his own agents already at St. Germain. Second, a recently arrived Cromwellian officer, who surprisingly was immediately appointed deputy to Lord Ashcroft and is seen regularly in conversation with the king, has begun another investigation into the murder of Lady Lucy Harman, which has some elements of the English Court very anxious. His enquiry may accidentally unearth my activities.'

'I am interested in that murder myself,' said the cardinal. 'Does the girl's death in any way bear on the security of France?'

'I doubt it. She was a naïve child. The general opinion is that she saw something or overheard something that led to her death. She had no contact with any French citizens since she arrived at St. Germain. Queen Henriette keeps close surveillance of her ladies-in-waiting.'

'Not too close a surveillance. I understand that an officer of the Rouen garrison is indulging in an affair with one of these ladies-in-waiting.'

'Only hearsay, I have never seen the said gentleman. Mistress Mortimer is at most times indiscreet about her lovers, and you have trouble separating fact from fiction. She was a stupid, carefree nymphomaniac. At one stage, she boasted that she had known Charles Stuart but quickly retracted the statement when she realised that if the Queen Mother had heard it, she would be dismissed.'

'My lady, I have called you here so that you will understand the changed situation that is emerging. From now on, you will report directly to me—and only to me. I have two tasks for you. As you said earlier, it is rumoured that Oliver Cromwell has an agent or more at the Royalist court. I want you to locate them and inform me. Do not tell the English king.

Your second task is more delicate. I have decided to appoint a representative of France to the English Court and to post a company of French musketeers to protect the English. My diplomatic representative and the commander of the musketeers are one and the same person.

You are to befriend him, but report every detail of his activities and statements to me. Be careful! He is a dangerous man who conceals his ambition and need for status behind a relatively humble appearance and charming manner. He manifests this false humility in seeking to be known as captain when he has many eminent titles—including Philippe, Vicomte Rousset. The man has been a trimmer and a turncoat in the past. I must know where his loyalties now lie.'

The agent saw her chance. 'In return for my assistance on these new matters, what does His Eminence have in mind regarding compensation?'

Mazarin's demeanour changed abruptly. His face revealed utter contempt for his spy, 'My dear, you are in no position to demand any consideration above that of a regular payment. You are not only a double agent in regards to the English factions, but, in addition to serving us, you are also in the pay of the Spanish. If these facts were made known outside this room, your life would be forfeit.

I have used your tenuous situation to convince your husband to change sides. He is currently recruiting Irish troops for the service of Spain. He will continue to raise the regiments, but, instead of serving Spain, he and his regiments will join the French army under Turenne. He will be in a position higher than that offered by Spain and on a pension double that offered by the Spaniards. You will immediately sow false information for the court in Madrid. Here are several pages of misleading news.'

The quadruple agent was quashed. The inhabitants of the English Court were babes in the woods compared with the guile and ruthlessness of the cardinal.

Mazarin had not finished. 'Do you suspect anybody as Cromwell's agent?'

'Initially, I suspected the recent arrival, Captain Lloyd, but his intimacy with Ashcroft and the king seem to negate this. He has taken a lover in Lady Catherine Beaumont who could be the spy.'

Mazarin dismissed his deflated agent and smiled to himself. With two separate representatives at the English Court, he would soon uncover the Cromwellian agent and impose French authority on the environs of the English Court.

15

English Court in Exile, Chateau St. Germain

HARRY QUESTIONED THE THREE LADIES who, for several months, had been constant companions to young Lucy Harman. He met Lady Jane Torrington in an enclosed garden of the chateau. Two servants accompanied her ladyship carrying with them an array of drinks and refreshments. Jane Torrington had charm and elegance. She was very tall, with long black hair, green eyes, a long aristocratic neck, and firm partly revealed breasts exaggerated by a tightly fitting emerald green bodice.

Lord Ashcroft doubted Jane's loyalty. She was the daughter of a parliamentary peer who, with his four sons, had fought against Charles I. Jane's four brothers continued to hold high rank in Cromwell's army.

Harry used this as his opening question, 'My lady, why is the daughter of Lord Colyton and sister to four Cromwellian colonels, two of which I know personally, a lady-in-waiting to the Papist former queen of England?'

'Captain Lloyd, my loyalty is not subject to interrogation, but as I have suffered similar innuendoes from Lord Ashcroft, I will respond. I am deeply in love with my husband, who is the second son of the Earl of Portismouth. My husband, Richard Lord Torrington, represented the late King in Spain for several years, and, with the outbreak of our civil war, rose to be a colonel of infantry in the Royalist army.

Until recently, he was fighting a rearguard action in Scotland on behalf of young Charles. He surrendered on the field of battle, and was so well thought of by his enemies that he was granted a licence to recruit Irish troops for the service of the king of Spain. I love my husband, and as he is loyal to the monarchy, I am loyal to him—despite my upbringing and the views of my father and brothers.'

'My lady, you are the most mature and experienced of the younger English women close to the old queen. What did you make of young Lucy Harman and her untimely death?'

'Lucy was so innocent; there can be only one explanation of her death. She knew something or someone thought she knew something that they did not wish revealed.'

'But if Lucy was naïve and childlike and watched over by the Queen Mother, when and where was she ever in a position to hear or see something that would endanger her life?'

'A valid point! That is why the fatal information was something she obtained before she came to court.'

'Where was she before she came here?'

'In convents in both Spain and France. Most recently, she was in the Abbey des Anges, near Rouen. It was from Rouen that her father brought her to the Queen Mother. Lucy's mother had been a lady-in-waiting during the thirties, and, above all, the Harman's were Papists particularly in tune with Henriette Marie's form of Catholicism.'

'Did you notice any changes in Lucy's behaviour in the weeks leading up to her death?'

'Yes, she was even more timid and withdrawn, scared of her own shadow. She was a very sad young woman. On many occasions, I found her crying, but she would never tell me why. One day, I was sent by the queen to fetch her from her apartment and found her stripped to the waist, engaged in vigorous self-flagellation, an art she learnt in one of the Spanish convents.

Blood was streaming freely from her macerated back. I told the Queen who instantly forbade the girl to resort to such self-mutilation. There was one aspect of that episode which I found strange. Spanish religious orders which indulge in this behaviour have a set ritual of precise words to be spoken during the activity, but Lucy was reciting words of her own, over and over again.'

'What was she saying?'

'Forgive those who covet; they have erred from the faith and have entangled themselves in many sorrows.'

'To what she was referring?'

'The words are vaguely familiar. I have not thought about them since, but I am sure they are part of Holy Scripture. Lucy would have used a Catholic version of the Bible.'

'I agree,' replied Harry. Both parties went quiet as each wracked their brains to locate the origin of young Lucy's plaint. Jane suddenly clapped her hands, 'I have it. Our local vicar based many a sermon around the text largely directed against my family. It's from Timothy I: *"For the love of money is the root of all evil,"* and it concludes with reference to those who have erred from the faith and pierced themselves through with many sorrows.'

'Great! This helps establish a possible motive for Lucy's murder. It suggests money is a key element. Was she scared of any one in particular?'

'No, it was pretty general.'

At that point, one of the female servants who had been refilling Harry's glass sought permission to speak to Jane in private. Harry diplomatically took his filled glass and meandered around the garden. He eventually returned to Jane who apologised for her servant's inexcusable behaviour.

'Young Edith knows better than to interrupt her superiors, but she believes she can answer your last question better than her mistress. Come on, Edith. Tell Captain Lloyd what you just told me!'

With her head down, the embarrassed servant rapidly mumbled her contribution, 'Lady Lucy was terrified of Mistress Mortimer. Several times, I saw Mistress Mortimer shaking Lady Lucy and demanding she answer her questions.'

Harry was delighted. 'Edith, did you hear what Mistress Mortimer asked?'

'No, sir, I was too far away, but I could see the terrified look on Lady Lucy's face and the speed at which she ran away the moment she could free herself.'

Harry's interview with Jane and her servant had been fruitful. Lucy was obsessed with the effect of money on someone and was being bullied by Mistress Mortimer to reveal information about something. The two aspects must be connected. He would question Bess Mortimer immediately.

His initial attempts even to contact the elusive lady-in-waiting failed. His messenger was told that she had disappeared from court for a few days to be with her French lover. Instead, Harry was forced to talk to Lady Mary Gresham.

Mary Gresham was unlike the other women of the court. She was not a professional courtier nor drawn from the middle to high aristocracy. Neither she nor her relatives had had any connection to the Stuarts before the king's defeat at Worcester.

Mary was a country gentlewoman who assisted Charles to escape Cromwell's men as they searched for the fleeing king. She shared many an adventure with him. She was a petite, lithe brunette, whose lack of stature was more than compensated for by her enthusiasm and energy. She was a feisty thirty-year-old who had developed a special relationship with Charles Stuart.

The gossips at court suspected she might have been Charles's lover. Charles had forced her on his mother as a lady-in-waiting to keep an eye on the intrigues of the aging exiled queen. Lord Ashcroft had told Harry that Mary Gresham was absolutely loyal to the king and was the only lady-in-waiting to the Queen Mother that he trusted.

As befitted her personality and country origins, Mary insisted that Harry ride with her through the forest that bordered the Chateau of St. Germain. They led their horses out into the forest and agreed to ride them home. Harry's first thought was how the small Lady Mary could possibly mount the horse she led. It was a large cavalry steed, and she was so tiny.

As they led their horses along a well-defined path through the forest, Harry began his questioning. 'My lady, the king told me that you would be the most reliable of witnesses. Did you notice anything amiss with young Lucy Harman in the weeks before her death?'

'Lucy was never well. Her pale complexion became more pallid by the day. Her self-flagellation, which the Queen forbade just before the girl's death, could not have helped.'

'Was she increasingly timid and scared?'

'I am not sure about timid and scared, but she certainly became more tearful and more prayerful. She cried at the drop of a hat, and she spent every spare moment in one chapel or another.'

'Was she teased or bullied by other ladies of the court?'

'Bess Mortimer was fed up with her behaviour, and I did see her shake Lucy on one occasion.'

'What was Bess saying as she shook the girl?'

'She was cruel; telling Lucy she was more fitted to the convent than to the court.'

'How did Lucy react?'

'Apart from crying, she showed a little spark, clothed in her religious view of the world. She spat defiance at Bess.'

'Can you remember her exact words?'

'Not exactly, but it was along the lines that, unless Bess reformed her evil ways, she would never know God's secrets or share his treasure.'

Harry was delighted. This confirmed the evidence that Jane's servant had provided. Bess Mortimer was trying to uncover a secret that she thought Lucy possessed.

Harry enjoyed the company of the petite Mary, who regaled him with stories of her adventures in helping the king escape England. Harry admitted that, at the time, he was probably leading the parliamentary horse in pursuit of the king. As they compared times and places, Harry realised that he had just missed capturing the king on at least two occasions.

Harry need not have worried about Mary's ability to mount her horse. She placed it close to a fallen tree trunk and, with the advantage of extra height, got her foot into the stirrup and leapt onto the horse. Harry was taken aback. Mary rode astride her horse like a man—no side saddle for this feisty woman. After ambling for some time, Mary challenged Harry to race to the edge of the forest. He was surprised that the gentlewoman kept pace with him, and if he were not such a good horseman, she would have beaten him.

As they trotted through the gates of St. Germain, Harry asked, 'Can you tell me about Bess Mortimer?'

'She was besotted by men. Most of the gallants at court claim to have slept with her. I am amazed that the Queen Mother keeps her on at court, but the King says that she is the illegitimate daughter of a powerful noble and that her unfortunate mother had served Queen Henriette in the past.'

'Did Bess Mortimer show any changes in behaviour or personality in the weeks leading up to Lucy's death?'

'Bess is not a religious person, but I saw her on several occasions, at the most odd hours, near an isolated chapel on the estate.'

'Was this the same chapel that Lucy Harman frequented?' Mary who had not made the connection until questioned replied to her own surprise, 'Yes, it was.' Harry probed deeper, 'Lady Mary, what were you doing near such a chapel at those odd hours?' Mary blushed. 'I was and am on a mission for Lord Ashcroft. He probably mentioned it to you. Your former commander, General Cromwell, has one or more agents at court. I discovered a possible spy going to this chapel.'

'How does a potential Cromwellian spy visiting an ultra Catholic chapel make sense?'

'I am not sure. She claimed she went to look at the stained glass window, which reminded her of one in her own village. You don't see much of such a window at night. She is hiding something in the chapel or meeting an accomplice there.' Harry gave an involuntary shiver as he thought of Cate's precarious situation.

16

'WAS THIS WOMAN IN THE chapel at the same time as Lucy Harman or Bess Mortimer?' asked a worried Harry.

'No, I never saw two, let alone three of them together, but Bess and Lucy visited the chapel at times that were not separated by more than a few minutes. Maybe they were fellow agents who communicated with each other by leaving notes in the chapel?'

Harry continued with his most important question, 'Did Bess Mortimer's behaviour change in the weeks before Lucy's murder?'

'Yes, the change was so remarkable that we all teased her about it. Up to a few months ago, the many men in Bess's life were all Englishmen associated with the court—relationships about which she boasted most indiscreetly. Then, suddenly, she put an end to these liaisons. She exuded happiness and was almost serene. Eventually, she confessed that she had taken a new lover, a French aristocrat. She was now often absent from court, presumably in the arms of this new lover—an absence we all lied about to protect her from the queen's wrath.'

'Did you ever see this man?' 'No.' As they reached the stables of the chateau, Harry lifted his companion from her horse and intuitively gave her a big hug. Mary could have been the sister he never had.

Harry's experience with Bess Mortimer was much less pleasant. She refused to be interviewed. After three days of noncompliance, Harry sent two armed guards to her apartment with a simple request—present herself at Lord Ashcroft's chamber at ten the next morning or be forcibly escorted there in front of the whole court.

At the prescribed hour, Harry, who had been given the use of the chamber by Lord Ashcroft, sat behind the desk awaiting Bess's arrival. She did not appear. Harry faced a dilemma. How long should he wait for this recalcitrant woman before sending his guards to arrest her?

Forty-five minutes later, Bess Mortimer arrived with a gaggle of laughing servants, who had obviously been given instructions to distract Harry. He had had enough. He ordered the guards to remove the servants from the room. Bess immediately responded, 'My servants stay with me, or you will answer to the Queen Mother.'

'Your servants leave, or you will answer to the king. Mistress Mortimer, you don't seem to understand. This is a murder enquiry ordered by the king himself, and you are a major suspect.'

The colour drained from Bess's face. 'How dare you, sir! You have no reason to consider me a suspect.'

'On the contrary, I have evidence from several witnesses that you abused Lady Lucy in the weeks before her death and that she was terrified of you.'

'Rubbish! I simply tried to shake some sense into that snivelling child who had no place at court. She never faced up to a single problem, escaping them by dissolving into tears and resorting to self-indulgent prayer. She was a wimp.'

'So much of a wimp that she whipped herself daily in an effort to obtain forgiveness.'

'Forgiveness for what?' sneered Bess. 'She knew so little of life; she could not have sinned sufficiently to warrant her obsessive behaviour.' Harry tried a little bluff. 'Oh, we know for what she sought forgiveness—the evil consequences of a large treasure.' Bess reacted too quickly. 'What would that child know about secret treasure?'

'Precisely, Mistress Mortimer, and, according to other witnesses, you were asking her that very question.'

'You live in a fantasy world, Captain Lloyd. I don't know why the king entrusted this investigation to a newcomer.'

'That should be obvious. You have woven such a web of possible intrigues through your many liaisons that there were few men he could trust.'

'Believe court gossip at your peril, captain! I have a powerful friend to whom I will report your conduct and spurious allegations.'

'Your friend will not prevail over the king, nor will your association with him be well received by the Queen Mother if she were to know.'

Bess laughed, 'How little you know! Queen Henriette will be delighted. My lover is of the highest French aristocracy, and the same Bourbon blood of King Louis XIV and of Henriette Marie flows in his veins. He only needs to speak to the king of France, and King Charles will dismiss you.'

'Thank you Mistress Mortimer! You have answered my next question. Apart from the murder mystery, I have been asked to uncover the secret agents who plague this court. You obviously act for the French government against our king. That is treason.'

Bess paled. She had never seen that her relationship with a French aristocrat had any political connotations. While her mind grappled inadequately with Harry's statement, he redirected his questioning. 'Why do you, who are in no way religious, spend so much time moving around the chapel at the far end of the estate. Is that where you deliver information to your contact?'

'I am leaving. This is an outrage. If I were a French spy, I would simply tell Philippe.' Harry cruelly seized on the unguarded remark, 'Is that a confession? You silly wench! Your lover is using you to gain information about the English Court. You cannot believe that a high-ranking French aristocrat would show any real affection for an untitled Englishwoman of lowly gentry status who has a very unsavoury reputation. Do you think the Queen Mother would really appreciate her kin associating with you?' Bess, unnerved and on the edge of tears, glared at Harry and ran from the room.

Harry hit the desk with clenched fists. He left the chamber equally angry. He had taken only a few strides down the corridor when a servant stopped him. 'Captain, you are required immediately by the king.' Harry had previously met the king in courtyards, corridors, and gardens, but had never been admitted to the intimacy of the king's inner chambers.

Lord Ashcroft was waiting for him at the door. 'Captain, remain standing in the king's presence. This is a formal meeting, and you may find His Majesty less friendly than usual.'

The king was seated in a large well-padded chair with extensive arms that almost encircled him. Opposite him on an armless stool sat a small corpulent man whom Harry recognised as the king's chief minister, Sir Edward Hyde. Facing the King but standing were Lord Ashcroft and himself.

The king spoke, 'Gentlemen, I have annoying news from Cardinal Mazarin acting on behalf of my cousin King Louis. I am no longer to approach the French government directly but put all my requests through a newly appointed French envoy to my court. A Vicomte Rousset will be the French envoy to us and will require several chambers in the chateau.'

Lord Ashcroft asked, 'Sire, why is Mazarin taking such a position. Surely, you should be able to talk to your cousin directly, king to king.'

'The cardinal is showing us that he is the real power in the land and that our relations with France will be completely supervised by him. It prevents my ten-year cousin making decisions that Mazarin opposes. It also provides him with an effective spy into the workings of this court and the opinions of its members.'

'Who is Vicomte Rousset?' asked Hyde. Ashcroft replied, 'Philippe, Vicomte Rousset is an illegitimate son of the former Prince of Condé. He has spent all his life in military service and prefers to be known as Captain Rousset.'

Charles resumed his statement, 'Lord Ashcroft touches upon an even more dangerous development. Cardinal Mazarin, for the better protection of our court, is to station a company of musketeers in the gatehouse of the chateau and will patrol the perimeter of the estate and escort any member of our court who wishes to leave the premises. The commander of this guard will be the same man, Captain Rousset.'

Sir Edward Hyde was irritated. 'A deliberate snub! We have become prisoners.'

The King continued, 'Mazarin claims he is protecting French sovereignty and that some of the enquiries made by Lord Ashcroft and Captain Lloyd have exceeded their powers and interfered in matters that are the responsibility of the French authorities. It is unfortunate that these changes will occur in my absence. Lord Ashcroft and I leave for the Low Countries in two days. Sir Edward will maintain our government, and, unfortunately, in the absence of my brother, control of the court reverts to my mother. Captain Lloyd you are the most senior military officer remaining and will assume command of our forces within the chateau.'

Charles rose, moved close to Harry and half whispered, 'On another matter, how is your investigation into Lady Harman's murder progressing?' Harry gave a brief outline and seized the opportunity. 'Sire, I suspect that Mistress Bess Mortimer knows more about the event than she admits. She abused the girl in the weeks before the murder, and when I pushed hard in my interrogation, she threatened me with retaliation from her French lover, whom I presume is this Captain Rousset. Could you question her under threat that she will be expelled from court?'

Hyde fumed, 'Captain, it is most impertinent to ask His Majesty to lower himself to undertake such a menial task.'

'Sir Edward, don't be so pompous! I will summon this Bess Mortimer. Her presence, until recently, has caused several duels amongst my gentlemen, and I know my mother has, from time to time, become distraught over this woman. To please mother will be a rare occurrence.'

Two days later, Harry received a note from the king. It read, *'No success with Mortimer, except a veiled threat that she would soon be protected by more powerful influences than an exiled king of England. You were right. Rousset, soon to reside here, is her lover.'* Harry was not displeased with the King's news. Depending on how affable Rousset appeared, he may be able to assist Harry in his investigation.

But Rousset completely ignored the lowly captain of the English troops within the Chateau of St. Germain. The Vicomte presented his credentials to the Queen Mother with an escort of black-and-gold-suited musketeers. A company of these men was accommodated in the far gatehouse of the chateau, and the land around this gatehouse was partitioned off from the rest of the estate by a temporary fence of hurdles.

Sir Edward Hyde informed Harry that the area beyond the hurdles, but within the Chateau's perimeter, was once again French territory. Harry must avoid any confrontation in the absence of the king and Lord Ashcroft.

Two weeks after the king's departure, Sir Edward asked Harry for an update on how the court was adapting to the presence of Rousset and his troops. Harry reported that there had been no contact, let alone conflict with them. As the Queen Mother had not invited him into her section of the chateau from which the formal court now operated, he had not met Rousset in his diplomatic role either.

Hyde nodded sagely. 'You will get no cooperation from the Queen Mother. We would have solved Lucy Harman's murder if the queen had allowed us to interview her precious ladies at the time of the offence. She is probably delighted with the presence of a distant relative and the French troops at her court. By the way, I have received a note from Lord Stokey. He has information that will assist Ashcroft and yourself solve that murder.'

'What does he say?'

'Only that he is certain of the motive.'

'When does his lordship return?'

'Within the next two or three days.'

Harry would not be there to welcome him.

17

HARRY WAS SITTING IN THE guardroom working on a duty roster when a French officer with four black-and-gold-liveried musketeers burst into the chamber. Harry was astonished. Speaking in perfect French, he demanded to know on whose authority they entered English territory. The officer replied that the English queen had asked Captain Rousset to provide her and her court with protection during the absence of her son.

'I provide that protection,' spluttered a fuming Harry. The French officer smiled. 'Her Majesty will explain. Come with us!' Harry's fury abated a little. At least, the Queen Mother was forced to recognize his presence. He was vaguely familiar with the apartments of the ladies-in-waiting, but he was now led into the inner sanctum of the Queen Mother's world.

As he approached an imposing door without which stood two French musketeers, his escort demanded his weapons. Harry was well aware of the protocol. No one entered a royal presence armed.

He entered the chamber and was confronted by a small middle-aged woman who sat on what appeared to be an imitation of a real throne. She was surrounded by a number of her ladies, three of whom he recognized—Catherine Beaumont, Jane Torrington, and Mary Gresham.

Standing at the queen's right hand was a very tall, well-built soldier, whose light brown hair had tinges of red, as had his square cut beard. He was an officer of the gold—and black-liveried musketeers, and his face reflected a permanent sneer of contempt.

The Queen spoke, 'This gentleman is Vicomte Rousset, the French government's envoy to my court, and as of this morning, captain of my personal bodyguard and that of the court. You, Captain Lloyd, are dismissed from your post and under arrest.'

Harry was taken aback and confused. Then he recognized the man standing beside Rousset. It was Captain O'Brien, the Irish mercenary who had identified Luke Tremayne on board ship and, later, informed the French naval authorities at Le Havre. Harry managed to raise a meek smile, fell on his knees and asked the Queen, 'And may I know Your Majesty's reason for this action?'

It was Rousset who replied, 'Captain O'Brien asserts that you entered France in disguise with one of Oliver Cromwell's most nefarious agents with the purpose of ingratiating yourself into the English Court where you would be in a position to assassinate King Charles. For that reason, my royal cousin, the Queen Mother, Henriette Marie, orders your arrest and removal from the chateau.

I have reasons of my own for complying with that directive. As a Cromwellian officer, you probably entered France also to spy on our military garrisons and positions, as a precursor to an English invasion to help the French Protestants or to assist our enemies, the Spaniards, who stupidly have recognized your republican government and disowned your king.'

'Your Majesty, I have explained all these matters to King Charles, and he was so satisfied with my answers that he appointed me as deputy commander of his bodyguard and of all English troops within the chateau. For reasons of state, I cannot reveal the details of my explanation. Place me under house arrest until the king's return when these matters can quickly be dealt with!'

Rousset responded firmly, 'No, Captain Lloyd! King Charles may accept your answers from his point of view, but I am responsible for the security of France. You will be detained until I am satisfied that you are no threat to France.'

His men took hold of Harry and bundled him from the room. Several of the ladies-in-waiting were aghast, and at least three were anxious to inform their clandestine masters.

Torrington soon had a message to Mazarin outlining what had happened and emphasizing that Lloyd was probably the Cromwellian agent he sought.

Mary Gresham made her way to Sir Edward Hyde who was apoplectic at the French presence and Lloyd's arrest. He immediately penned a letter of protest to Mazarin, which was as quickly returned, as it had not been sent through Rousset. Cate Beaumont had to wait for most of the day before she could obtain her codebook and send an account of the affair to Oliver Cromwell.

Harry was stunned by his mistreatment. Rousset's musketeers bound his hand and foot and threw him onto a small wagon. It was a bumpy and uncomfortable ride. One musketeer drove the wagon while four others escorted it. They were on the main road to Paris.

Harry was alarmed. He could be murdered or disappear forever into some minor filthy French prison. His only hope were Mary Gresham and Cate Beaumont, but he was not sure what they could do as the king and Oliver Cromwell were both out of the country and had no authority within France.

The driver asked the nearest horsemen why they had not taken the prisoner to the nearest gaol at the Abbey de St. Germain. 'He is an English spy and should be going to the Bastille, but Captain Rousset has given our sergeant secret orders,' replied the wagoner.

Harry's mood worsened on hearing the soldier's concluding remark. Simultaneously, the sergeant ordered that he be blindfolded. A musketeer wrapped a square of fabric neatly and tightly around Harry's face, completely obscuring his vision. He lost sense of time and direction.

The wagon eventually stopped, and he was led stumbling across a courtyard and up a steep, winding stone staircase. Orders were shouted and the blindfold, removed. Harry was in a prison cell at the top of a high tower. He had a small window, a bed of strewn straw, a bucket—and a companion.

A person, who wore part of the livery of the musketeers that had escorted Harry to the prison, rose and greeted him. 'Pierre Rougemont, until recently, a lieutenant in a regiment of the line currently garrisoning the fortress at Rouen!'

'Harry Lloyd, deputy commander of King Charles II's bodyguard stationed at the Chateau St. Germain!'

'You speak very good French for an Englishman. You must have upset a very important person to finish up here.'

'Where is here?'

'The worst prison in Paris—the Bishop's Prison.'

'What do you mean "the worst prison"?'

'For centuries, this tower block was the prison for those under the ecclesiastical and secular jurisdiction of the bishop of Paris. Thirty years ago, when the status of the incumbent was raised to archbishop, the French government abolished any secular jurisdiction of the archbishop and severely reduced his ecclesiastical powers.

The prison fell into disuse until other jurisdictions began to use it as a dumping ground for people who they had illegally imprisoned or for those that they wished to torture—a practice banned in most French jurisdictions. Even the old king, when he wanted to avoid his own edicts or those of his magistrates, sent victims here.

It has nothing to do with the archbishop of Paris anymore. Its governor is a minor nobleman who receives financial support from a range of authorities and individual aristocrats who want to use his facilities.'

'Am I to be starved to death and my corpse tossed in the Seine?'

'More likely, you will be tortured until you expire. Several floors below us is one of the most feared torture chambers in France. A Spaniard, a master of his craft who can extract a confession from the most difficult of prisoners, controls it. Why are you here?'

'I am accused of being a spy for the English Republic.'

Rougemont looked pained. 'Alas, my friend, spies are automatically tortured. Even in the Bastille, where torture is severely proscribed, you would experience it.'

'Cheer me up! And why are you here?'

'I annoyed one of my fellow officers who just happened to have royal connections. I am being taught a lesson about minding my own business.'

'What serious busybodying did you indulge in?'

'I had the temerity to joke about this officer's latest lover and suggested a range of motives he found distasteful.'

'Hardly a serious offence.'

'I would feel better in any other Parisian gaol. The law is no protection in here,' moaned Rougemont.

Harry's gloom slightly dissipated when a gaoler opened the door of the cell and placed two large bowls of food on the ground. It was a lamb stew with turnips, carrots, and parsnips. Even Rougemont was impressed, 'Harry, you must know someone important. This is the best meal since my arrival.'

Harry emptied his bowl and, partly as a joke, shouted out for more food. He was amazed when the gaoler returned with a small pot and ladled out more of the delicious stew. Rougemont declined any further offerings.

Another gaoler appeared with two goblets and a flagon of wine. Both prisoners sat against the wall imbibing what Rougemont described as passable, sweet, white Rhenish wine. With nothing else to do, Harry emptied the flagon.

Ten minutes later, he felt queer. He had over indulged in the past but had never felt like he did now. He thought he saw a third person in the cell and asked Pierre to help him control the intruder. Pierre had a strange look on his face, and before Harry passed out, he vaguely realised that he had been drugged. No wonder Pierre had not asked for a second helping and had drunk very little.

When Harry regained consciousness some time later, he was being manhandled down several flights of stairs. Eventually, he reached the torture chamber. One of the gaolers spoke, 'Come sir, let me show you what lies ahead. Here is a Spanish Barrel. You will kneel inside it, and we will fix you to it permanently. You will then rot in your own filth and among the vermin. They feed initially on your excrement then on your living flesh and, finally, on your rotting corpse. If you are lucky, boiling oil or water will be thrown in—to keep you warm.'

The torturer laughed at his weak joke and, to emphasize the horrors of the barrel, thrust Harry's head into it. The smell was nauseous, and a rat jumped at his face.

He was then dragged to a long table and the gaoler, delighted in picking up instruments and pretending to use them on Harry. He relished the opportunity to describe their exact purpose. 'This is an iron boot. Once your foot is inside, I will hammer wedges into it until your bones are crushed.' The torturer enjoyed his game showing Harry instep borers, denailing devices, crushing implements, cat o' nine tails, and a heretics' fork which could be placed strategically to penetrate chin and breast simultaneously.

Eventually, he was forced to confront a spiked iron chair, a spiked coffin-shaped iron maiden, and, finally, the strappado. Harry tried to block out of his mind the thought of being suspended from this instrument by his arms tied behind his back and then dropped suddenly several feet, dislocating his shoulders. Even more painful, the final drop could be onto a pointed stool gleefully described by the gaoler as the Judas Cradle.

After hours of relentless inspection of these instruments of torture, Harry was allowed to sit on a bench while another gaoler, who exuded authority and confidence and spoke with a decidedly Spanish accent, fired question after question at him. Harry resolved not speak.

Another tour of the torture chamber ensued. As the hours wore on, the drugs and a growing tiredness combined to demand a relaxing sleep. But it was not to be. He was kept awake, subject to constant questioning and experiencing hallucinations, which made it difficult to distinguish fantasy from reality. Harry had no recollection of what happened over the next few days.

18

Three Days Later, the Bishop's Prison, Paris

THE GOVERNOR OF THE PRISON welcomed his guest profusely with an array of sweetmeats and drink. 'It's great to see you again, Philippe. In the early days of the late rebellion, we had many an adventure together, and both of us have survived the change in fortunes.'

Rousset ignored the civilities of his former comrade-in-arms. 'Did you get any information from the English spy I sent you?'

'Of course! A combination of drugs and sleep deprivation renders most prisoners incapable of resisting our interrogation. This man was no exception.'

'And what did he reveal?'

'In answer to the questions you wanted asked, he is no threat to France. There was nothing to suggest he is here to plan an invasion or to liaise with our Protestant brethren or Spanish supported rebels at Bordeaux.'

'Good! So what did he confess to?'

'He is a loyal servant of the English Republic and devoted to the service of his general, Oliver Cromwell, and to his immediate superior, a Colonel Luke Tremayne.'

'I know Colonel Tremayne very well.'

The governor looked confused but continued, 'My conclusion is that Lloyd is a threat, not to France but to the English king.'

'Well done! You have given me information that should enhance my standing with the cardinal. He is very anxious to uncover the Cromwellian agents at the English Court. I will return Lloyd to St. Germain.'

'Not so fast, my friend! You may wish to rethink that approach.'

'Why?'

'You also asked me to probe about English treasure hidden in France. His answers were very specific. Lloyd linked this alleged treasure to the murder of an English gentlewoman and named you as a possible suspect in her death and in the race for the treasure. You cunning one! Are you on the brink of unearthing a hoard of gold and silver?'

Rousset did not respond to the governor's question. He was silent for some time weighing up the advantages of freeing Harry and gaining kudos from Mazarin for uncovering an agent that the cardinal would undoubtedly use for the benefit of France but risking closer probing of his role in the murder of Lucy Harman and the search for the treasure.

He had no choice and declared, 'Lloyd cannot be freed or returned to the English—at least for the time being.'

'He can stay here,' suggested the governor.

'No, the English are already asking questions and will soon persuade the cardinal to search every Parisian prison. I will send a troop of my men to escort Lloyd to an ancestral dungeon in the south of France. It has cells that are more secure and horrifying than yours. Was Rougement of any help?'

'No, he claims he has had too little time to gain the confidence of the prisoner.'

'Continue to use him. My men will take both of them south. Tell him to encourage Lloyd to escape then my men will legitimately kill them both.'

Harry was informed that he would be moved south as soon as an escort arrived. Nothing happened for days, except Rougemont's inquisitive nature began to irritate him. He would feed this obvious spy false information.

Three days later, he heard the tread of marching feet outside the tower. Within a few minutes, the noise of gaolers dragging an unwilling victim up the narrow stairs was deafening. The cell door opened and another prisoner was thrust through the doors. Harry was astonished.

It was Simon, Lord Stokey. Stokey threw his arms around Harry and exclaimed, 'Thank god you are alive. The ladies of the court thought the nefarious French had murdered you. Lady Torrington verbally attacked the Queen Henriette on your behalf, but then she accepted Rousset's word that you were a Cromwellian spy.'

Harry took advantage of Rougemont's argument at the cell door with a gaoler over the supply of fresh water. He placed a finger to his own lips and then pointed it at the French officer. 'Simon, I am amazed that you have joined me here. I would love to hear your story, but there is something I must do first.'

Harry walked across the cell to the door, swung Rougemont around, and, without warning, hit him with a clenched fist. The man fell to the ground hitting his head on the hard cobbled floor.

When the gaoler returned with fresh water, Harry took it and threw it over the prone Frenchman and declared, 'Get this man out of here, or I will kill him. Does Rousset think I am a fool? This man is a hopeless agent.'

The gaoler disappeared and returned later with the Spaniard who had conducted Harry's interrogation. He entered the cell and, also without warning, clubbed Harry with his truncheon. 'You are lucky that the governor wants you kept alive, at least for time being.' He turned to his assistant, 'Drag Rougemont out of here and take him to our quarters!'

Harry had a very sore head, but he was determined to hear Simon's story. The Catholic peer obliged. 'I returned home to attend the funeral of one of my nephews. Most of the leading Catholic peers of England and Ireland were there. They are divided on how to react to the rising power of the English army.

One group is inclined to support Cromwell, as a better defender of Catholics than the republican parliamentarians or the religious sects. Lord Harman, father of the unfortunate Lucy, leads this group.

Other peers, including myself, refuse to deal with Cromwell and are worried about Harman's rumoured overtures to him.'

'Why are they worried?'

'Many wealthy Catholic families placed their moveable valuables—money, silverware, and precious jewels into Harman's care. This treasure contained in several coffin-sized chests was smuggled out of the country and hidden in an unknown location. Only Harman knows its whereabouts, and it is rumoured that he is prepared to use some of that treasure to bribe Cromwell into a better deal for Catholics.

As soon as I returned from England, I went in search of you and Ashcroft to relate what I had uncovered as a plausible motive for Lucy Harman's murder. Someone thought she knew the location of the treasure left in her father's care.'

'This information led to your incarceration here?'

'Yes. When I failed to find you, I told Queen Henriette that I had discovered a motive for the murder of young Lucy. She listened carefully and concluded that we must all work together to prevent the treasure falling into Protestant and Cromwellian hands. I returned to my apartment. Within the hour, French guards arrested me. They placed a hood over my head and brought me here.'

'We are both here for the same reason. We are asking questions about Harman's treasure and linking it to Lucy's murder. Someone, and I suspect it is Rousset, does not like it.'

Before the men could continue their conversation, a group of gaolers appeared. They shackled each man around the feet and, with their hands behind their backs, bound the wrists. There was just enough length within the foot shackles for the prisoners to slowly descend the winding staircase.

Once in the courtyard, Harry could make out a large wagon and six mounted guards all in the black and gold livery of Rousset's men. Harry whispered to Simon, 'Speak only English! Don't let on that we understand French. It may help us pick up some vital information.'

The wagon was laden with supplies for man and horse and just enough spare room along the railings to shackle a prisoner on each side. The head gaoler demanded that the leader of the escort, a large overweight sergeant, sign papers formally relieving the prison of its two English spies.

The gaoler asked where his former prisoners were being taken. The sergeant replied, 'To the dungeons in the Chateau Rousset near Toulouse.'

'That will take you a couple of weeks with this large wagon.'

'We are in no hurry. Captain Rousset has paid us extra to take our time and get the prisoners well away from Paris. Given the reputation of the dungeon at Chateau Rousset, they will never see this city again.'

'They must be dangerous for the Captain to go through so much trouble, yet if they were major English spies, why were they not taken to the Bastille as is the custom?'

'If they had been in the Bastille, their English friends may have had legal means to assist them. The English Court has already sent men to the Bastille to see if our prisoners were there. We must get them out of Paris before they are found by the English and their French friends.'

Ten Days Later, Nearing Toulouse

Harry and Simon readily adjusted to a daily routine. The escorts took it in turn to tether their horse to the back of the wagon and become its driver. Each evening, while most of the escort enjoyed themselves eating and drinking in the inn chosen for the evening, the two prisoners were shackled to a post in the barn or stable and were watched over by the remaining guard.

The prisoners were reasonably comfortable as they managed to steal sufficient straw from their overnight stops to cushion the bumps of the wagon. Their escorts were not ungenerous when it came to the evening meal. Whole chickens, and plenty of red wine were brought to their barn by the women of the establishment, some of whom took pity on the prisoners and brought them extra food and drink—and offered additional comforts. Neither man was interested, nor did they have the wherewithal to pay for anything.

From the first day, Harry and Simon planned to escape. They were effectively fixed to the wagon as they travelled, and, except for periods of rain, it was uncovered. They were in full sight of the escorting musketeers.

The same difficulties applied at night. The fetters holding their arms behind their back were removed, but they were shackled to each other by one wrist and to an upright post by chains attached to their feet shackles.

One advantage of the overnight sojourn in a barn or stable was that they were not watched all night. The guard who supervised their eating joined his companions in the inn around ten o'clock. For the rest of the night, Harry and Simon were free to escape undetected—if they could remove their fetters.

19

NIGHT AFTER NIGHT, NO SUCH opportunity arose. Then after ten days, Harry sensed a chance. As he was thrown heavily against the barn post for the inevitable nightly shackling, it moved considerably. When their guard withdrew, he left behind a nearly exhausted taper.

The two men scraped away at the base of the post and were delighted to see that it was rotted in several places. They began to throw their combined weight against it and then stood and pulled with all their might. As they rocked the post back and forth, it moved further and further.

Eventually, just as the taper flickered out, the post snapped at its decaying base. The broken post to which they were still shackled was heavy and awkward and their fettered feet did not permit long steps. The two men made their way very slowly out of the barn dragging the massive wooden pole after them.

Once outside the barn, they moved behind the inn to avoid the main road. It was still busy with customers, the worse for wear leaving the establishment. By the light of an intermittent moon, Simon saw an open field and, beyond it, dense woodland. He pointed in the direction of the forest, but Harry shook his head. 'We will not be free until we can rid ourselves of these shackles and the post. We cannot get very far in our present state, and the mark the post is gouging into the ground will make it easy for us to be followed.'

'What do you suggest?' asked Simon.

'As we entered this village, I saw a blacksmith's shop. We must cut our shackles and get rid of this log.'

Fortunately, the woodland, which the Englishmen had first seen across the field, also swept around and bordered the blacksmith's house. The men edged their way along the open field towards the conjunction of the woodland and the edge of the village.

The journey was slow. The fetters and post continued to hamper them. They only moved when clouds covered the moon. At this pace dawn would break before they reached the safety of the forest. They spurned a shorter route along a pathway at the back of the inn because the small ditch that the post dug was clearly visible. In the adjacent ploughed field, they tried with some success to keep the gouging propensity of the post aligned with a recently cut furrow, which to some extent concealed their progress.

Harry and Simon finally reached the blacksmith's shop. In front of his small cottage was a large awning, which protected his furnace and workshop. This was good news. They would not need to break into the house to find what they wanted. Unfortunately, it was still difficult to manipulate the post around collections of metal pots, pans, harrows, and a string of horseshoes that played a deafening tune when accidently struck.

Following such a noise, the two men froze. They sensed movement behind them and prepared to swing the unwieldy post at the unwelcome guest. To their relief, a cat bounded away from its sleeping position near the warming embers.

A blacksmith's fire always contained sufficient red coals overnight to enable him to quickly reach the heat he required next day. Harry found a ceramic container and filled it with glowing embers. Simon filled a metal basket with charcoal. They found a sledgehammer and a cold cutter.

With the heavy hammer and awkward containers of coals and charcoal, moving was an increasing strain on both men. They had to be well into the woods before they could begin the process of freeing themselves. They could not use the sledgehammer until daylight because the noise would travel miles through the silent night air. The trained ear of the blacksmith would be immediately alerted.

As soon as they reached the forest, they lit a fire and moved the post into a position where the iron ring by which they were shackled to it was directly above the flame. Eventually, the iron hoop fell away from the burning pole. Harry found the thinnest and weakest part of the shackle uniting him with Simon. He applied the cutters, which ate into the metal as if it were a piece of cheese.

At dawn, the forest came alive with the noise of axes and saws, and Harry felt safe to swing the hammer carefully down on Simon's fetters without alerting the neighbourhood. Simon uttered a cry of pain as the chain broke asunder, and in the process cut into his foot.

Simon soon returned the compliment; however, the aristocratic diplomat did not have Harry's brute strength. Nevertheless, after many blows with the hammer and efforts to further weaken the join with the cutters, the chain finally broke.

The men were free. They quickly moved deeper into the forest. As the noise of axes, saws, and crashing timber became louder, Harry and Simon fell on their knees and crawled slowly towards a clearing that some woodcutters were creating.

One man, clearly an overseer, directed operations. He had left his horse tethered nearby. Simon, who had a special knack with horses, gently whispered to the animal. Amazingly, it moved towards him. He severed its extended tethering rope with the blacksmith's cutters. It was a large horse capable of carrying both men.

As they trotted on through the forest, Harry asked where they were going. Simon, who during his diplomatic missions had spent some time in the area, listed the options. 'We are a day or two away from Toulouse in the south, eleven or twelve away from Paris in the north. Our guards will assume we would try to return to Paris. So we will but not by travelling north. We must move west then turn south to reach the Garonne. We can then obtain a riverboat and reach Bordeaux, from which we can ship ourselves back to the Le Havre and then on to Paris.'

Harry was pessimistic. 'Bordeaux it is, but how do we get there? We have no money, no weapons, and no food. Whom do we trust? Are we in territory still loyal to the Prince of Condé, or are the inhabitants now devoted subjects of King Louis? Is the rebellion in the city of Bordeaux finally crushed?'

Simon was pragmatic, 'Ignore the politics. We have to make a strategic decision immediately. Do we go west through the woodlands for as long as we can or make straight for the river now and steal a boat?'

'What do you recommend?' asked a confused Harry.

'Getting to the river would be the quickest, but we would need luck to find a boat and steal it without discovery. Movement through the woods would be very slow, but there are a number of castles with outhouses and stables that would furnish us with what we lack. We could introduce ourselves to an owner as lost gentlemen.'

Harry was getting anxious. 'Are we English or French gentlemen?'

Simon smiled. 'We are French. In most parts of rural France, all Englishman are seen as spies. In the heated tensions of this region, with remnants of the Frondeurs and strong protestant centres already creating anxiety for the average villagers, the arrival of two English subjects could be the last straw.' This comment was to prove prophetic.

Harry found that despite his egalitarian Puritan gentry upbringing, he fell easily into the social customs of his class. Simon was a peer and had been a major general. Harry readily followed his lead. Luckily for Harry, Simon's status had not pickled his common sense nor dulled his natural ability. He quietly suggested, 'We keep to the woods and hope to find a hunting lodge or woodcutters hut that might provide us with some weapons.'

They followed a well-defined path through the forest. Around midday, they smelled a slight whiff of smoke and the tempting aromas of a rabbit stew. In a clearing off the path, two woodcutters and a young girl were sitting on a log.

As Harry and Simon approached, the taller of the cutters grabbed his staff and demanded, 'What are you doing in his lordship's woods? Does the Sieur de Vassey expect you?'

Simon lied, 'I hope the Sieur received my message, but we are a few days late as we were attacked on our way here. Our weapons, money, and one of our horses were taken. We were not even sure that this was the right path to Lord Vassey.'

The other woodsman invited them to join in their meal as he quickly skinned and quartered another rabbit and placed it in the large pot. His companion replied, 'You are out of luck. The seigneur is in Bordeaux, and I do not know when he will return. These are troubled times as the rebellion there still festers, and the Protestants are restless. They expect an English invasion to restore their old privileges. Our master does not get involved but, in recent months, we have had detachments of the rebels and a troop of mounted musketeers from the king's army searching these forests, looking for each other.'

'Where are the nearest Royalist garrisons and soldiers and the closest rebel stronghold at the moment? Like your master, we would wish to avoid both,' asked Simon.

'There is a large Royalist garrison at Toulouse, which has recently been supplemented by Marshal Turenne's infantry of the line. They expect a Spanish incursion. The master heard that several of Turenne's troops were already moving up the Garonne to Bordeaux, which still harbours some rebels. If the English try to help the Protestants at La Rochelle, Turenne will be ready.'

'It would be foolish for Cromwell to send troops into such a trap,' commented the unthinking Harry. The woodcutters looked at him quizzically. Simon was worried that the remark would make them suspicious, but, almost immediately, they smiled and invited their visitors to tuck into large chunks of rabbit. At the end of the meal, the girl, the taller woodsman's daughter, handed them some dried fruit and nuts obviously the produce of the previous autumn.

Simon probed, 'Is your seigneur's household in residence? Perhaps I could speak to his steward?' The woodsmen looked at each other before replying. 'The master lives alone, and all his in-house servants have left with him. Our immediate overseer, the head forester, looks after the estate in their absence. There is no point going to the chateau. It is empty.'

Harry replied, 'We will catch up with the seigneur in Bordeaux, but we would appreciate a horse and some weapons to defend ourselves but we do not—'

Simon interrupted him. 'All I have to pay you for your help is this gold pendant.' Simon undid a small gold crucifix from around his neck and handed it to the taller woodcutter. Harry was amazed that their gaolers had not confiscated it.

The woodsmen wandered out of earshot and argued. Eventually, they returned, and the leader said, 'We have a horse tethered at our hut. Take it! We shall tell the head forester that our horse wandered away and could not be found. My friend here will go to the old blacksmith's shop attached to the stables. There are several old swords there, which he can sharpen, and my daughter will bring you some cheese from the dairy.'

As darkness approached, the woodcutter and the girl returned with weapons and provisions. Harry asked, 'The quickest way to Bordeaux?'

'The quickest route is to return the way you came. Head for the big river and follow the road that runs parallel with it. But, for strangers, it would be very dangerous. It is full of highwaymen and marauding soldiers. Take the longer but safer path deep into the forest. This is the one always taken by our master.'

20

THE ENGLISHMEN TRAVELLED WEST FOR three days surviving on rabbits stolen from the traps of the locals, few of whom they encountered. Around noon, on the third day, their path turned sharply left and they suddenly emerged from the forest. They were entranced by the vista that opened up before them.

In the distance, they could see the river and the lowlands that surrounded it. The forest path had joined a road that climbed up from the valley and, turning at right angles, continued to their left along the edge of the forest.

A hundred yards up this road was a small village. Coming up the hill towards them were a group of peasants heading home. All were on foot, except for a man driving a wagon full of market goods that the villagers had just purchased.

Suddenly three horsemen burst out of the forest and attacked the peasants who were no match for the armed and aggressive highwaymen. One villager used his staff to defend the group but was soon cowered by the carbines directed at him.

Harry and Simon looked at each other and mutually nodded, but the latter held up his hand. 'Wait until these braggarts discharge their carbines.' The highwaymen methodically ransacked the peasant cavalcade and, as Simon anticipated, eventually, fired shots into the air to celebrate their success.

At this signal, Harry and Simon charged. Harry killed one robber with the initial thrust of his sword. The man was so obsessed with rifling the purses of the women and taking liberties with them that he did not see Harry coming. It took only a few minutes to subdue the two remaining villains. Harry and Simon wielded their borrowed swords with only moderate effect, but the peasants tripped up one highwayman with their staves and rendered the other unconscious by pounding a large rock into his head.

The robbers were immediately stripped and their hands firmly secured behind their backs. Space was made on the wagon, and, once supine, they were tied together by the ankles. Their dead comrade was placed next to them.

The peasants reclaimed their possessions. Harry examined the saddlebags of the highwaymen. He found the proceeds of earlier robberies—a considerable amount of silver coins and jewellery.

After a short discussion, with the peasant leader, it was agreed that the peasants would take the highwaymen back to their village and administer justice to the living and a Christian burial to the deceased. They also took three of the horses—the steeds that Harry and Simon had ridden and that of the deceased robber. In addition, Harry gave them all the jewellery and plate found amongst the loot. The Englishmen took the two remaining highwaymen's horses, all their weapons, and a small fortune in gold and silver coin.

Harry worried about handing the villains over to the peasants whom he thought might be too lenient. Simon put his mind at rest. 'These people will extract their revenge. The women in particular will punish them severely. They may not survive their torment, if not torture.'

Harry and Simon felt good. They were well armed, rode good horses, and were cashed up. All they needed was a good meal, a wash, and a change of clothes. Harry was all for taking the fine clothes removed from the highwaymen, but Simon was adamant. 'Don't be a fool! We have their horses and part of their loot. If we wear their clothes, we might be mistaken for them. It would be silly to escape apprehension as English spies to face death as highwaymen.'

They farewelled the peasants and trotted down the hill through an area of intense cultivation and finally reached the main east-west highway that followed the northern bank of the Garonne. This was a busy road. Wagons and drays were carting a wide variety of goods, and a multitude of travellers were moving in both directions. Some vehicles were taking goods to and from the several ships anchored along the river.

Harry became anxious as several troops of soldiers passed them moving west. Simon explained that the grey-liveried men were Turenne's troops of the line, moving to enforce the government's control of Bordeaux. Others appeared to be local militia moving in the same direction. Whether they would supplement Turenne's men or oppose them was the question.

As dusk approached, Harry and Simon reached a large inn with extensive stables where they decided to stay for the night. They could afford the best room. They ordered tubs of hot water, and each man had a soaking, soothing bath—the first cleansing for nearly three weeks. They sent their clothing to a laundress who promised they would be washed and dried by the morning. The inn provided shirts and trousers to be worn in the interim.

The next item on the agenda was a large meal—whole roasted chickens, legs of pork, a special spiced sausage, and litres of local red wine. Neither man remembered the latter part of the evening. They had such a relaxing alcohol-induced sleep that they did not awake until mid morning.

They had missed breakfast, but, apart from a slight headache, they felt good. Harry thought that it might be time to approach one of the many boats they could see unloading and loading along the riverbank. One of them might be destined for northern ports. If they obtained a passage here, it would avoid the dangers of approaching Bordeaux on horseback.

They were so engrossed in assessing the ships that they did not notice a large troop of cavalry approaching them. As the group drew level some of the horsemen cut across in front of Harry and Simon, and the rest quickly surrounded them. They pointed their primed carbines at the duo.

Their leader was direct. 'Gentlemen, you will accompany me to the nearest magistrate, the governor of the fort at Cadillac. I am not sure whether you are the English spies that have been cried up and down the Garonne valley or the highwaymen that have been causing havoc locally.'

'What makes you think we are either?' asked Simon. 'A laundress at the inn noticed that your clothes were foreign and probably English, and she was anxious for a reward that has just been posted for your apprehension alive. At the same time, a stable boy said that the horse you ride with the distinct white diamond facings was that ridden by a hooded highwayman that robbed him and friends the day before yesterday. An additional white dot on the left ear made him certain it was the same horse.'

'The stable boy is very observant. It is the same horse, but we are not the highwaymen,' Harry replied. He went on to give a highly edited version of their confrontation with the robbers, implying they took the horses and left everything else to the victimized peasants. The militia lieutenant stopped the conversation. 'That might be true, but the Governor and his lawyers will decide.'

The fort at Cadillac was hardly worthy of the name. It was a small chateau with a thin wall on the landward side and backed on to the river, towards which were mounted three large guns. Its purpose was to defend the river against marauding pirates. Its governor was not a military man, but a local magistrate who was new to the position.

The previous governor had sided with the defeated rebels and had been summarily executed. The present governor surprisingly received the English prisoners with a magnificent spread of food and drink. Harry wondered why. His question was answered immediately.

'Gentlemen you are very important fugitives. I received news from Toulouse that two dangerous Cromwellian spies were at large and must be captured dead or alive. Almost at the same time, a statement from Paris countermanded that order. You must now be arrested but in no way harmed. Detailed descriptions of you were also issued. Welcome to Cadillac, my Lord Stokey and Captain Lloyd. What impressed me was that the order was not only signed by the chief minister Cardinal Mazarin but countersigned by King Louis himself.'

'What happens now?' asked Simon.

'I will ship you to Le Havre from where you can move up the Seine to Paris. When you see the cardinal, have kind things to say about me.'

'When do we leave?' queried Harry. 'There is a problem. Rumours of continued trouble around Bordeaux have forced the government to blockade the mouth of the Garonne. No ships are being let in or out of the estuary.

My own infantry and cavalry detachments have been sent to join Turenne's troops surrounding Bordeaux and La Rochelle. Our fort is unmanned except for artillerymen ready to blast enemy ships out of the water. When the emergency is over or hopefully sooner, a royal ship of the line will move up the river to take you on board. Until then, enjoy my hospitality!'

Simon sought the latest news from Paris. The governor responded, 'Gentlemen, I only hear what is relevant to my position. We have been put on alert. Local authorities have been ordered to arrest a former confidant of Cardinal Mazarin and a one-time leader of the rebellion, who may be hiding in one of his many estates in this area. He is one of the late Prince of Conde''s bastard brood, Philippe, Vicomte Rousset.'

The Englishmen gave a spontaneous cheer and slapped each other forcibly on the back. The joy on their faces was clearly evident. The governor was intrigued. 'You are acquainted with this renegade aristocrat?' Harry answered, 'He is the man who arrested both of us on trumped up charges. He took advantage of the absence of our King to illegally interfere in English affairs.'

Harry and Simon spent pleasant afternoons soaking up the sun, and watching small boats sail up and down the river. Two days after their arrest, the tranquility was suddenly broken by a rising crescendo of voices shouting outside the gates of the fort. They took little notice until Simon understood their catch cry—'Death to the English murderers!'

A few shots were fired, and the artillerymen primed their muskets and ran to the main gate. At the same time, a servant ran from the chateau and shouted to Harry and Simon to follow him. Once inside the building, the doors were latched, but the governor could not put them at their ease. 'I am sorry. The front door will not hold for long. There is nowhere to hide.'

A confused Harry asked, 'Why are these people so incensed? Why do they want to kill us?'

The governor replied solemnly, 'I understand their anger. The recent rebellion severely disrupted their lives. Now, when everything appeared settled, the rebellion appears to have been reactivated. Everybody blames the English. They have listened to rumours that Cromwell will invade to help both the Protestants in La Rochelle and the radicals in the city of Bordeaux. All their miseries of the last five years are projected on to you.'

'Is there any hope of saving us from their wrath?' asked Simon. 'There is a slim chance. One of my men has left by a small boat. I hope he can reach Turenne's army in time.'

'What do you mean "in time"?' asked an apprehensive Harry.

21

'IF YOU LOOK THROUGH THE window, you will see that the mob carry rocks with which to stone you and ropes for a ritualistic hanging. Unfortunately, there is a gallows in the courtyard. My men are not skilled marksmen, and each of them will only get one shot off before the two hundred or more rioters subdue them. Given these odds, I have ordered them not to fire on the crowd. It would only inflame the situation.'

'What about your own safety?' Harry asked the governor. 'They will not harm me. I led them against the previous governor. I will try to calm them but anti-English sentiment is overwhelming. They believe that the fleet that lies off the coast is Cromwell's invasion fleet, even though Turenne has had it proclaimed in all churches that it is the king's fleet that comes to assist in containing the remnants of the rebellion.'

'Can we escape by boat as did your man?'

'Yes, if the tide was moving rapidly downstream, but, unfortunately, it is now moving back up river where you would quickly be recaptured. Our only hope is to delay the rioters until rescue comes from outside.'

The main gate collapsed, and the mob surged into the open courtyard. There was a massive cheer from the rioters and a few desultory shots from the artillerymen who withdrew and formed a cordon around their cannons. The mob ignored the guns and moved to the main door. It splintered after a few blows from men armed with axes, and the rioters spilled into the entrance hall. The governor met them. He spoke briefly but was gently manhandled and tied to a chair.

Harry and Simon resolved to die like true Englishmen. Their weapons had been removed on their initial arrest. They marched unarmed into the invading mob. Harry remembers little of what happened. They were both felled by swinging cudgels.

When they regained consciousness, they were in the courtyard, standing on a small wagon located beneath a scaffold. Ropes attached to the scaffold's crossbar were placed around their necks. They were about to be hanged.

The self-proclaimed executioner stood beside the dray with whip in hand, awaiting the signal to drive the horse and wagon away from his prisoners. A wagon was a useful substitute for a trap door.

Harry looked at the man who led the mob with mournful anticipation. He was about to order the execution when Simon spoke, 'As God-fearing Catholics, you would not wish a man to go to his eternal destination without the blessings of a priest. I am a fellow Catholic. Before you hang me, for the sake of the Mother of God and the blood of our Saviour; bring me a priest!'

After a short discussion, a woman left the courtyard to fetch the priest. The mob became silent, and the ropes were temporarily removed from around the men's necks. A compassionate girl in the crowd placed a flask of water in Harry's hand, which he half emptied and passed on to Simon. Simon whispered, 'Think of another delaying tactic when the chaplain arrives.'

He arrived too quickly, and Simon, kneeling in the cart, received the last rites. The priest spoke to the leader of the mob asking that Simon as a fellow Catholic be spared. After a shouting match between several of the rioters and a tearful intervention by at least two women, the plea was rejected.

The ropes were replaced around the necks of the two victims and hoods pulled down over their heads. Harry tensed as he felt the hangmen adjust the tension on the ropes. At the top of his voice, he recited in English the twenty-third psalm. He was hardly audible amid the jeering and shouting of the enraged mob. Then there was silence. Harry waited for the sound of the whip, encouraging the horse to pull the cart away and leave him swaying in the breeze.

Instead, the silence was broken by artillery fire. Harry was hit in the chest by a piece of shrapnel. His already-bruised-and-battered body ached with pain and bled from many a wound.

The crowd screamed, and Harry sensed panic amongst his tormenters. The cannonade was quickly followed by intense musket fire. The lack of individual cries suggested that the shots were being fired as a warning, rather than as part of a massacre.

As his hopes rose, he heard the potentially fatal whip, and the cart began to move. Simultaneously, he felt someone bound into the cart beside him—he expected a deathblow at any minute. Instead, the rope slackened as it was cut. His hood was removed, and he saw in the wagon with them, the priest and the woman who had given him the water.

Panic-stricken by the gunfire, the horse stampeded out of the courtyard. Harry and Simon jumped from the moving vehicle as the priest grabbed the reins and guided the distressed animal away.

In front of them was an amazing sight. At the fort's wharf was a royal ship of the line, whose guns were trained on the courtyard. Landing in organized fashion with muskets fully primed was a company of French marines. Harry had encountered the marines previously, but this company was not led by one of their officers but by a tall man in a bright red livery and cape. The marines fixed bayonets and moved slowly towards the mob, which quickly dispersed.

The man in the red livery approached Harry and Simon. 'Lord Stokey and Captain Lloyd?' The duo nodded, and Simon expressed his gratitude. The commander of the rescue force suggested that they find and free the governor. He handed the marines over to their own officers who deployed them as guards around all landward sides of the fort.

An hour later, the governor, the man in red, the marine commander who introduced himself as Lieutenant Heritier, and the naval captain gathered with Harry and Simon around a table laden with food and drink.

The Governor spoke directly to Harry and Simon, 'I am not sure that you realise what an honour it is to be rescued by this gentleman in red. He is France's leading swordsman and commander of France's most elite military unit, the household guards of His Eminence, the cardinal. This is Colonel Marcel Guarin.'

'And why are we so honoured?' asked a thankful but bemused Simon.

Guarin responded, 'The cardinal will explain in detail when he meets you. But, as soon as he heard of your unauthorized arrest, he took steps to have you rescued and remove any disharmony between France and England. He was surprised that both the English Court and the government of the English Republic reacted so dramatically. Charles II was livid and promised an alliance with Holland rather than France, and Cromwell threatened his fleet would bombard the French coast—an overreaction if you are simply who you say you are.'

Guarin looked both men in the eye, expecting his concentrated glare would provoke a confession. Harry who was tucking into a pork dish of exquisite taste and tenderness ignored the visual request and responded prosaically, 'What happens now?'

The naval captain replied, 'When the tide turns, we sail for Le Havre. From there, the Comte Guarin will escort you to the cardinal; after which, you will be free to return to the English Court.'

Simon asked, 'What is the latest news of Vicomte Rousset, the author of our plight, and, I imagine, an embarrassment to the cardinal?' Guarin was thoughtful before replying, 'Rousset was dismissed by the cardinal from all his positions, and I was ordered to arrest him for treason. Sadly, he disappeared. The cardinal believes he is in the south of France trying to resurrect the rebellion with his former allies among the Frondeurs.'

Guarin lowered his voice and addressed the Englishmen in a confidential manner, 'Why were you arrested?' Harry spoke for both of them, 'We believe that Rousset is implicated in the murder of one of Queen Henriette Marie's ladies-in-waiting, Lady Lucy Harman.'

Guarin tensed, 'Well, gentlemen, Rousset may have added another victim to his tally. Just before I left Paris, the cardinal was informed that another lady-in-waiting to the English queen had been found dead—an Elizabeth Mortimer.'

Harry almost choked on his spiced pork. 'Damnation, I was just about to interview her again when I was kidnapped. She was Rousset's lover. She was probably killed to hide what she knew.' 'Knew about what?' asked the ever alert Guarin. 'That is what we hoped to discover,' replied a cautious and suspicious Simon.

The group took their goblets and wandered out into the courtyard to enjoy the cool breeze wafting from the river. The naval captain led Harry aside. 'I have some very good news for you, which my commanding officer, Captain Sauvel, thought you might wish to keep confidential. Your former commanding officer, Colonel Tremayne, is alive and reasonably well, but he has one major disability. When you jumped from the boat, he cracked his head on a large rock and has completely lost his memory. He is apparently learning French and engaged in inquisitorial work for his new master, Henri St. Michel, Marquis des Anges.'

Tears ran down Harry's face. 'Thank god! Will his memory return?'

'No one knows'.

'Where can I find him?'

'He is living on the Marquis's estate near Rouen that you entered after leaving the ship.'

Harry shook the captain's hand and then sat on one of the bollards and reminisced about his many adventures with Luke. Nostalgia for the Cromwellian army overwhelmed him. His latest mission appeared like a dream in which he did not really participate. He was brought back to reality as, in the darkness, a white barn owl swept past his face.

Simon had noticed the discussion between Harry and the sailor and innocently asked, 'What was that about? He seemed to cheer you up. Had you met him before?'

'No, I have never met him, but his commanding officer, who controls the fleet outside the estuary and I, are old friends. On a previous occasion, he acted for France, and I for England in a very delicate matter. The captain was passing on his commander's greetings.'

Before first light the next morning, Harry and Simon were aboard the French frigate that drifted out into the river and allowed the tide to turn her a full 180 degrees. The captain did not bother to put up sail until Bordeaux had been passed. It did not take long for the ship to be well out to sea, and as the sun rose higher, the might of the French fleet could be seen riding at anchor on the edge of the Garonne estuary.

Simon had been a little surprised with the naval captain's one to one conversation with Harry. He was further troubled when his fellow adventurer spent some time alone with Colonel Guarin. Simon was increasingly suspicious. Was his friend, Harry, a French spy? That would explain the excellent treatment they had received and the presence of Cardinal Mazarin's right hand man at their rescue. King Charles himself did not receive such friendly assistance from the French.

Simon would have been further troubled if he had overheard what Guarin had said. The Frenchman warned Harry that the cardinal would put a number of proposals to him.

Harry too was troubled.

22

Mazarin's Apartment Two Weeks Earlier

THE CARDINAL WAS LIVID. TO trust the irresponsible aristocracy was dangerous. He knew that Vicomte Rousset was a political trimmer, but he had assumed that the man understood that his thwarted political ambition could best be realised through loyal service to Louis XIV through his chief minister. Rousset had been given a simple task to uncover the Cromwellian agent at the court of the exiled English king. He had been given unprecedented power and status to accomplish this, being made both France's official envoy to Charles II and commander of a large body of troops to impose French sovereignty outside the walls of the St. Germain estate.

The cardinal had just learnt that Rousset had exceeded his authority and arrested the acting commander of Charles's bodyguard—and the officer commanding all troops within the English enclave—and had whisked him off to parts unknown. Even worse, he had taken over security within the English compound. The cardinal had just ended a fiery interview with Charles's usually placid chief minister, Sir Edward Hyde, who had accused him of abducting an English officer from within the English Court and infringing English sovereignty by imposing French troops within its confines. The enraged English minister demanded the immediate release of Captain Lloyd and the withdrawal of French troops from within the Chateau St. Germain.

The cardinal denied any infringement of English sovereignty as Rousset had not acted on his orders but at the express wish of the English Crown, as represented by the Queen Mother. Sir Edward should take up the matter with Henriette Marie. Whatever face Mazarin put on developments, his plan to win English support had suffered a setback—much more serious than he had anticipated. A week later, he was staggered to receive an ultimatum from the English government in London threatening military reprisals along the French coast if the English officer was not found and released.

Rousset had become a problem. Mazarin summoned his confidant, Marcel Guarin, who was not only a soldier of integrity, but also a trained lawyer. The cardinal outlined the relevant events and was just about to ask Guarin his views when a servant interrupted them. 'Your Eminence, there is a courier from the English Court who insists on seeing you as a matter of urgency.'

The servant entered the room, bowed extravagantly to the cardinal, and explained. 'My mistress sends me here to deliver a verbal message.'

'Which is?'

'Viscount Rousset has committed another outrage. He has arrested Lord Stokey, King Charles's leading courtier, and a man well known to you as an able diplomat, and one of the highest ranking peers in the British Isles.'

'Is Rousset insane? Why has he committed this atrocity?' asked an incredulous cardinal. 'Lord Stokey returned from England, and informed Queen Henriette, in the absence of the King, that a large hoard of English Catholic treasure in some way associated with the late Lady Lucy Harman was hidden at court. My mistress speculates that Rousset wants to get his hands on that treasure,' replied the well-informed courier.

Mazarin raised doubts, 'Rousset is a very wealthy man in his own right. He is seigneur to dozens of estates in the south of France and as an army officer, spends a lot less than most aristocrats by not maintaining a minicourt for his retainers.'

Marcel kept focused on obvious. 'We must find both these Englishmen and return them to the English Court, hopefully unharmed—and Rousset must be withdrawn immediately from St. Germain.'

Mazarin dismissed the messenger and turned to his friend, 'Agreed, but how do I handle Rousset in the longer term?'

'Question him before you decide. I will take a troop of your men to St. Germain to escort him to an urgent interview with Your Eminence.'

'You will do more than that. I will withdraw Rousset's company from St. Germain forthwith and return them to garrison duties at Rouen. You will take a company of my men and replace Rousset's troops but only in regard to the external protection of the English Court. You are to return control within the conclave to the English authorities. Bring Rousset here tomorrow afternoon. Let's not alarm him! Give him the impression we are very pleased with his work.'

Next afternoon Mazarin received Rousset with a show of friendship and congratulated him on his achievements at the English Court. 'My dear Rousset, I have received a constant stream of reports from St. Germain. I understand you accepted the offer of the English Queen to take over security within the English Court?'

'Yes, Your Eminence! The Queen felt insecure. The man responsible for her security, a Captain Lloyd, was revealed by an Irish visitor as a Cromwellian spy.'

'Did you confirm this Irishman's allegations?'

'Eventually! I thought it best to remove Lloyd from the English Court immediately in case he should assassinate their King.' Guarin bristled. 'A strange reaction! There was no urgency. The English king is in the Netherlands for weeks.'

'Where did you take Lloyd?' asked the Cardinal.

'To the Bishop's Prison.'

'If you considered him a spy, why not take him to the Bastille?'

Rousset hesitated for a moment and then confided, 'I assessed that a man of Lloyd's experience would not confess to his crimes without the application of torture.'

Mazarin nearly fell off his chair. 'Rousset, don't tell me you tortured an English courtier-soldier on the say so of an Irish mercenary?'

'Yes, and with great success! As a result, I can report two things for sure. Captain Lloyd is an agent of Oliver Cromwell, fanatically loyal to his immediate superior, a Colonel Luke Tremayne, and to the general; and he is no threat to France. He and Tremayne are in France to achieve a mission at the English Court. They are not concerned with assessing French military positions nor naval deployment, nor were they involved in any plans to assist the Protestants nor the remnants of the Frondeurs.'

'Excellent work, Rousset! You have acted brilliantly in the interests of France. However, the English are understandably more than annoyed by what they see as interfering in English affairs, and it was probably undiplomatic to have accepted the English Queen's request to take over the security of the English Court. You should have consulted me before taking that step.'

'What happens now?' asked an unsuspecting Rousset.

'You have given me the information I needed regarding the Cromwellian spy at the English Court, and as a bonus, you have cleared him of any intention to harm France. All we need to do is to return Lloyd to the English and remove you from the situation. You are promoted to the rank of colonel. You and your men will return to garrison duty in Rouen. I am also withdrawing you as France's envoy to the Charles's court. Where is Lloyd? He must be freed immediately.'

Rousset was slow to reply. 'Good god,' exclaimed Mazarin. 'You have not had him killed?'

'No, he lives, but I do not know exactly where he is. He is somewhere on the road to Toulouse. My men are taking him for safe custody to a dungeon on one of my estates. I did not want the English to find him before Your Eminence was ready to release him.'

'Thank you Rousset! You deserve a rest. Do not return to the Rouen garrison for four weeks. Enjoy your break!'

Rousset was almost out the door when Guarin at Mazarin's instigation asked, 'And where is Lord Stokey?' It was Rousset's turn to be agitated and cross. 'That, Colonel Guarin, is a personal matter involving a code of honour.'

The Cardinal rose from his seat and advanced towards Rousset. 'I am afraid that any actions of yours involving the English Court is a matter of state. I will not push you to elaborate the code of honour that forced you to abduct Lord Stokey, but I must know where he is and return him to the English forthwith.' 'He is with Lloyd, both of them are heading towards Toulouse under escort.' Mazarin waved Rousset away.

After the Vicomte had left, Mazarin turned to Guarin. 'It is interesting that he did not mention any treasure or any innuendos involving himself in the affair.'

Guarin smiled. 'Is that why you gave him four weeks to report to Rouen? You hope he will act in that period to find the treasure.'

'Yes, but I want you to have him followed until he finally reports to Rouen.'

'And how do we recover the two Englishmen?'

'I will send orders to all the authorities along the Paris-Toulouse road to have these men detained but in no way harmed. I will also send a similar order to Le Havre to be delivered by ship to all authorities along the Garonne. And I want you to accompany a frigate from Le Havre up the Garonne and move towards Toulouse with a company of marines to find our two victims. These are dangerous times, and two Englishmen alone in that troubled area will need all the protection available. I can only pray that no harm has befallen them.'

The following midday, Guarin, just before his departure for Le Havre, reported that he had placed Rousset under surveillance and that for the moment, the quarry showed no hurry to leave his accommodation at the Chateau de St. Germain, although all his men had gone and their places taken by the cardinal's musketeers. Their conversation was interrupted by a servant who announced, 'Your Eminence, the same courier who came the other day from the English Court wishes to see you urgently.'

The courier did not dwell on formalities. 'There has been another murder at the English Court. The lover of the Vicomte Rousset, Mistress Elizabeth Mortimer has been found dead in the forest adjacent to the Chateau de St. Germain.'

'Was her death suspicious?'

'As she was found outside of the boundaries of the chateau, the officer in charge of your musketeers is investigating, but the rumour running wild through the court is that the Vicomte Rousset is involved.' Mazarin dismissed the courier and indicated to Guarin that he would follow up this investigation that fortuitously was now in the hands of his own musketeers.

Two days later, he received the report, which stated that, a week earlier, Bess Mortimer went riding, as was her practice. She regularly met her lover, Vicomte Rousset, in the forest. When she did not return, her friends assumed she had gone off with Rousset for a day or two—a not infrequent happening.

Sir Edward Hyde, who had temporarily taken command of the English soldiers, assisted the cardinal's lieutenant. Hyde ascertained from the other ladies-in-waiting that, on the day of her disappearance, they had seen the Vicomte around the court, and Lady Gresham heard him order four of his men to follow Bess Mortimer into the forest. She innocently assumed that it was to protect his irresponsible lover from her spur of the moment escapades.'

23

Three Weeks Later

HARRY AND SIMON WAITED IN an antechamber in the Louvre for Cardinal Mazarin to return from his daily discussion with young Louis XIV. After almost an hour, the cardinal arrived and, with an imperious wave, indicated that Simon should follow him into his inner chamber.

Mazarin spoke as he removed his cape, 'Lord Stokey, I wish to interview each of you separately, so that I can get the most accurate picture possible of your adventures and the role played in them by Vicomte Rousset. Tell me all!' Simon did.

The Cardinal responded, 'I have apologized both to King Charles and to the English government in London, but I pointed out that Rousset was not acting on my instructions and completely overstepped diplomatic boundaries when he accepted your Queen Mother's request to take over the internal security of the English Court. King Charles has spoken severely to his mother. One of my guards will escort you back to St. Germain.'

'That will not be necessary, Your Eminence. I will wait for Captain Lloyd, and we will find our own way back.'

'You may wait for Captain Lloyd, but my man will escort both of you nevertheless. He is now located at St. Germain. I have replaced Rousset's large number of musketeers with a company of my own elite guards to protect the perimeters of the English Court. I have yet to decide on a new envoy to replace Rousset.'

Harry's interview started dramatically. The Cardinal announced, 'I told Lord Stokey that I wished to see you independently so that I could get a clear picture of what happened. That was a lie. I wanted to see you alone to put a proposition to you.

You work for General Cromwell. One of the few positive achievements of Rousset was that, under torture, you confirmed that fact. It explains why Cromwell threatened France with a naval bombardment. It was not to help a low ranking Royalist officer but one of his own top agents. I want good relations with the English Republic through the man who is in control—General Cromwell. You will act as my go-between in these negotiations.'

Harry blustered, 'Your Eminence, your intelligence is astray. Yes, I was, until recently, an officer in Cromwell's army, but I am now deputy commander of the King Charles's bodyguard. Our young king is not stupid. He would see through any double agents at his court.'

Mazarin smiled. 'Have it your way, young man, but I am sure you will pass on to Cromwell my suggestion.' The Cardinal signalled the end of the interview, and Harry rejoined Simon in the antechamber.

The interview was so short that Harry felt he had to explain to Simon. Harry told him that Mazarin had sought to recruit him as a French agent, and when he refused, the Cardinal terminated the meeting. Simon's reaction was predictable. 'Tell the King as soon as he returns!'

Mazarin's next visitor was Marcel Guarin. Guarin reported on the rescue of the two men. Mazarin nodded approvingly and then asked, 'Was there anything unusual in the behaviour of Stokey or Lloyd?'

'Lloyd talked earnestly with the captain of our frigate. I was intrigued as to what these men might have in common, so I later asked the naval officer for an explanation. His answer was interesting. He brought greetings from the commander-in-chief of the king's Atlantic fleet. Apparently, our naval chief and the young English officer were engaged in a joint enterprise quite recently.'

Mazarin paled, 'Is Sauvel a traitor?'

'No. During your enforced absence, Queen Anne, on behalf of the English Queen Mother, sent Sauvel to England. The result was the safe return to France of one of our long-standing agents in London.'

A meeting with Lady Jane Torrington, his spy at the court of the English king, completed Mazarin's busy morning. 'My lady, what is known about the latest murder?'

'Sir Edward Hyde in the absence of the king's party in Holland, and the abduction of Captain Lloyd and Lord Stokey took personal control of the investigation. His assessment is clear. He is certain that Mortimer was murdered because of her knowledge of the death of Lucy Harman. Hyde says that Lloyd suspected that Harman had been murdered because of something she knew. He had established that Mortimer bullied Harman and seemed to be acting in concert with her lover, your recent appointment to our court, Vicomte Rousset.'

'Do the English believe that Mortimer was murdered by Rousset?'

'That will certainly be Captain Lloyd's conclusion when he resumes his enquiry.'

'Did Lloyd's disappearance upset any of your fellow ladies-in-waiting more than the others?'

'Yes, two of them were particularly overwrought. Lady Catherine Beaumont is Lloyd's constant companion. They are lovers. She was distressed and understandably so.

The other was a surprise. Lady Mary Gresham, who is very close to King Charles and to the Queen Mother, was utterly devastated. She left the Queen's presence when Lloyd was arrested before being excused by Her Majesty and ran across the courtyard to inform Sir Edward Hyde. But, as you know, I did the same to get the message to you—your man at court went berserk.'

Mazarin ignored Jane's scarcely concealed rebuke and asked, 'Tell me again. What charge did Rousset proffer to Queen Henriette to justify Lloyd's arrest?'

'That he was an agent of General Cromwell.'

'Did Rousset indicate why he held such suspicions?'

'Yes, he had the word of an Irish officer who had served in Cromwell's army and who was aboard the ship in which Lloyd and his commanding officer, Colonel Tremayne, entered France. This officer immediately reported the presence of Cromwell's men to the naval authorities in Le Havre. The navy pursued the two spies, who disappeared in the vicinity of Rouen. If Lloyd was one of these men, he somehow convinced King Charles and Lord Ashcroft that he was a genuine deserter to the Royalist cause.'

Or, as Mazarin mused to himself, he is a special agent of Cromwell's appointed to deal directly with King Charles. The English government in exile was not a fool, but they were playing a very dangerous game.

After Lady Jane had departed, the cardinal turned his attention back to Rousset. The man had betrayed him and had seriously embarrassed France's relations with England. If a disgruntled Rousset rejoined the almost-extinguished rebels, he posed a threat to French security.

Of more immediate concern was that Rousset might be a serial killer and, as Lord Stokey implied, on the trail of a large fortune in English Catholic treasure. After a considerable time lost in thought, Mazarin rubbed his hands together and smiled. He had a plan to kill several birds with the one stone.

The cardinal took some light refreshments that passed for his midday meal. He did not look forward to his afternoon of receiving members of the public who all claimed they had information that was vital to the security of France or needed the cardinal's help to achieve a specific objective. Several levels of bureaucrats had previously interviewed these people, and Marcel Guarin and his men had investigated the final six. There were still plenty of people who would assassinate the cardinal given the opportunity.

Guarin provided background information for the first supplicant. 'Your Eminence, Georges Livet who awaits your summons mentioned the same location and personalities that were raised this morning by Lord Stokey and Captain Lloyd.'

The now-interested cardinal indicated to Guarin to admit Livet and was somewhat taken aback by the man that confronted him. Livet was a well-built man whose face was almost completely covered by brown hair with the occasional streak of grey. His hair fell well below his shoulders, and he had a fringe that covered his entire forehead reaching to his eyebrows. A beard that started below each ear was wild and woolly and reached his chest. An equally unkempt moustache obscured much of his top lip and arched down to join his beard.

Mazarin thought instinctually of a wild man of the forest that permeated much of Italian and French literature. This not unreasonable reaction was countered by the extravagance of the man's dress. The supplicant had money and knew how to use it in presenting himself. Given Mazarin's obsession with status, he immediately noticed that the embroidery in Livet's doublet was of gold thread, a privilege reserved exclusively to the high aristocracy. Mazarin saw his opportunity to humiliate this petitioner and give himself the initiative in the interview.

'My man, you risk imprisonment coming before me decked out in gold embroidery. A Rouen merchant and shipper has no right to wear such finery.'

Livet was not ruffled and responded aggressively, 'Your Eminence, I do have that right, and it explains why I have disguised my appearance and needed to see you. Georges Livet is a name I gave myself in Canada and have continued to use since my return a few years ago. I made a fortune in New France trading with the Iroquois and, subsequently, as a ship owner transporting Canadian beaver pelts to France and most of the needs of the Canadian settlers—spades, picks, clothing, and, sometimes, grain to New France. I am now established in Rouen society and wish Your Eminence to right a severe injustice and to install me in my rightful place.'

'And what would that be?'

'I am Emile St. Michel, younger half brother to Henri St. Michel, Marquis des Anges, one of France's highest ranking nobles outside the Royal family.'

'And why would I replace your half brother and give the title to you?'

'Twenty-five years ago, my father banished me to Canada for being overfamiliar with my brother's young bride. Years later, I received a letter from my sister to inform me that my brother's wife had died in tragic circumstances; and, at the same time, her son, Alain, had gone berserk, murdered some peasants, and was confined to a dungeon in southern France. Neither events concerned me at the time as I was engrossed with my frontier life and building up my fortune.'

'What changed your mind?'

'When I relocated to Rouen as Georges Livet, I made enquiries of the Rouen magistrates, whom I got to know socially, of the events surrounding the Chateau des Anges in my twenty-five-year absence. One of them revealed where Alain had been sent. I also struck up an acquaintance with a man I knew before my exile who had resumed his regular visits to the Chateau, Philippe Rousset.'

Mazarin sucked in a deep breath. 'What did you do with this information?'

'I went south to where Alain was incarcerated. The gaolers, helped by a significant inducement, turned a blind eye while I helped the unfortunate lad to escape. I did not reveal that I was his uncle but made clear that I was an enemy of his father, and, given his unfair detention, we should work together to get justice for both of us.

Alain revealed a story that shocked even me. He claimed that his father, the marquis, had murdered his wife, destroyed the evidence, and convinced the magistrates not to investigate the matter further and that he, Alain, had been detained to prevent him revealing such an atrocity.'

'Bring forward Alain with any evidence he has, and I will order the magistrates at Rouen to investigate the matter.'

Emile fell silent and finally announced, 'I cannot. Alain is dead. He was celebrating his release with me at an inn in Toulouse when he suddenly took a fit and died.'

'Without evidence it is not a matter that I can concern myself with.'

'Your Eminence, at least order an enquiry! The magistrates may discover the truth. My half brother is a murderer and as such, should be removed from his position. Then the title will revert to me.'

'I am afraid it will not. The marquis has long been remarried and has an heir by his second wife. There are only two ways you could receive the title—if Henri St. Michel is removed from his position as a murderer and his heirs die, or if you can prove that the marquis is a traitor. Then the Crown can confiscate his titles and lands and could bestow them upon you. In the Crown's current impoverished state, it is highly unlikely.'

Emile left the interview with a smile. He already knew that Henri had remarried and that there was a young heir. Their removal would not prove a difficulty, and the cardinal had also given him another line of attack—convince the authorities that Henri was a traitor and rely on the Crown's generosity.

24

English Court, St. Germain, Several Weeks Later

HARRY SETTLED BACK INTO HIS role as acting head of security and commander of English troops within the Royal Court with clear priorities. He must complete his investigation into the murder of Lady Lucy Harman and clarify what had happened to Bess Mortimer. Rousset must be captured and his role in the deaths of both women and in the search for English Catholic treasure established.

Harry's determination to settle the personal score of his false imprisonment gave the hunt for Rousset added intensity. Harry also awaited instructions from Cromwell concerning Mazarin's proposal for him to provide a direct link between the cardinal and the general. Last but not least, he would visit Luke at the earliest opportunity.

On the Mazarin proposal, he soon received a coded order—a code deliberately leaked to the French authorities. Cromwell required Harry to accept the cardinal's offer. He would be Oliver Cromwell's personal but secret representative to Cardinal Mazarin, as well as to the English king. Cromwell's true wishes were relayed some days later through Lady Catherine.

The secure coded message reiterated the acceptance of Mazarin's suggestion but included the condition that Harry should inform Charles II of his double role immediately on the king's return from the Netherlands. There was a further order that took Harry by surprise. He was not to see Luke. Cromwell would personally take care of that matter. Harry was to concentrate on his dual roles at the English Court and with the French government.

Harry invited the three ladies-in-waiting—Mary Gresham, Cate Beaumont, and Jane Torrington for a general discussion on the two murders and the behaviour of Rousset. Jane and Cate added nothing to the information concerning the Mortimer murder already provided to Sir Edward Hyde and the cardinal's lieutenant.

The three women were all convinced that Rousset ordered the murder of both Lucy and Bess in order to discover or to conceal knowledge of a Catholic treasure. Lord Stokey, who on his return had regaled the court with his views on this matter, only confirmed their perception of Rousset's involvement.

New evidence came from Mary Gresham who revealed that, during his stint as Henriette's bodyguard, Rousset ordered his men to examine, after dark, every outbuilding on the estate. And, during the day, on the excuse of uncovering more spies, they thoroughly searched most of the rooms in the chateau itself. Mary believed they were looking for the treasure, but after such intensive, uninterrupted searching, Rousset concluded it was not there. Jane who had listened to Mary's information added, 'But there were two places they did not search—The queen's bedchamber and the Chapel of St. Magdalene.'

Cate Beaumont blushed. It was the chapel in which she hid her codebook despite Harry's suggestions that she keep it closer to herself. Harry asked, 'Why didn't Rousset search the chapel?' Jane replied, 'At the time, the body of a leper was left there. The chaplain would not bury the victim until he was paid, and the gravediggers refused to work. Rousset's men also refused to enter the chapel until the victim was buried and the chapel, physically and ritualistically cleansed.'

Mary nodded. 'That's true! I went to the chapel one evening and was told of the problem by the sexton. I sat in the shadows on the seat beneath the statue of St. Magdalene when I saw Rousset approach the chapel. He pushed the sexton aside and entered the building. Within minutes, the chaplain, waving part of the leper's clothing under Rousset's nose and abusing him in words not fit for a priest, ejected him. Rousset was not amused.'

Next day, Harry was pleasantly surprised by a visit from Colonel Guarin. The two soldiers greeted each other cordially, and Guarin handed Harry a document that contained the evidence gathered by Guarin's deputy into the murder of Bess Mortimer. She had been shot in the back while riding in the forest. She had fallen from her horse, and her body was dragged beside a fallen tree trunk and lightly covered in leaves.

The horse was never found, but Guarin's man assumed it was returned to Rousset's then stable attached to the coach house. It could not be used to prove their complicity in the murder because Rousset had permitted Bess Mortimer to take any horse she wished from the military stable. She apparently never picked the same horse twice.

As Harry accepted the report, he asked, 'And why are you really here, Marcel? Your lieutenant, with whom I deal daily, could have given me this dossier.'

'True. I bring you the latest news concerning Rousset. Before I went south to rescue you, I had my best men follow him. The cardinal gave him a break of four weeks, hoping that he would reveal something of interest to our various investigations.

When I returned to Paris and took over the surveillance personally, I was surprised to find that when he finally left his apartment in the Chateau St. Germain, Rousset made his way to the Chateau des Anges near Rouen. He stayed there for little more than a day. My men reported yesterday that he is back in Paris staying at an inn in St. Germain where he met four of his men who have obviously deserted, as they should have been on garrison duty in Rouen.'

'Your men have done well,' exclaimed Harry.

'Better than you think. One of my men got so close that he could hear their loud conversation reflecting the amount of drink they had consumed. They meet tonight at the Chapel of St. Magdalene; after which, according to their drunken boasts, they will all be extremely wealthy.'

'Excellent, this fits my intelligence that the only places that Rousset did not search in the Chateau de St. Germain were the queen's bedchamber, which I have asked her ladies to discreetly search, and that chapel.'

'As the chapel is within the English Court, I will leave this operation to you, Harry. My men will continue their surveillance of Rousset should he escape your clutches. However, when you capture him, hand him over to me.'

As soon as Marcel departed, Harry sent two of his men to ascertain the situation at the inn. Rousset was nowhere to be found, but his four henchmen were still there openly wearing their gold and black livery and consuming immense amounts of Normandy cider.

As dusk fell, Harry placed his men in strategic positions around the chapel. Within the hour, five hooded men emerged from the shadows and entered the chapel unimpeded. There was some noise as the drunken rabble overturned statues and forced open coffins in their search for the treasure, which Rousset had promised as the guarantee of their recruitment. Harry had given orders not to move until Rousset's men had time enough to search the chapel. He would capture Rousset and recover the hoard in the one operation.

Harry's hand was forced prematurely when a distraught chaplain came fleeing from the chapel screaming murder and arson. Harry moved in with Simon by his side. Four men were quickly located and arrested. Their failure to find substantial treasure and their inebriation had led them to settle on the few precious objects contained in the chapel.

Harry froze. He suddenly realised he had been duped. 'Damn, that varlet Rousset has escaped. Five men entered the chapel, and we have captured only four.' 'And the fifth one ran past us disguised as the chaplain,' deduced an angry Simon.

A thorough search of the chapel uncovered the real chaplain. He had been half strangled, stripped of his outer clothes, and placed in a sepulcher with just enough of an opening to allow him to breathe. The treasure was not in the chapel, and Harry had allowed Rousset to slip through his fingers.

As one of his men bustled, a shackled and inebriated would-be robber passed him. Harry managed a smile. 'Well, well, well, it is nice to meet you again, Rougemont. I see your commander has run out on you, and as the senior officer amongst the men we have caught, you will suffer the most severe of penalties. This time, your incarceration will be for real. Take him away!'

Next day, Mary Gresham reported on behalf of the ladies-in-waiting whom he had asked to search the queen's bedchamber. No treasure was found. He then interrogated Rougemont who initially was stupidly aggressive. 'I am a Frenchman. You have no jurisdiction over me.'

Harry could not conceal his contempt, 'Never fear, I will eventually hand you over to the French authorities where you will be charged with complicity in the illegal abduction and torture of Lord Stokey and myself. Even more damning, you will be charged with sacrilege for your ransacking of the Chapel of St. Magdalene and the attempted murder of its chaplain. The chaplain who is not a young man is in a bad way, and, should he die, you will be charged with his murder. A minimum of twenty to thirty years in the Bishop's Prison lies ahead—unless you can persuade me to be more lenient.'

'How can I do that?' asked the wretched man, who suddenly realised the seriousness of his situation.'

'Answer my questions honestly! Why did Rousset arrest Stokey and myself? Why did he move us both out of Paris so quickly? Did he have any part in the murder of Harman or Mortimer? And what do you know about the treasure?'

Rougement tried to delay the inevitable, 'Can I have a drink and my fetters removed?'

'Your fetters stay, but I will send for water.'

'I need something stronger than water.' Harry was willing to oblige. A slightly intoxicated person might be encouraged to reveal more than an uptight sober prisoner. Harry poured him a large ceramic mug of brandy and indicated he would return in a couple of hours to begin the interrogation. The mug was refilled on several occasions by obliging gaolers.

When Harry eventually returned, Rougement was relaxed and ready to talk. He began without prompting. 'Captain Rousset's lover heard one of the other ladies-in-waiting praying about a treasure. This lover, Mortimer, bullied the girl, certain that the wench knew its whereabouts.

Rousset was convinced that it was hidden at the English Court. He knew that when she came to court, Lucy Harman received a large casket brought to her by her wealthy father. Rousset assumed that this very rich Catholic peer had smuggled the family wealth out of England to prevent it being confiscated by the Protestant Parliamentarians. He became even more obsessive when Stokey revealed that the treasure was not limited to the wealth of one family.'

'Did Rousset kill Lucy Harman?'

'No! Her death was an accident, but he implied that his lover Mortimer was over zealous in her interrogation of the girl. Mortimer later turned on the captain threatening to say that he had murdered Harman because the girl refused to reveal the location of the treasure. He always denied any responsibility in the Harman death and was rightly furious with his lover. He eventually ordered four of his men to follow the blackmailing wench into the forest and kill her.'

This candid confession took Harry by surprise. He asked, 'Are you personally confessing to the murder of Bess Mortimer?' Rougemont had been too clever by half. 'That is not what I said.'

Harry went for the kill. 'No, but four men rode out to murder Bess; four men were ready to rob the chapel and assault the chaplain. It is not unreasonable to suspect they were the same four men, of whom you are the leader, whom Rousset trusted implicitly to do his dirty work.'

Rougemont ignored the accusation and ploughed on with his exposition. 'Your arrest was not planned, but the arrival of that Irishman at the English Court gave the captain a perfect opportunity to ingratiate himself with the cardinal who had ordered him to uncover any Cromwellian agents. Queen Henriette's request to take over the security of the English Court put him in an even better position to act. Your arrest as a spy provided him with the opportunity to discover what you knew, or did not know, about the murder and the treasure.'

'Did he get such proof?'

'Oh yes, under a combination of drugs and sleep deprivation, you revealed all—namely you were a spy for Oliver Cromwell and, much to Rousset's concern, that you suspected him of involvement in Harman's murder. You were shipped out of Paris because he could not risk you continuing your enquiries.'

'And what about Stokey?'

'He was unlucky. He returned from Britain with more evidence of a Catholic treasure, which he was determined to find before others misused it. In all innocence, he told Queen Henriette, who immediately informed her then head of security, Rousset. He acted very quickly. Stokey was in the Bishop's Prison before he had unpacked from his English visit.'

'And what was going to happen to us in the south of France?'

'Our men had orders to encourage your escape so that you could lawfully be shot. Failing that, your new gaolers would be informed that Rousset would be grateful if you never left their dungeon alive.'

Harry paled and felt slightly ill.

25

Six Weeks Earlier, Chateau des Anges

NORMAL LIFE AT THE CHATEAU ceased for six weeks. The marquis and marquise, accompanied by Mathieu Gillot, visited their other estates along the German frontier. Father Morel used the period in retreat within the family's Abbey des Anges, and Pascal de Foix went to see his relatives in La Rochelle. The household heard from Philippe, Viscount Rousset at his last dinner with them before everybody dispersed that Cardinal Mazarin had summoned him to Paris.

Luke's improved standing in the household was evident in the Marquis's decision to place him in control of the estate. Mathieu briefed Luke on the immediate issues but made clear that he should leave important decisions until the family returned. Luke was left with the pleasant company of Josette St. Michel and Odette Bonnet. He thoroughly enjoyed five weeks of relaxation, good food, and visits with them to Rouen. His casual conversations with them revealed little that helped with his investigation, an investigation for which he had lost his appetite following the discovery of the marquis's button in the tower.

In the fifth week of this idyllic existence, the chateau received a surprise visitor. Rousset returned, anxiously wanting a meeting with the marquis. He became agitated when he discovered that the marquis would not return for at least another week. Luke scrutinized

Rousset as he shared a sumptuous meal of a dozen courses with the reduced household.

Rousset revealed flashes of extreme anger, mixed with overweening trepidation. As part of the social chitchat, Luke asked, 'How is your assignment in Paris progressing? Is the cardinal using your talents?'

Rousset gradually relaxed as he told a selective version of recent events. He had been sent to guard the English Court and to uncover a Cromwellian agent therein. He was successful and the cardinal had promoted him to the rank of colonel and reassigned him back to the garrison at Rouen.

Luke responded, 'Congratulations! So you are back at the garrison?'

'No, not for a week or so! The Cardinal gave me several weeks between assignments.'

'But we will see quite a lot of you again?'

'Not necessarily, I may be sent to England or the Low Countries. I wanted to see Henri urgently in case I have to depart for overseas unexpectedly.'

'In the marquis's absence, can I help?' asked Luke.

'No, I will return to Paris; and, pending the results of that visit, I may not need Henri's help. If things go badly I will be back within the fortnight to complete my business with him.'

Luke knew he should feel some sort of negative reaction to Philippe's uncovering of a Cromwellian agent. From what he has been told, he was himself a Cromwellian agent, but he had absolutely no recollection of the fact or what it meant. If he really was such a person, why had the English army done nothing to rescue him? On the other hand, perhaps he should take the initiative and return to England. When he had completed his assignment for the St. Michels, he would seek their assistance to facilitate his homecoming.

These investigations were almost complete. Did Henri murder his first wife, and who was trying to kill his present spouse? So far, he had reached the opposite conclusion on each case. He accepted Josette's word that Henri did not kill Antoinette, but, on the basis of the button, the marquis was the prime suspect in the attack on Charlotte.

Within a week of Rousset's departure, everybody returned to the Chateau des Anges and life quickly reverted to normal. Luke reported Philippe's visit and the probability that he would soon return. And he did. Henri had been home a week when Philippe arrived. He looked even more desperate than on his previous visit. This was not the Philippe of old. He appeared in serious trouble.

During the evening meal, Luke noticed that Henri constantly observed Philippe. At the end of the repast, the former announced that Philippe needed to see him urgently and that Luke and Mathieu should wait in the antechamber as he may need their advice. Luke and Mathieu frowned at each other. Henri always conducted business on his own—a habit that Mathieu had not been able to stop. To be on hand in case he was needed was a first. Did Henri expect Philippe to be troublesome?

As Luke and Mathieu sat in the antechamber, the latter pointed to another change in routine. The door to Henri's chamber was left open. Henri, when discussing business, always shut the door himself. Henri was also speaking loudly, and Philippe's volume increased rapidly as Henri resisted his demands. Luke and Mathieu moved closer to the half-open door where they could hear every word of an escalating argument, which had been Henri's intention.

'I want my half yearly income but six months in advance,' shouted Philippe.

'I cannot give you what I do not have. Your income for the last six months has not been forwarded to me, let alone funds to pay you in advance. You know full well that your family needed every livre it could obtain from the Bourbon-Conde´ estates to finance its uprising against Mazarin and the Queen Mother. You are lucky that your income is protected by the special deed drawn up by your father. The delay in the provision of these funds is temporary.'

'Henri, I must undertake a long mission abroad and would like to have my coffers filled with the monies owed to me. I do not trust a regular flow of income while I am out of France. If my family money is not immediately available, lend me the equivalent! You are the wealthiest man in France.'

'No, Philippe, I will not lend you the equivalent of your allowance.' Henri tapped his desk with his fingers for an annoying length of time and then announced, 'But I can advance you two thousand livres, a third of the monies owed to you.' Philippe relaxed visibly and muttered, 'Well that is better than nothing.'

Henri then shouted, 'Mathieu and Luke come in!' He continued, 'Philippe and I have just reached an agreement. I will advance him two thousand livres against monies that are owed to him. Mathieu draw up the required paper work here and now, and we will all sign it!'

Henri offered everybody a brandy as they waited for Mathieu to complete the necessary documents. Henri wandered into a corner and did not speak. Luke tried to start up a conversation with Philippe, who appeared to be slowly regaining his composure. Luke asked, 'Are you likely to visit England on your next assignment?'

'Yes, colonel, I will be going to England. You may be able to help me. I have to go to Hampshire. Is it far from London?'

'Hampshire is a large county. It would depend on which end of it you are going to visit.'

'Near Winchester.'

'In that case, avoid London and save yourself a couple of days. There is a regular packet that sails from Le Havre to Portsmouth which is only a few hours from Winchester.' Henri suddenly rejoined the conversation, 'Luke, do you realise what you just said?' Luke looked confused. Henri smiled. 'Your memory is returning. You remembered the geography of England and the details of a regular shipping timetable across the channel.'

Before Luke could comment further, Mathieu presented the agreement for Henri and Philippe to sign and Luke and himself to witness. Henri asked all of them to wait in the antechamber while he counted out the money to be given to Philippe. After ten minutes, Philippe began to worry. 'The crafty old villain has my signature, and I have no money.'

Luke, hoping to set his mind at rest, went to the door of Henri's inner chamber and gently eased it open. The room was empty. He would not tell Philippe and instead lied, 'He is counting the coins over and over again.'

Eventually, Henri emerged from the room with a fabric drawstring bag. He emptied it onto a small wall table. There was not a silver coin to be seen. They were all gold coins, worth some twenty livres apiece. To Luke's mind, there should be one hundred coins. There were. Philippe was satisfied and nodded agreeably as he left the room.

Mathieu, who had held himself back during the negotiations suddenly exploded, 'What is this about? Can you afford to give away two thousand livres at this time? And from whom do you receive monies to pay Rousset?'

Henri held up his hand, 'My father made a deal many years ago with the Prince of Conde´ that continues until my death. I act as banker for Rousset.' Mathieu was irritated. 'Your estate has a stream of income that is unknown to your steward?'

'Mathieu, calm down! You know of all incomes that relate to my many estates, but the deal with the Bourbon-Conde´family required that the details be kept secret. Another brandy anyone?'

Luke had so enjoyed his inspection of the forest when he was acting steward that he joined Mathieu the following morning to continue this pleasurable activity. Mathieu was still smarting that Henri had kept a major financial interest secret from him.

'If Henri has acted as banker to the Bourbon-Conde´family, he has not done it for nothing. Some of the inconsistencies I discovered over years can now be explained.'

'For example?' asked Luke.

'There were often bursts of expenditure that were not accompanied by an explanation of how they were to be paid. In the end, the other accounts tallied. He always explained discrepancies in terms of unexpected legacies. The massive expenditure on that part of the chateau occupied by Lady Josette was listed as being paid out of a fund that her ladyship owned. And, another thing, where did Henri get those golden coins? I have access to the safe in his room. There are no golden coins there—just papers and silver currency.'

'You are right; the money was not in his room. When I poked my head around the corner yesterday, the room was empty. The money is stored somewhere else, a hiding place that can be accessed through some secret passage from his room.'

As Mathieu's party reached a part of the forest close to one of the small hamlets, they were confronted by a group of agitated villagers. 'Monsieur Gillot, take care! Our people have seen a bear wandering in the forest.'

'Don't be silly man! The last bear in this forest died two hundred or more years ago.'

'I know that, but perhaps one escaped from the bear pits that the English have introduced into much of Normandy.'

'It's a possibility. Were your people sure?'

'No, it was dusk, and all they could vouch for was that they thought they saw a large hairy creature move quickly through the trees.'

26

DURING THE EVENING MEAL, JOSETTE whispered to Luke, 'Tomorrow, I take you to our abbey. The superior, Mother Evangeliste, has some interesting gossip about Morel and Rousset.'

Later in the meal, she commented to the whole table, 'Philippe was not himself yesterday—and he has disappeared this morning without a word.' Henri responded coldly, 'He has a few problems at the moment. We may not see him again for sometime.'

'That might be for the best. He upset the nuns at the abbey,' Josette replied. 'When was he at the abbey?' asked a now-suspicious Henri. 'A few weeks back, when you were away,' answered Luke. 'What in the world did Philippe want from the Abbey?' continued a puzzled Henri. 'Father Louis knows,' said Josette with malicious intent. All eyes turned to a flustered Morel.

'What do you mean Lady Josette?' he mumbled.

Josette was enjoying the situation. 'While you were in retreat at the abbey, you disturbed the pious nuns by engaging in a shouting match with Philippe. Why did Philippe visit you at the convent?'

Louis replied with a more pronounced stammer than usual. 'He-he-he wanted me to break-break the con-con-confessional.' Luke diplomatically intervened, 'Father, no one expects you to break the confessional, but as Philippe was not confessing to you, tell us what questions you were asked.'

'He wanted to know whether in my association with the nuns any of them mentioned an English girl called Lucy Harman and whether this Lucy ever talked about a treasure hidden within the abbey. He told me he had asked the same questions of the abbess. She can tell you more.'

'I am sure she will. Luke and I are seeing her in the morning,' said Josette with a gleam of triumph on her face. Luke watched Louis for any reaction, but he could not ascertain anything significant.

Henri surprisingly showed a keen interest in the discussion and asked, 'Philippe is looking for a hidden treasure supposedly located in our abbey? He is certainly in need of money. Let me know, Luke, what you and Josette glean from the abbess! And, Father Louis, I trust you have told us all you know. If Mother Evangeliste makes a formal complaint, I will have to reconsider your role as chaplain to the abbey and, consequently, your position in this household.'

Louis was shaken. Henri was convinced that the priest knew more than he revealed, and the former was determined to use the ultimate sanction, the threat of dismissal, to get to the truth. Louis squirmed but retained his dignity, 'My lord, before God, there nothing more that I can tell you.'

Next day, Luke and Josette walked slowly through the woods to the convent. Luke had not completely regained his confidence and every rustle in the undergrowth conjured up memories of a rampaging boar. He was perspiring profusely by the time they reached the convent.

There they were greeted by the abbess and ushered into a large chamber filled with refreshments. At this time of day, only the abbess could speak, and the midmorning silence was eerie.

'Luke, this is my old friend, formerly Angelique Montmorency who entered the walls of this establishment on the same day that my father dumped me here. For five years, Angelique was my best friend. Since I left the Abbey, we have kept in touch almost weekly. Evangeliste, unlike myself, entered the institution with a spiritual mission, and combined with her common sense, my brother appointed her the youngest abbess in the history of the convent.'

Formalities completed, Luke immediately asked, 'What can you tell me about Lucy Harman?' Evangelique answered slowly and quietly, 'Lucy spent her life in one convent after another. At one time, she was enclosed in a Spanish abbey that emphasized physical punishment. Lucy, a thin sickly girl in the first place, became an obsessive self-flagellant. Her arrival here was also unusual. Her father, an English peer, arrived with several wagonloads of possessions. I pointed out that, while the nuns could live a life of luxury with their own goods and possessions, three wagon loads was a little excessive.'

'Most interesting,' commented Luke. Evangelique smiled. 'Even more so! The girl came from Spain penniless but her father arrived from England independently with an abundance of goods. He took me aside and asked if I could conceal three additional caskets that he admitted were independent of Lucy's possessions.'

'And did you?'

'Yes.'

'Are they still here?'

'Yes. Harman's men took them to the crypt of our chapel and placed them beside the rows of caskets containing the bodies of our deceased sisters.'

'Did Harman explain their contents?'

'Yes. He said he had been entrusted with the religious and secular valuables of many Catholic families, which he had to remove from England before Parliamentarians and Protestants confiscated them. These caskets contained those valuables. He made me promise not to open them in any circumstance.'

'And you kept your promise?'

'Yes, although I had my first moment of self-doubt regarding my promise when Harman arrived six months after his first visit and removed one of the caskets. It was taken with Lucy to the court of the English Queen Mother at St. Germain. He returned only a few weeks ago on his third visit with another more elaborate casket that contained the remains of his daughter Lucy. He asked that we keep the casket here, and he would send an entourage from England to collect it.'

'Can I look at the three caskets, starting with the two that Harman deposited on his first visit?'

'Before we do, I must tell you about Rousset. I have known Philippe since the days of my novitiate. After Josette left the convent, he occasionally came with her to visit me. Some weeks ago, he arrived here in an agitated state. He had gone to the chateau only to find everybody was away. He sought to stay in our gatehouse until Henri returned. Unfortunately, it has been tenanted. We had a meal, and then Philippe departed. Or I thought he had.

After Compline was finished about ten o'clock, I retired. However, I rose well before midnight for vigils. I had some worrying problems with some of the younger nuns. I went to pray in the chapel. There, I heard noises coming from the crypt below.

I made my way, in almost total darkness, down the steps and could see a glimmer of light coming from under the door of the crypt. I knew I could not open the door without alerting whoever or whatever was there. Fortunately, the door contains a small window. Despite the distortion of the glass, I saw Philippe loosening the lid of a casket. I was distressed. If he were looking for the Harman caskets, it could take him weeks to find them, but, with luck, they could be among the first he attempted to open.'

'What did you do?'

'As punishment for a minor indiscretion at vigils, I ordered three nuns to spend the rest of the night in the crypt with their hands on a casket contemplating their mortality. Philippe was forced to cease his investigation and hide behind some newly constructed coffins at the back of the crypt. He emerged at daylight and apparently went to argue with Father Morel. I had to speak to both of them as they upset the nuns during their time of required silence.'

'Did Lucy Harman say anything about a treasure when she was here?'

'Yes, all the time! But to Lucy, treasure was spiritual, and she would only find it through flagellation and prayer. The girl, through self-imposed malnutrition and flagellation was slowly driving herself mad. I was delighted when she left. Given her health, I was not surprised to hear that she had died at the English Court but that she had been murdered, at first, seemed incomprehensible. But, now, everything fits into place. People thought she knew the whereabouts of a real treasure and killed her in their effort to recover it.'

Luke perused the large crypt. Behind a screen at its far end was an ossuary but most of the space was taken up with rows of wooden caskets and stone sepulchers. Evangeliste led him to the two coffins left behind by Lord Harman on his original visit.

Luke prized open the lid as Evangeliste and Josette watched intently. Evangeliste was the first to realise the nature of its contents. It was stacked full of calico bags. As Luke began to take out the contents of the first bag, Evangeliste fell on her knees, crossed herself, and asked God for forgiveness. The first bag contained a black painted statue of the Madonna; a second had a lock of hair contained within a glass tube. Several more contained assorted bones of various saints.

Evangeliste took Luke by the arm. 'There is no need to undo the other bags. These are indeed priceless treasure but not what Philippe expected to find. These are sacred relics that English Catholics preserved in their private homes after they were banned from churches when England became Protestant one hundred and twenty years ago. They probably feared that, with the victory of an extreme Protestant army, these relics would be destroyed.'

Luke re-placed the lid and moved on to the second casket. Its lid was already loose. There was no need to rifle through this coffin. It was filled with elaborate and richly ornamented ecclesiastical robes and a few icons of the Mother of God.

Back in Evangeliste's reception chamber, a perplexed Luke suddenly thought he saw the light and asked, 'When Lord Harman and his men moved the three caskets in and then a second time when they moved one of them out, did they spend any time alone in the crypt. Could they have transferred coins and plate into another casket?'

'No! I was with them the whole time on both occasions. If there was a casket of coins, jewellery, and precious plate, it was the one transferred to the English Court.'

'Could there be additional coffins? You say you were present when Harman's men moved coffins in and out on three occasions. Is it possible that they moved more coffins either way than you saw?'

Evangeliste thought for some time. 'It's possible. Harman had a lot of men moving about and while I was talking to his lordship, they may have brought in or removed an extra coffin.'

'On the other hand, the coffin with the treasure may still be at the English Court,' said Josette.

Luke was silent for some time and then commented as if to himself, 'Rousset was transferred there with much authority. I will go to St. Germain and try to uncover what he discovered there, if anything.'

27

EVANGELISTE EXPLAINED THAT SHE MUST return momentarily
to her duties. There was a wave of hysteria sweeping through some of
the younger nuns, and she had imposed a supervised penance to put
an end to it. 'That is unlike the Mademoiselle Montmorency I used
to know. It must be serious for you to impose harsh penances. What
is it about?' asked Josette.

'It is rather weird. Three nuns, on separate occasions, claim they
have seen a bear in the abbey grounds. A fourth, Sister Hilary, who
looks after our pigs in the forest, swears she saw it moving between
the trees.'

Luke could not contain himself. 'Mother, these young women
should not be punished. Several villagers have also seen a bear in the
forest. It has probably escaped from a bear pit. May I talk to these
women?'

'No, Luke, given their vows, they may not talk to you or any
man.'

'Can they write?'

'Yes.'

'May they write a detailed account for you of what they saw, and
then could I read those accounts?'

'No problem with that! I will immediately rescind the penance
I prescribed and replace it with the requirement to write a narrative
of what they saw. Wait here! I will return in a few minutes. There is
another aspect of these bear sightings that I must relate.'

During Evangeliste's absence, Luke helped himself to the last remaining pieces of chicken and refilled his goblet with the finest of Bordeaux red. This was an extremely wealthy abbey.

Evangeliste started talking as soon as she reentered the room. 'When the nuns told me about the bear, I questioned them thoroughly. One thing stood out. The bear was seen at dusk and heading towards our gatehouse.'

'Does anybody live in the gatehouse?'

'Yes, at the moment, a Rouen merchant who trades with Canada has taken a long-term lease of it. He has also given the abbey a substantial donation.'

'Do you know anything about this man, or will I have to ask Gillot?'

'Mathieu knows nothing of this. When I first became superior, Mathieu helped me with the finances of the abbey and demanded that we become self-sufficient and not be a drain on the chateau. He offloaded the legal aspects of our financial situation to a group of lawyers in Rouen.

For an annual fee paid by the lawyers and by us to the Marquis des Anges, we are completely independent of Gillot's frugal hand. The gatehouse is regularly leased at a substantial rent, but all the details and the income are in the hands of the Rouen lawyers. The women in this abbey bring substantial dowries with them, or their fathers pay heavily to keep them in this secluded environment. I have also invested well.'

As Luke walked back to the chateau with Josette, she suggested that she approach Henri and Charlotte about Luke's trip to Paris and the English Court. Charlotte was English and had once been lady-in-waiting to the queen.

'She would be an ideal person to introduce a Cromwellian officer to the Royalist court. You would not be welcome on your own.' Henri was receptive to the idea that Charlotte accompany Luke to the English Court.

Charlotte was quite excited about meeting the queen, whom she had served loyally years earlier and who was the cause of her meeting with Henri.

The marquis insisted that the visit should be arranged according to protocol. A letter was sent to the English Court seeking permission for Charlotte and Colonel Tremayne to visit—in Charlotte's case, to renew her acquaintance with the Queen and in that of Colonel Tremayne, to enquire into the fate of Lucy Harman and the existence of English Catholic treasure.

Two Weeks Later, English Court, St. Germain

With the return of Charles and Lord Ashcroft, morale at court greatly improved. The Queen Mother was delighted that they brought with them her youngest son, Henry, Duke of Gloucester, whom the English Republic had released into the hands of his sister, the wife of the late Prince of Orange.

The arrival of Henriette's youngest son, in part, made up for the humiliation she suffered from the tirade delivered by her eldest son, Charles. He threatened to expel her from court and have her confined in some isolated monastery for her abject surrender of English sovereignty to the French and her callous mistreatment of Lord Stokey and Captain Lloyd.

Two days after the king's return, he summoned Harry to a meeting with Sir Edward Hyde, Lord Ashcroft, and Lord Stokey. The king asked both Simon and Harry to recount their adventures, and Hyde briefed the king on events at court during their enforced absence. The King listened and asked again for details regarding the murder of the two ladies-in-waiting.

Harry summed up, 'Both women were probably murdered on the orders of Rousset, and his motive concerned a hidden treasure of English Catholic gold and silver of which Lord Stokey has personal knowledge.' Simon explained the decision of English Catholics to protect their moveable wealth by having some of it moved out of the country.

The King smiled. 'Then I have some relevant news, especially for you, Harry. Waiting for my return was a letter from the Marquis des Anges, France's highest-ranking noble below those troublesome

Bourbon princes. He seeks permission for his wife, an English gentlewoman, to visit my mother whom she served a decade ago and for a man who has been investigating problems on his estate to talk to people here.

Apparently, he also suspects Vicomte Rousset, who seems obsessed with hidden English treasure. Lady Lucy Harman, who was murdered here, previously lived at the Abbey des Anges. Their investigator, Harry, is your former commander, the Cromwellian agent, and a known adversary of mine, Luke Tremayne.'

Harry nodded, 'Unfortunately, I understand from French sources that the colonel has completely lost his memory. He hit his head on a rock in the Seine, while I believe on a mission to you. I only recently became aware of his whereabouts through the French navy.'

Sir Edward Hyde spoke, 'Your Majesty must reject the request for the colonel's visit. I am well aware from correspondence over the last five years of this man's abilities and his dedicated loyalty to the nefarious regicide, Oliver Cromwell. His visit and apparent loss of memory could be a fiction to inveigle him into this court to your physical and political detriment.'

'My dear Edward, for reasons which I am not yet ready to reveal, I have nothing to fear from Luke Tremayne. In fact, he could prove a great asset regarding my political future. Now, what do we do about Rousset?'

Simon replied, 'Harry and I wish to pursue him in terms of our own honour and England's reputation.'

Sir Edward disagreed. 'Sire, we are at a difficult time in our negotiations with the French. Their Queen Mother, Anne, who was favourable to our cause, no longer rules on her son's behalf. It is with Cardinal Mazarin that we must deal. He is putting out feelers to General Cromwell for an alliance with England. These murders should be left to his jurisdiction and in the person of his right hand man, Colonel Guarin. He has a very capable officer.'

'By all means, work with Guarin, but I must take a stand on this issue. The treatment of Stokey and Lloyd was abominable. They have my permission to track down Rousset and bring him to justice. I will also protest to my cousin King Louis about Mazarin appointing such a man to our court.'

'Well, he was a Bourbon, even though illegitimate,' muttered Sir Edward.

The king closed the meeting.

Harry asked for a few minutes alone with Charles and Lord Ashcroft to discuss Luke's visit. He was concerned. 'Your Majesty, this visit will not be easy given that the colonel has no memory of events before he hit his head on the rock several months ago. We do not know whether the Marquis des Anges has filled Luke's mind with the true facts from the past or created an almost-fictional character. He may not be the man both of us knew.'

'What do you suggest Harry?'

'That I see him alone and assess the situation before I present him to you and before I reveal any of the information we have regarding the murders, the treasure, and Rousset.' The king agreed.

'Your Majesty, I have another problem, and I have been ordered by General Cromwell to inform you fully of the situation.'

'And what is it that my father's murderer wishes me to know?'

'When I was tortured, Rousset's stooges used drugs and sleep deprivation forcing me to reveal that I was Cromwell's agent. Sir Edward is quite right. The cardinal wishes to develop friendly relations with England, which may run counter to your interests. The cardinal wishes me to become a go-between for him and Cromwell. The general has ordered me to accept but to inform Your Majesty.'

Ashcroft was not impressed. 'Inform His Majesty of what? That you will become a double agent or that you inform him of all the details that pass between Cromwell and Mazarin?'

Harry lied. He could not contemplate Cromwell wanting the King to know the details of negotiations between himself and Mazarin. One major condition demanded by the army might be to have Charles expelled from his safe haven in France. He replied insincerely, 'Sire, as long as you accept me here as a go-between for yourself and the general, I will keep you fully informed of all developments with the French.'

'Can I believe you, Harry? Cromwell's experiment with these rampaging religious fanatics is failing, and there are rumours even at the Dutch Court that the English Republic may soon return to monarchy. Are these rumours true, and would it involve me?'

'The first half of your question I can answer in the affirmative. The general is well aware of the overwhelming sentiment within the English people for the return of monarchy, and his legal advisers are strongly in favour of it. Your young brother Henry was kept in England until very recently as a possible new monarch. His loyalty to you was admirable. You were the rightful king, and he would not accept any offer. That is why Cromwell pressured the Parliament to permit him to leave the country.'

'What then are my chances of returning to the throne backed by the English army?'

'With Cromwell, personally, they are very high. That is why he sent Luke and myself here. Luke has spoken to the general on several occasions as to your personal qualities.'

'But?'

'There are many in the army who are dyed-in-the-wool republicans or fanatical sectarians. Cromwell will have trouble convincing the army as a whole to seek your immediate return.'

'What will happen if he cannot?'

'Only God knows,' was Harry's pathetic but honest reply.

28

LUKE WAS USHERED INTO A spacious but unadorned room. A young officer rose from behind the desk, bounded forward, and shook his hand. Luke was confused and embarrassed. Harry apologized and led him to a window bench and sat beside him. Three hours later, Harry called for refreshments.

He had briefed Luke on his life before he lost his memory and especially of the events immediately prior to their ejection from the ship. Then for another three hours, Harry updated Luke with events at court and the adventures caused by Rousset's intrigue. Harry then sent a servant to inform Lady Charlotte that Luke would be staying with him overnight. Charlotte would not be alone as, at the last minute, the Marquis des Anges decided to accompany them to Paris with a large entourage. Luke could not help comparing the threadbare apartment of an English officer at court with the magnificent structure and furnishings of the Palais des Anges, the St. Michel's Parisian townhouse.

Next morning, it was Luke's turn to talk. He outlined the events that had occurred since he awoke on the bank of the Seine and was rescued by the St. Michels. Harry was spellbound by Luke's detail of murder and intrigue—and especially the role that Rousset may have played in it.

Harry invited Simon to join them for the midday meal and introduced Luke as 'my former commanding officer Colonel Tremayne who has been pursuing similar investigations to our own

166

into Rousset, Lucy Harman, and the Catholic treasure.' Simon was initially alarmed by Luke's account of the discoveries in the crypt and asked anxiously, 'And what has the abbey done with the relics and ecclesiastical robes?'

'The abbess has displayed the relics on and around the side altar of the chapel. She has also hung many of the ecclesiastical robes and fabrics around the walls.'

Simon relaxed. 'The ecclesiastical treasures are in safe hands until the time comes for their reclamation. Rousset must have been disappointed. Another Harman coffin was left here in the Chapel of St. Magdalene. It was filled with dismantled triptychs and altar cloths. But I know for certain that a collection of gold and silver coin and plate and expensive jewellery exists awaiting recovery. All these items were entrusted to Lord Harman for safekeeping.'

The three men went over the facts relating to the murders, the treasure, and the activities of Rousset. Finally, Luke asked, 'What next? My employer, the marquis, feels that the Rousset problem should be left with the French authorities.'

Simon ignored Luke's last remark. 'I will find the treasure and Rousset.' Harry was quiet for a time and then announced, 'I half agree with Luke. We must include the French in our activities. One man has already been helpful and could overcome any legal or political difficulties we might experience as foreigners.'

'Who is he? asked Luke.

'Colonel Marcel Guarin, commander of the cardinal's musketeers! He is not only an excellent soldier, but he is also a confidant of his master. Above all, his men have followed Rousset for weeks.' Harry did not announce it, but he felt such cooperation would also assist him in developing closer relations with Mazarin.

The following day, the three Englishmen brought Lord Ashcroft and Marcel Guarin up to date with developments. Harry asked the latter, 'Have your men followed Rousset since he escaped from me disguised as a chaplain?'

'Not all the time! Like you, my men did not see through the clerical disguise. However, only yesterday, they picked up his trail in Le Havre where a man answering his description was about to board a ship headed for Portsmouth, but the weather led to the cancellation of the service.'

Luke jumped to his feet. 'Pittikins! I gave him that advice myself. He wanted to get to Winchester and had contemplated going to Calais and London.'

'My god!' added Lord Stokey. 'I know where he is going—Harman Hall. It is a few miles outside of Winchester. Rousset is no fool. If you cannot find the treasure or torture its whereabouts out of people who might know, you go to the person who does know—James, Lord Harman. I fear for his safety.'

'Rousset has several days lead on us, even if we rode post haste to Le Havre using the navy's express horses,' concluded Harry. 'Nevertheless, I must go,' announced Simon. 'I am Catholic. I know Lord Harman and am a distant cousin to Lady Harman. Our hope is that the family is not at Harman Hall, and Rousset has to wait for them.' 'I'll come with you,' announced Harry. Lord Ashcroft concurred, 'I will seek the king's permission immediately for both of you to depart from court.' He left the room while the others continued their discussion.

Harry was enthusiastic. 'We can get a message to the English authorities and Lord Harman's servants before we arrive if we use the French naval intelligence network to get a warning to Le Havre and the English army's system from Portsmouth to Winchester. I still remember the name of the army's man in Portsmouth who can facilitate this.'

Marcel gave approval for a message to be sent by the naval network and suggested that as both men were able riders, they could use the same network to get themselves to Le Havre as quickly as possible. Ashcroft reentered the room conveying the king's approval.

Harry and Luke returned to the former's apartment. He used his own codebook, which had been leaked both to the French and to the Royalists, to inform Cromwell of the plan and to ask that he send elite forces into Hampshire to protect the Harmans and to apprehend Rousset.

Luke left for the Palais des Anges, and Harry quickly visited Cate Beaumont and instructed her to send a coded message to Cromwell.

He was returning to England, not only to help save Harman and his treasure and to apprehend Rousset, but also to seek clarification of his position at the Royalist court. Charles was no fool and could not be strung along for much longer regarding his restoration by the army to the English throne.

This long coded message also gave Harry's assessment of Luke and recommended that Cromwell should take action to return Colonel Tremayne to England as soon as possible. He confirmed that Luke had completely lost all memory of events before his fall into the Seine but, otherwise, was in excellent health.

Hampshire, England, Five Days Later

Harry and Simon were in a good mood. They reached Le Havre to discover that no packets had left the port for a week due to extreme weather conditions in the channel. Rousset was not aboard the first boat to sail, which included Simon and Harry. Rousset, rather than wait, had moved north to Calais or south to Bordeaux where larger ships could have crossed to England despite the adverse conditions. These ships would have likely docked at Dover or up the Thames estuary at London, adding further to Rousset's delay.

The good mood turned to desperation later that day as they galloped up the drive to Harman Hall. Servants were running everywhere, and a retinue of horsemen sped past them. Lord Stokey knocked loudly on the large ornate door and was confronted by an obviously distraught servant. Simon introduced himself and asked, 'Good man, may I speak to your master, Lord Harman? It is a matter of life and death.' The man choked up and finally replied, 'My lord, both Lord and Lady Harman have just been abducted by four Frenchmen.'

'What happened?' asked Harry.

'Less than half an hour ago, his lordship received a Frenchman into his library. The man claimed he had known young Lucy.'

'What happened next?'

'After ten minutes, they began to shout. The Frenchman came to the door and delivered an order in French to his men who were waiting in the antechamber. The meaning became clear when one of them grabbed me and placed his dagger against my throat and indicated that I must take them to Lady Harman. I refused, but, unfortunately, at that very moment, her ladyship appeared.

One of the men thrust her through the door into his lordship's reception chamber. Another tied me to a chair and roped my ankles together. The two of them then left the antechamber and mounted guard at his lordship's door, forbidding anyone to enter.'

'Forget the details,' pleaded an increasingly anxious Simon. 'Where are Lord and Lady Harman now?'

'Eventually, the Frenchman emerged from the room with a dagger pressed against Lady Harman's throat. Lord Harman shouted to his servants not to move nor try to save him, or Lady Harman would be killed. The Frenchman ordered horses for my master and mistress. The kidnappers rode off, firing their pistols at the nearest of our people. Servants alerted our steward, who immediately organized a party of horsemen to follow the French. They passed you as you came up the drive.'

Simon and Harry looked at each other, and the latter asked, 'Are there any fresh horses? Ours are exhausted.' 'Unfortunately not! The steward took all the horses in the stable. Our other horses are grazing in a field some miles away.'

'What will be, will be,' said Harry philosophically as both men remounted their tired steeds and moved down the drive to follow the steward's troop. Eventually, they reached a substantial rise, and, looking down at the plain below, they saw a crossroad.

Three horsemen were coming up the hill towards them. Riding behind one of them was a woman. Simon immediately recognized her as Lady Harman. He dismounted and ran towards her. Her escort raised their muskets until Harry heard a female voice shout that the approaching man was a friend. While Simon and Lady Harman renewed their acquaintance, Harry questioned the leader of her rescuers.

He was brief. 'When we reached this very spot after leaving Harman Hall, we saw the six horses we were chasing below us on the plain. When they reached the crossroads, they divided into three groups. Two horsemen went straight ahead; two went to the left, and two to the right. There was no way of telling from this distance which pair included Lord and Lady Harman.

I knew a short cut that could get me ahead of the two horses travelling left. We reached the intersecting point well ahead of our quarry, moved back along the road, and concealed ourselves on either side of it in a small wood. I began to panic. The two horsemen travelling in my direction should have passed us some time earlier. Eventually, a sole pedestrian appeared. It was Lady Harman. Her captor had forced her to dismount, took her horse, and disappeared across country.'

Later that evening, after Lady Harman had rested, she and her two visitors ate together as they waited the return of the other two troops of pursuing servants. Lady Lucinda, after whom her daughter was named, was eager to describe her ordeal.

'The Frenchman threatened to kill me if James did not reveal the whereabouts of English Catholic treasure. James suggested an alternative approach. If Rousset spared me, James would take him to the treasure. James refused to tell him where it was because he claimed that as soon as Rousset had the location, he would kill both of us.'

'My lady, do you know where the treasure is?' asked Harry.

'No, Captain, but James left a cryptic message for its retrieval should he die suddenly. It makes no sense to me.'

'What was it?' continued Harry.

She passed him a small book that had scribbled on its frontispiece. *'French blood confused with angels.'*

The other groups returned. They had not found Lord Harman nor any Frenchmen. Lucinda began to cry, and, as Simon comforted her, Harry diplomatically took his leave.

29

SIMON AND HARRY ASSUMED THAT Harman would lead Rousset back to France. Cromwell confirmed this to Harry three days later. He had reluctantly lied to Simon that he had a secret message from King Charles to deliver to the hated army leader. Simon was happy to wait for his companion in a nearby Whitehall inn.

The general reported that persons who were most likely Harman and Rousset had left Dover bound for Calais two nights earlier. By the time the news reached the French authorities, the travellers had disappeared.

Harry had lost any fear of stating his mind in front of the general. He was fired up over two issues. He told Cromwell bluntly that the pretext for staying at the English Court to act as go-between for the general and the King was wearing thin. 'Charles is beginning to doubt that you have any intention of supporting his recall to the throne. In such circumstances, he may soon see no point in keeping his hated enemy's agent at the centre of his court. Is there any morsel I can feed him that may keep him content for the next month or two?'

'Captain Lloyd, you have done an excellent job so far, but I cannot give you any reassuring information for the king. Our experiment with the godly has been an absolute failure. My generals are pushing me to sack them, as we did the rump. My legal advisers want the return of monarchy.

The army, however, is deeply divided—some want a parliamentary republic strengthened by bringing back many of the former

Presbyterian members to the House of Commons; the hot heads want a military junta; and the sycophants even suggest I take on the trappings of monarchy as a protector of the nation. Unfortunately, only a few of my senior comrades want a fully fledged monarchy and even less one with young Charles Stuart at its head.'

Harry was not impressed, but he moved on to his other worry. 'General, we must assist Colonel Tremayne. He should be brought home now. Familiar surroundings may help him regain his memory. At the moment he is of no value to the English army and is happily working for a wealthy and powerful French aristocrat.'

'And doing what he does best—solving murders.'

'True, General, but it is not helping your cause.'

'Lloyd, now that you have made contact with Tremayne and exchanged information of your experiences in France over the last few months, continue to cooperate! Keep me updated on Luke's situation. He will capture this Rousset before you do.'

'So you will not order Luke home?'

'No, but I will give both of you familiar help. You will return to France and the English Court with Sergeant Andrew Ford as your assistant. In addition to the duties that come his way in such a role, you will send him regularly to see Luke. Knowing their past together, a close association with Andrew might bring back his memory. If, from close quarters, Ford agrees with you that Luke should be brought home, I will consider it. For the moment, all of you will be kept busy finding Harman, Rousset, and the elusive treasure.'

'Sir, may I raise an issue about Harman and yourself?' Cromwell nodded, and Harry asked, 'Is Lord Harman negotiating with you for a better deal for Catholics, and is the missing treasure the price he is asked to pay you for such a deal?'

Cromwell went red in the face and fumed. 'You forget yourself, captain. Harman and I have spoken on the matter of better treatment for Catholics for some years. You well know that the army is more tolerant of Papists than the politicians.

We have discussed what Catholics might contribute in return for concessions. The payment of a vast donation has never been raised. The payment of a small but regular additional tax is my preferred

173

option. It is in the English army's interests that this Papist treasure be preserved and returned to the rightful owners, so they will be in a position to contribute financially to the English government over a long period of time when such a tax is imposed.'

While they had been talking, Cromwell had sent his adjutant to find Ford. Andrew entered the room and was delighted to see Harry. 'And how is our beloved colonel?' he asked, being completely ignorant of Luke's position and condition.

Cromwell raised his hand to prevent an answer. 'Sergeant, prepare to leave immediately for France with Captain Lloyd. You will be his assistant and act under the cover of a deserter to the Royalist cause. Lloyd will update you on Colonel Tremayne. I will inform Charles Stuart of my reasons for adding a man to my mission.'

By the time Andrew and Harry rejoined Simon in the inn, the sergeant had received a crash course on what had happened in France over several months. Simon remained unaware of his companions' true allegiance.

The English Court, a Week Later

Harry and Simon reported to the king who readily accepted Andrew's presence. His meeting a week earlier with Luke Tremayne had persuaded him to accept such a proposal. Charles admitted he left his meeting with Luke quite saddened. 'It was obvious he had no recollection of meeting me previously and of saving my life. It is good that your man will regularly visit the Chateau des Anges to be with him.'

A few days later, Marcel visited Harry. 'Sadly, my men have been a day or two behind Harman and Rousset. Rousset is being led back to the areas that he and we have already searched. They are somewhere in the vicinity of Rouen.'

'That information will give my new man his first job. He can take that information and what Simon and I uncovered in England to Colonel Tremayne.'

Cardinal Mazarin's Apartment, Same Day

The cardinal, who had been away for three weeks, was most interested to hear Marcel's report of what had been a joint enterprise between France, the English republican army, and the exiled English king to track down a person that he had just formally declared an enemy of France. Marcel noted the cardinal's irritability and asked, 'Is something amiss, Your Eminence?'

'Yes, Marcel. In my attempt to punish Rousset for his treachery, I have been thwarted in my main thrust. It is common practice in such cases to declare the culprit a traitor and an outlaw. This I have done. The final step is for the Crown to confiscate all his lands and income.'

'What's the problem? Rousset was never short of money.'

'But it was not his. I assumed that Rousset was bequeathed dozens of estates in the south of France by his father, the late Prince of Condé. When our lawyers delved into the matter, none of the properties are actually in Rousset's possession.'

'How can that be?' asked an incredulous Marcel.

'The late Prince of Condé was no fool. While his illegitimate son was given the various titles related to these properties, the land and its income were given to someone else.'

'The older Condé was not known for his generosity. To whom did he grant such munificence?'

'That is the most intriguing aspect of this whole mysterious arrangement. The estates were granted to a family who is already of great interest to us, the St. Michels. The late Marquis des Anges and, now, his successor, the current marquis, provide, from their massive additional income, a small portion as an allowance to Rousset. The agreement ceases on the death of the current marquis, and the titles, land, and income revert to the main Bourbon-Condé line.'

Marcel was speechless. Finally, while shaking his head in disbelief, he commented, 'The plot thickens. Rousset is totally dependent on des Anges for his income and must ensure that nothing threatens the life of the marquis.'

'I want to know why the late Prince of Condé made such a deal.'

'They were both among the highest ranking nobles in the land,' Marcel replied.

'But there was never a close relationship between the St. Michels and the Bourbons! I can, nevertheless, use this information against Henri St. Michel. If the marquis paid Rousset his allowance throughout the recent uprising, then I will be able to charge Henri with aiding and abetting a traitor—especially if this assistance continues now that Rousset has been outlawed. I will have this arrogant aristocrat for treason.'

'Your Eminence, there may be a way to discover the answer to these questions without us acting openly against the marquis who still has friends in high places.'

'And what do you suggest?'

'I have just left Captain Lloyd. He now has a sergeant to assist him, but the man is also to keep an eye on Colonel Tremayne who is employed by the marquis to track down Rousset and find the treasure. Ford is about to visit the Chateau des Anges. I will inform Lloyd that his man should ask Tremayne to find out why the late Prince of Conde´ drew up such a document and whether the current marquis has paid Rousset during the periods of crisis.'

The cardinal agreed but added, 'Now is the time to strike at the St. Michel dynasty and their ilk throughout the nation. The local magistrates must investigate the accusations of that Canadian merchant from Rouen. Find out everything you can about what has been happening at that chateau. See how much you can find out from the Englishmen. At the right time, I will arrest the marquis and place him in the Bastille for aiding and abetting Rousset. And if the accusations of that Canadian merchant are proved, he will be tried for murder.'

Marcel fidgeted with the hilt of his sword and nodded his head disapprovingly. He then took the unusual step of confronting his master. 'On reflection, my suggestion is too devious. Why not be more direct yet, at the same time, more cautious. Send me with the newly arrived Englishman to visit the marquis. I can approach him directly and tell him that charges of murder have been made against him and that his loyalty during the Fronde is in question given his support of the rebel Rousset and that he is about to be indicted for treason because he still aids and abets this man, now an outlaw and traitor.

I will emphasize that you do not want such a noble family to be discredited on false hearsay and have sent me to establish the truth. If the marquis has a reasonable explanation, I will guarantee in your name that no formal charges will be laid. My presence in the Chateau des Anges will also enable me to cooperate with Colonel Tremayne who, despite his memory loss, is a useful ally.'

Mazarin placed his hand on his friend's shoulder, 'Marcel, my Italian nature suggests that I should adopt a more byzantine approach, but your simple suggestion is eminently sensible—and politically foolproof. Nevertheless, as the marquis is in Paris at the moment, I will visit him and stir the pot. I will let him know of the possible charges against him and my intention of sending you to the Chateau des Anges.'

30

LUKE RETURNED FROM PARIS A troubled man. The long briefing from his apparent deputy filled in the details of his life before the accident. It was a surprise to have some of that past confirmed by the king, whose life he had saved from a Scottish madman. It was now more difficult to reconcile the competing images of what others told him he was with what he knew he had been for the last few months. Was he essentially the Cromwellian colonel of his revealed past or a senior member of an aristocratic French household employed to investigate its domestic murder, assaults, and mysteries?

As the marquis and marquise remained in Paris, Luke ate in Lady Josette' apartment, and he shared with her his concerns about his identity. Her warmth, friendliness, and plain common sense convinced him to concentrate on matters that involved the chateau. He must discover who attacked Charlotte and search every nook and cranny for the missing treasure.

In addition, Josette directed his attention to the case of the mysterious bear. While he was away, there were more sightings of the animal, some close to the chateau, others concentrated around the gatehouse of the abbey.

This was the easiest of Luke's problems. He seconded five of Mathieu's gamekeepers to track the animal. The men hid in the forest, radiating out from the point where it impinged on the gatehouse of the abbey. Luke stayed overnight in the abbey in a position to observe the gatehouse in relative comfort.

He saw nothing out of the ordinary. At dawn, he made his way to the men he had stationed in the woods. The first two had nothing to report, although Luke suspected that they had been drinking heavily and had probably dozed off.

When Luke finally found the last gamekeeper, he could not believe his eyes. The man was in a state of shock. It took Luke with the aid of his flask of brandy some time to restore a modicum of normality. The distraught gamekeeper slowly recounted his night's activities.

'You placed me at the crossroads of the two most used paths in the forest. One path runs from the abbey to the wharf on the Seine and the other from near Rouen to the chateau. Not long after you left, I saw a creature walk along the path from the abbey. At first, I thought it was you returning with changed instructions.

Clouds covered the moon from time to time, and, during those periods, I could see nothing. When the cloud cleared, the creature had passed my hiding place and appeared in silhouette to be a bear. I crept out onto the path to follow it. I was surprised. Its gait was that of a man. Then I trod on a dry stick, and, instantaneously, the creature ahead of me disappeared. Remembering your orders, I tried to return quickly to my original position.'

'That does explain your traumatized condition.'

'No, colonel. On the way back to my hiding place, I realised that the bear was now stalking me. One moment, it was on my right then, later, on my left; at another time, it was behind me. I primed my musket many times and fired shots in all directions. I was scared.

Then I heard something very close in front of me. It was hideous. The face of a bear was inches from mine. Before I could do anything, the creature hit me across the face. I was knocked out for some hours. I came to just minutes before you arrived.'

'You are sure it was a bear?'

'Although, at times, it had the gait of a man, the face that thrust itself into mine was definitely a bear, and the strength of the strike was immense.'

'You are very lucky,' announced one of his comrades. 'Normally, when a bear strikes, its sharp claws rip you apart. I've seen what they do to dogs in the pit. You probably received a gentle cuff.' He and his friend laughed at the supposed timidity of their comrade.

Luke turned to his men. 'As gamekeepers, you track the prints of the animals that inhabit this woodland on a daily basis. There was rain early last night. If your friend is right, then there should be tracks of a heavy bear through this area. Search it!'

Later that day, the men reported back. They found the prints of deer, the scratching of rabbits and squirrels, and a surprising number of boot prints. There were several near where their comrade confronted the bear, and they were not those of the gamekeepers. The strange prints were made by a heavy male's expensive shoe.

Luke discussed the situation with Mathieu. 'Our bear is a man. Pascal's schoolroom has a drawing of American Indians wearing the heads and skins of various animals as masks. The gatehouse of the abbey has something to do with the bear's appearance. Evangeliste said that the leasing of it was subcontracted to some lawyers in Rouen who have leased it to a Canadian merchant. Verify to whom it is leased and any details regarding the tenant's background!'

Mathieu nodded. 'I go to Rouen tomorrow, but the answer is already clear. The tenant of the gatehouse has either brought with him a bear from Canada, or he is skulking through the woods wearing a bear mask and skin. Either way, he is a person of interest.'

Next evening, after supper, Mathieu and Luke remained behind finishing a carafe of Bordeaux red. 'Did your Rouen visit provide any information about the tenant of the abbey gatehouse?'

'He calls himself Georges Livet. Until a year or so ago, he lived in Canada and made a fortune shipping beaver skins to the merchants at Rouen. Apparently, he used his wealth to buy two ships that now trade with the Americas. He lives in Rouen as a shipper-merchant, exporting the goods needed by the settlers and importing beaver pelts.'

Luke was puzzled. 'Why then does he lease the gatehouse which is within walking distance of his residence in Rouen?'

'This Livet is not a desirable character. According to the information provided by my favourite tavern owner, Livet illegally exports arms and ammunition to the Iroquois Indian—weapons used to kill French settlers and which he obtained corruptly from officers in the Rouen garrison. One of the names mentioned as a supplier was Captain Rousset.'

'Well done Mathieu! How old is Livet?'

'In his late forties or early fifties.'

'Is anything else known about him?'

'His appearance has been hard to clarify as his face is reportedly covered almost completely by his long hair, exaggerated moustache, sideburns, and woolly beard.'

'As if he wishes to conceal his real identity?'

'It would appear so.'

Both men looked at each other knowingly. Mathieu asked the obvious, 'Is Georges Livet, Emile St. Michel, the marquis's exiled half brother? There is one way to find out. Josette is Emile's full sister. Even after all these years, she should be able to recognize him. Let's ask her! With luck, he may have a childhood scar that will make identification certain.'

'No,' cautioned Luke. 'I want to know more about Georges and what he is up to at the abbey before we involve Josette. After all, we have nothing to link Georges with Emile except he is the right age and has been in Canada. That would fit hundreds of men. No, his activities at the abbey may give us the evidence we need.'

'How are you going to obtain that?'

'I will visit the gatehouse,' replied Luke.

Luke's plan to interrogate Livet had to be put on hold. Next morning, the marquis and marquise arrived home from Paris. The marquis was livid. He issued orders that he would see every member of the household throughout the day. They should cancel all engagements and be ready to report to him when summoned.

Mathieu, who joined Luke in Josette's apartment for the midday meal, was surprised. 'I have never seen Henri so cross. He had me rummage into the family archives for a whole range of documents. I persuaded him to change his mind about talking to everybody separately. He will talk to the whole household during supper.'

There was an air of tension as they gathered to eat, and the sight of a strained and drawn Charlotte set alarm bells ringing in

Luke's mind. Josette immediately asked, 'For god's sake, Henri, what's wrong?' The marquis explained, 'While I was in Paris, I had an unexpected visit from the king's chief minister, the Cardinal Mazarin. This apparent social visit soon revealed its true nature. It was a warning and a preliminary hearing of serious charges against me—charges that could threaten my life and the future of this family. An unnamed person has accused me of killing my first wife and of supporting the now-declared outlaw, Rousset, in his treachery. Specifically, I am charged with supplying him with funds during and since his rebellion against the Crown.

This two-faced Italian cleric claims he does not believe any of these charges, but he must be seen to act fairly, especially against the great nobles, some of whom think they are above the law. As a sign of his generosity and fair-mindedness, he asked me to entertain, for several weeks, one of his senior aides who will peruse our archives and question us all. He will assess whether I should be formally charged and tried.'

'Who is Mazarin sending?' asked Luke.

'An acquaintance of yours and the commander of his musketeers—Colonel Marcel Guarin.'

Luke responded, 'A good man! The English Court, the English government in London, the French government, and I, representing your lordship, have recently acted together to track down Rousset. Marcel Guarin represented the French. He also rescued a former comrade of mine now at the English Court and a senior peer from the clutches of Rousset. He continues to supply most of the information against that fugitive.'

Henri remained tense and muttered, 'Just because you know this man, and he is an enemy of Philippe Rousset, it does not follow that he is a friend of the St. Michels. His master, the cardinal, hates all branches of the high nobility equally, whether they be Bourbon or St. Michel.'

Josette intervened, 'Calm yourself, brother. I know you can defend yourself successfully against the charge of murder. I will tell all to save you. Luke has accepted my word, and maybe this Marcel Guarin will do likewise. But can you defend yourself against the other charges? I can swear that you took no part in supporting the rebels throughout the years of the aristocratic uprising.'

'Thank you dear sister! Unfortunately, there is a major problem to my defence. The Italian fox could have me legally arraigned for aiding a declared traitor, and he would be within his legal rights. Only a week or so ago, I advanced Rousset a very large purse of gold coins. My reasons for doing this lie in a family secret, which I promised father I would never reveal. Unfortunately, Mazarin has unearthed most of it, which he will use to destroy me. It involves the Prince of Condeˊ.'

'Philippe's father?' queried Josette. Henri whispered a soft yes and withdrew rapidly from the table, quickly followed by a tearful Charlotte.

The remainder of the company sat in stony silence.

31

TWO DAYS LATER, GUARIN ARRIVED. He sought out Luke and acknowledged his achievements. 'The cardinal is impressed with the report of your investigations here with regard to Rousset; and your colleague, Captain Lloyd, has spoken glowingly about your past exploits.'

'Thank you, colonel! It's a pity I have no memory of them.' Both men uttered an awkward half laugh. They soon graduated to first names as Luke recounted the detail of his investigation into the murder of Lady Antoinette. Marcel probed, 'What makes you sure that Henri St. Michel is innocent?'

'His sister Josette was a very close friend of the Lady Antoinette. On the day of the murder, Antoinette asked Josette to precede her to this hunting lodge, where a rendezvous, supposedly with Mathieu Gillot, was to take place. Four people saw the dead body of the marquise—the murderer, Josette, Henri, and Mathieu. I have a feeling that both Josette and Henri saw the murderer and decided to shield him or her from the authorities.'

'Given that, they still wish to maintain their silence, even when Henri is under investigation suggests it was someone close to both of them,' commented Marcel.

'Don't waste time on this aspect of your investigation! When Henri's life is in danger, Josette will tell all,' advised Luke. Marcel noted the comment and continued, 'What is Henri's relationship with Rousset?'

'In the short time I have been here, Philippe has visited often and stayed sometimes for weeks. I was never sure of the nature of the relationship. I was told Philippe was a friend from Henri's childhood, who had drifted away during the Fronde. It was only since his reconciliation with the Crown and his appointment to the garrison at Rouen that their acquaintance was renewed.'

'There is a much closer relationship which the cardinal discovered when he took legal steps to seize Rousset's property for the Crown. Despite appearances, Rousset owns no property. His father gave him a string of titles, but the lands were bestowed instead on the late Marquis des Anges and his immediate successor, the current marquis. The St. Michels receive the income from these lands and use a little of it to pay Rousset a fairly large allowance. The lands and income revert to the main Conde´-Bourbon line on the death of Henri St. Michel.'

'So Rousset is totally dependent on Henri for his income and must ensure that he stays alive or his income ceases totally. That makes for a very complex relationship. If the cardinal has all this information, what more does he wish to know?' asked Luke.

'The Cardinal is a very astute man, but even a staid conservative Englishman must be curious. Why would a senior Prince of the Blood bestow a considerable portion of his lands for two generations on another aristocratic family and bind his illegitimate son to their generosity for that period?'

Luke was troubled. 'These issues must be cleared up immediately. I will ask Henri to call a meeting of the household, and forewarn him that you will ask him why the Prince bestowed Bourbon-Conde´ estates and income on his father and also that you will question Josette on the murder of Antoinette.'

Henri was in no hurry to oblige. The fateful midday meal began three days later with an air of apprehension. Josette had been apprised of what lay ahead, and Henri belatedly informed Marcel that he and his sister would cooperate.

The French colonel waited until well into the meal and then announced, 'My lord, the government of France has been asked to arraign you for the murder of your first wife and for treason, in that you aided and abetted a declared traitor and outlaw, Philippe, Vicomte Rousset—both during the late rebellion and since the recent declaration of his treachery. How do you answer to these charges?'

Henri began. 'Regarding the murder of my first wife, I plead guilty to distorting the evidence and lying to the magistrates and my family, but it was to protect someone very close to me. On that fateful day, Antoinette, Mathieu Gillot, and I all received notes suggesting we meet at the hunting lodge where, in my case, I would see something of importance.

Antoinette and Mathieu received letters, purportedly coming from each other, arranging a secret tryst. As both parties were suspicious of each other, they both took precautions. Mathieu decided to arrive much later than the designated time, and Antoinette had Josette go ahead of her to the designated meeting place and hide in the building. Josette will explain the events of that horrible day.'

Josette calmly recounted the details of the murder. 'I reached the hunting lodge ahead of Antoinette. There was no one in the building. This intrigued me. Perhaps Gillot's letter was genuine, and he had dismissed his servants for the period of his meeting. I hid myself in a small antechamber next to the bedroom that I knew was Antoinette's destination.

Antoinette arrived, and I heard her undressing. Eventually, there was a knock on the bedroom door, and Antoinette began her well-rehearsed seductive invitation. The bedroom door was flung open, and I heard a voice denounce Antoinette as a conniving whore who deserved the judgment of God. Antoinette then gave as good as she got, attacking the visitor as a misshapen dwarf, a pitiable excuse for a male, and a good-for-nothing son. It was Alain St. Michel.

I moved away from the adjoining wall as I did not wish to eavesdrop on mother and son. I poured myself a drink from a container resting on a small table against the far wall. I then heard a torrent of hysterical abuse from Alain, amidst considerable sobbing from him. Then I heard a muted scream from Antoinette that was cut short.

I grabbed the poker from the fireplace and burst into the room to see Alain choking his mother. Alain stood up from the bed. He seemed in a trance and appeared not to see or hear me as he took up one of Antoinette's hatpins and stabbed her incessantly.

I hit him relentlessly with the poker, but he was only slightly shaken and advanced on me with hatred in his eyes. At that moment, Henri burst through the door. Alain ran at Henri, pushed him aside, and disappeared into the forest.

Henri and I partially cleaned up the room and placed Antoinette on the bed. We both returned to the chateau to consider our options. Soon after, Mathieu arrived to tell us that he had found Antoinette's dead body in his bed. Henri decided that Mathieu would say he had found the body in the forest. There was some confusion as to whether she would be shot by arrows or gored to death by a wild boar. In the end, Henri declared the latter to be the official version and imposed a vow of silence on us all.'

Henri took up the story, 'The more urgent task was to find Alain. Later that day, the headman of one of the hamlets in the forest came to me severely wounded. Alain had run amok and slaughtered many of the womenfolk of his village in a blind rage against all women. With the help of the villagers and my servants, Alain was finally apprehended. I persuaded my fellow magistrates that with regard to the murder of the peasant women, Alain was of unsound mind and should be detained in the south of France.'

Josette concluded the confession, 'Henri and I promised for the good name of the family and Antoinette's reputation that we would never mention the situation again. The recent reported disappearance of Alain from his place of detention and the current charges about to be brought formally against Henri forces me to break my oath of silence.'

Henri interposed, 'Let us enjoy several more courses before I answer Colonel Guarin's second question. Drink up, as what I have to reveal will come as a shock to all, although it will answer a question many of you have asked me over the years—what precisely was my connection with Philippe Rousset? Some of you are also closer to Philippe than you could possibly imagine.' Henri was coping with the difficult predicament by trying to inject some mystery into the situation.

An hour later, Henri recommenced his exposition. 'Most of you believe that Philippe, an illegitimate son of the late Prince of Conde´, was given many estates in the south of France by his father. In depriving Philippe of these estates as a declared traitor, Cardinal Mazarin discovered that Philippe possessed none of these properties. They are all mine.

Conde´ drew up an agreement with my father that for two generations the St. Michels would draw the income from these estates, and, from this income, my father and then myself would pay Philippe an allowance. Philippe was regularly here to receive his monies and, most often, to encourage me to increase its amount.'

Marcel interjected, 'My lord, what you have just said has been verified by the lawyers. The cardinal wants to know why Conde´ selected your father as the banker and financial guardian of his illegitimate son?'

'I trust what I am about to reveal does not go beyond these walls and that my explanation will satisfy Mazarin.' Marcel replied that he could not speak for the cardinal but anticipated that if the answers were satisfactory, any record of this confession would disappear. It was the cardinal's practice.

Henri poured himself a brandy and downed it immediately. He crossed himself and asked his father to forgive him. 'You ask why this family was chosen to act for the Prince of Conde´ with regard to his illegitimate son?' There was a long pause. Henri continued, 'Philippe's mother was my father's second wife.'

His listeners were stunned into absolute silence. 'The prince seduced her just after my father married for the second time. Within a short period of time, my father had lost his first wife, my mother; and his second wife had made him a cuckold. It was rumoured that the prince had slept with my stepmother on her wedding night. Nevertheless, the prince was a gentleman and regretted the humiliation he had brought to my father. He was open about his affair with my stepmother, and the two men reached the agreement explained earlier. We were chosen as compensation for the liberties that the prince had taken with the new Marquise des Anges.'

Josette fainted and slowly slid from her chair. When she recovered, she asked, 'Philippe Rousset is my half brother?'

'Yes, I am sorry, Josette, to have kept this from you, but father was determined that his disgrace should never be revealed.'

Marcel continued, 'Thank you, my lord. It is a painful and fully plausible explanation. And, finally, to the charge that you aided and abetted Philippe during the rebellion and in recent days, how do you plead?'

'To these charges, I plead guilty in that I provided Philippe with a substantial income during both these periods, as I and my father have done throughout his life. I would in my defence argue that I was bound by my father's agreement to continue to provide the monies to Philippe whatever his circumstances and political loyalties.'

The household was in a state of shock. Charlotte led a weeping Josette back to her apartment.

32

LUKE AND MARCEL REMAINED AT table, and the former commented, 'That should answer your questions. Mazarin must drop the charges. Set Henri's mind at rest!'

'Come on, Luke, you have worked for politicians. I cannot anticipate how the cardinal will react to my report, which will exonerate Henri. Technically, he has continued to finance a traitor, and Mazarin may concentrate solely on that Achilles heel.'

Luke sat silently for a while and then asked, 'At least you can reveal who informed on Henri so that we may build a legal defence if it is needed.'

'I cannot tell Henri St. Michel anything, but I will inform you in the strictest confidence. The man who claims that Henri murdered his wife is a Georges Livet, a merchant from Rouen who made his fortune in Canada. He says that Henri's son, Alain, had given him the details.'

'Has Alain been interrogated?'

'No. Livet freed him from his confinement and was going to use him to confront Henri, but the young man had a seizure and died.'

Luke grinned. 'This is more pertinent that you think. Georges Livet is the tenant of the abbey gatehouse on the edge of this estate. I have already begun to investigate him. Your information will help me tie up a lot of loose ends.'

Luke decided to speed up his investigation into the abbey gatehouse and its tenant. Next morning, as he sat planning his first move, he was interrupted by a well-armed mounted horseman wearing clothes similar to those Luke had worn when he first stumbled ashore on the des Anges estate. It was Andrew Ford. Luke knew of Andrew's major role in his past from the detailed briefing he had received from Harry, but the figure before him struck no cord of recognition.

Andrew handed Luke a letter from Harry. It outlined the events that had taken place in England and the latest reports Harry had received on Rousset's activities. Philippe, with his prisoner, Lord Harman, was moving towards either the Chateau des Anges or the English Court, and Lady Lucinda Harman was also on her way to France to reclaim her daughter's body from the Abbey des Anges.

Harry did not believe this. Simon had convinced him that James Harman had placed Lucy's body in the family crypt at Harman Hall months earlier. Luke, as a matter of urgency, must verify if her remains were in the abbey coffin or not. Harry suggested that Luke use Andrew as his assistant in pursuing the enquiries from his end and send him back to St. Germain when he had something significant to report.

Although he had no recollection of Andrew, to have a fellow Englishman share his apartment and activities dramatically improved Luke's mood. He immediately sought the marquis's approval for the additional guest. The marquis was happy that Luke had an assistant who was above suspicion and hoped that this extra help would speed up Luke's enquiries into the attacks on Lady Charlotte.

The marquis's gentle reminder forced Luke to think through what he knew about the attack on Charlotte. Suddenly, he saw the light—or some light. If the bear wandering around the estate was Georges Livet, and Georges Livet was really Emile St. Michel, he could be the person who had assaulted Charlotte. A fragment of bearskin had been snagged on a bramble bush next to the tower. If Josette knew about the secret passage in the tower, then it was likely that her brother Emile also had that knowledge. Maybe he found or stole Henri's button and left it in the tower to incriminate his half brother.

Luke and Andrew's visited Evangeliste. The abbess was delighted to receive them and used the occasion to display her sisters' cooking skills and her own proficiency in English. Luke explained, 'Mother Evangeliste, I have several questions regarding the tenant in the gatehouse, the sightings of the bear, the missing treasure, and the body of Lucy Harman.'

The nun paled at the last question and was overeager to volunteer further information about the bear. 'Colonel, we have had further sightings of the bear, and the hysteria has not abated. Sister Clare and Sister Anne now claim the bear was in the kitchen. It's impossible! There is no way into this convent after the doors are shut and locked.'

'Perhaps it wandered in during the day and slept in some secluded spot and started to move about at night,' suggested the practical Andrew.

'Even more impossible! Immediately on the reported sighting, I had every sister out of bed, and the premises were searched from top to bottom. The outside doors were still locked. There was no bear. The sisters are undergoing punishment for their troublemaking and to discourage other outbursts of such inanity.'

Luke trusted Evangeliste. 'Reverend Mother, I agree. There has been no bear within the convent or in the woods. The figure which your sisters saw was a man, maybe wearing the mask and skin of a bear or just with a very hairy appearance.'

'The same applies whether it was a man or a beast. There is no way in or out when the doors are locked,' replied the abbess. The discussion was halted by what sounded like a riot within the convent. Female voices were raised as sisters shouted at each other.

Evangeliste turned from the friendly hostess into the stern disciplinarian. 'This behaviour is unseemly and quite without precedent. For once, the presence of men may be conducive to good order. Follow me!'

The uproar came from the kitchen. Evangeliste, Luke, and Andrew strode into the room. The two soldiers could not conceal their amusement. One nun had another on the ground and was slapping her face. Yet another had a small skillet and was about to apply it to the head of the face slapper.

As the abbess's presence was noticed, all of the nuns lapsed into absolute silence except for the slapper who shouted, 'If you touch

Sister Josephine again, you will answer to me. The devil has possessed you. First, you see a bear, and then I catch you pushing and bullying the aged sister.'

'Stop this at once Sister Mary! Why is my deputy assaulting a fellow sister?' Sister Mary, the prioress, was not intimidated. 'Reverend Mother, I came into the kitchen a few minutes ago and found Sister Anne and Sister Clare pushing, if not punching, Sister Josephine who is, as you know, well into her nineties. I asked them to stop, but they ignored me. I then stepped in between them and Sister Josephine. They are possessed by Satan.'

Luke was attracted to Sister Mary, a well-built woman who had obviously spent much of her life in physical labour. She had held her own against the two younger and fitter nuns.

Evangeliste restored peace, ordering the nuns back to their duties except for Clare and Anne who were to follow her. There was no doubt that these renegade nuns were overwrought. Perhaps the discipline of the convent had finally overwhelmed them, and they were striking out at the weak point of the convent's establishment, the oldest of the nuns.

Evangeliste ordered the recalcitrant sisters to kneel and seek the Lord's forgiveness in silent prayer. After what seemed to Luke like an eternity, she spoke to them, 'I have put your disruptive behaviour down to youthful high spirits and, more recently, to your bouts of hysteria and hallucinations regarding the bear. Perhaps Sister Mary is right, and you have become possessed. What do you say in your defence?'

Sister Clare responded. She was small, olive-skinned, with a bubbly personality. She was not cowered by Evangeliste. 'Reverend Mother, we meant Sister Josephine no harm, but she has information that will prove we did see a bear in the kitchen.'

'What information? You cannot take what Sister Josephine says as truth. Her memory went years ago; and, now, her mind, in general, is confused,' replied the abbess. Luke could not contain himself and gently asked, 'But what was it that she said that led you to believe she could validate your fantasy of the bear?'

Sister Anne took up their defence, 'As punishment for claiming to have seen a bear in the kitchen, the Reverend Mother sent us there as scullery maids. The other sisters continually teased us about seeing things, which increasingly annoyed us. We started to argue with them. Sister Josephine, who is too old to work, spends her days near the kitchen fire to keep warm.

Suddenly, in the middle of the arguments, her shrill and wavering voice broke through the noise. She said, "Stop teasing the young ones. They have seen a bear. And I know how it entered the abbey." Then she fell back into a deep sleep, as was her want. I was so mad that I began shaking her awake. At that point, Sister Mary came into the room and dragged me away from Josephine. I resisted, insisting that Josephine could free us from the taint of hysteria and hallucinations that you, Reverend Mother, have laid upon us.'

Sister Clare reentered the discussion. 'Anne and Mary began to wrestle, and Anne slipped and fell on her back. Mary threw herself on top of Anne and began slapping her face. I picked up a skillet to help Anne, just as you entered the room.

We were only trying to obtain evidence to prove to you that we do not deserve the punishments that you have imposed. Anne was not punching or even pushing Sister Josephine. She was shaking her awake and trying to get her to focus on how she knew that we could have seen a bear.'

Evangeliste indicated that Anne and Clare could return to their duties in the kitchen, and she would speak to them later. After they had left, she turned to Luke, 'Well, what do you make of that?'

'I'm inclined to believe them. To me, neither appears to be the hysterical type. They reflect more the spirit of rebellion of young women placed in an environment that is alien to their personalities,' replied Luke.

Andrew broke his silence, 'Reverend Mother, is it possible to talk to Sister Josephine?'

'No. I will speak to her, but, to Josephine, I am still the young novice in the days when she was in charge of us, as deputy to the then abbess. She lives in the past.'

Luke's face brightened. 'I have a suggestion. Impose a simple disciplinary punishment on Clare and Anne. They must take it in turns to read to Sister Josephine as she sits, half asleep in front of the kitchen fire. They may use the opportunity to gently prod the old lady's memory as to the bear and how it appeared and disappeared. Maybe there was a similar experience in the deep past.'

Evangeliste surprisingly agreed and then apologized for this riotous interruption to their conversation and asked, 'Were there other matters you wished to discuss?'

'Reverend Mother, you and your sisters are in great danger. Philippe has kidnapped Lord Harman, and they are headed here to retrieve the treasure. Is there anywhere in the convent where Harman could have hidden the hoard? Could he have concealed it in the gatehouse?'

'Lord Harman did stay in the gatehouse, both when he brought Lucy to us in the first place and then when he helped her to move to court. In fact, he stayed on three occasions. He was there overnight when he escorted his daughter's coffin from the English Court on the first part of its journey home to England.'

'And where is that coffin now?' asked Luke.

'I took a solemn oath not to reveal its whereabouts until it ceased to be in my charge. That is about to happen at any time. Lady Lucinda Harman will arrive soon to accompany the body of her daughter back to England to be buried in the family's church.'

'So the body of Lady Lucy is still here?'

'Yes, but that is all I can say.'

33

LUKE HOPED THAT SOMETHING WOULD come from the gentle prodding of Sister Josephine's memory by the two young nuns. His confidence was rewarded sooner than he expected. He received the news in a way he did not anticipate.

He returned to the hunting lodge to find several domestic pigs rooting through his garden beds. Making little attempt to control them was a nun, Sister Hilary, who indicated that she could not speak. She drew a letter from within her habit and gave it to him. Within minutes, the pigs and clerical swineherd had disappeared.

Luke called Andrew to listen to the letter as he translated it from the French.

> *Dear Colonel, We seek your help because the abbess may not believe us yet again and punish us unfairly. We did see a bear, and, now, we know how it appeared and then disappeared from the kitchen. Reverend Mother asked us to read to the elderly Sister Josephine and surprisingly suggested we could gently question her about how we could have seen the bear. Gradually, the old lady revealed that sixty or seventy years ago, when there was little discipline or religious commitment at the abbey, men used to visit some of the nuns, unknown to those in authority. According to Sister Josephine, there were two secret tunnels leading into the convent—one came from the gatehouse and the other, from somewhere in the woods. The bear could have stumbled on the*

*forest entrance and followed the scent of food and found itself in
the kitchen. Unfortunately, Josephine cannot remember or refuses
to tell us where the tunnels finished up within the abbey. Clare
and I have searched most of the building but cannot find any
hidden entrance. Please help us! At least tell Reverend Mother
that there are secret tunnels into the abbey and that you need to
find them. Bernadette de Coligny (Sister Anne).*

Luke was excited. The nun's revelation supported his hypothesis
that Emile, based in the gatehouse, was the bear seen by various
people. His experience in the Canadian wilderness would explain
his ability to move through the forest virtually undetected. Luke
would find the tunnels and unmask Emile's intentions. In addition
to attacking Lady Charlotte, Emile must have other plans to bring
grief to his half brother.

Next morning, Luke and Andrew returned to the abbey. Luke
was surprised. Evangeliste had gone to Paris and would be away for
at least a week. Luke explained to Sister Mary, the prioress, that
the tension regarding the bear in the kitchen and the resultant
disharmony among the nuns might be explained by the existence of
secret entrances to the abbey.

He asked permission to examine every inch of the convent.
Mary's reply surprised him. 'That brings back memories. When I
first came here, before the moralistic reforms of Evangeliste, there
were rumours that nuns entertained men who came at night through
secret passageways.'

'Did you ever mention this to the other nuns or to the Reverend
Mother?' asked Luke.

'No, it was not a fit subject to raise with your superior, especially
in the climate of reform that was then sweeping France.'

Luke and Andrew began their inch-by-inch examination of the
abbey. They started with the public places—the kitchen, the refectory,
the library, the reception rooms, the chapel including its crypt, and
several storerooms. They found six secret panels that led to adjoining
rooms and narrow passages that provided a short cut to the chapel.
No long tunnels leading in or out of the abbey were discovered.

Mary did not feel she had the authority to allow them to search Evangeliste's apartment. While Luke and Andrew searched the interior of the convent, Mathieu's gamekeepers searched the forest in the vicinity of the abbey, looking for a hidden entrance.

Next day, a disappointed Luke joined the equally unsuccessful gamekeepers as they gradually closed in around the abbey. All of a sudden, one of the dogs pulled heavily on its leash and began to bark. The keeper let the dog loose. It bounded ahead of the men and stopped in front of a large rock. It began to scratch at the lichen that covered the ground adjacent to the monolith.

Luke reached the site and called for a spade. He was perspiring with anticipation. The lichen rolled back like a rich carpet, revealing a stone that had an iron ring attached to it. Luke sent one of the gamekeepers in search of tapers. The rock was lifted. When the tapers arrived, Luke, Andrew, and the senior keeper descended down a metal ladder into a wide tunnel.

It had been recently used. Cobwebs had been destroyed. There were footprints in the wet ground at the beginning of the tunnel. The floor dried as they progressed, and Luke sensed that they were walking up hill.

Then the tunnel stopped. At first appearance, it seemed blocked by large boulder that had been left *in situ*. The gamekeeper pointed out handprints in the dust that covered the topside of the gigantic rock. Luke climbed over it and found a small wooden door, half the normal size. Luke squeezed through the entrance and immediately realised where he was. He was in the short hidden passageway that ran from the kitchen to the chapel, which his earlier search of the abbey had revealed.

When Andrew arrived, Luke jokingly upbraided him, 'What fools we were! We did not examine the walls of the secret passageways in as much detail as we should have. The secret door we found in the kitchen, which we concluded led only to the chapel, in fact led also to an external tunnel. Let's not make the same mistake again. We must test every inch of these secret walls. There must be another tunnel that comes in from the gatehouse.'

Luke noticed that the secret passage from kitchen to chapel was encased in wooden paneling that was decorated in several types of wood. He noticed that the aperture through which they had crawled was cleverly concealed in the paneling as a square in which several angels had been inlaid in a lighter-coloured wood. Further along the passage, on the other side from where they entered from the forest, Luke found a similar piece of paneling.

He pushed and prodded. As he did so, the centre portion popped open, and he was able to get his fingers around the edge and open it completely. Luke sent the gamekeeper back to inform Mathieu. Luke and Andrew crawled through the small hole until they could stand upright. Luke believed they were now heading for the gatehouse.

Towards the end of this tunnel, wooden panels replaced the dirt and stone surrounds. They were now within the gatehouse, probably in the walls between rooms as the passage way had narrowed considerably. Before they reached its end, Luke held up his hand. He could hear voices—and they were very audible.

Luke was astonished. It was Rousset who was speaking. 'Thank you, Georges! It was fortuitous that I saw you at a distance in Rouen and was able to confront you without being seen by others.'

'Philippe, we had a good business partnership for the last two years. You obtained for me muskets, pistols, and ammunition at a very low price. I exported these to Canada at an immense profit in which you shared. Why have you destroyed our mutually beneficial arrangement? You have been outlawed and the cardinal's men are hunting you down. You must have done something very stupid.'

Rousset ignored the implied criticism. 'Thank you, Georges, for hiding me here! I have lived at the Chateau des Anges on and off for decades, and my prisoner has led me back here by a circuitous route.'

'Don't thank me, Philippe. I am not a charitable man. You agreed that if I hid you and the Englishman, I take a share of the massive fortune you claim is hidden in the abbey.'

'Yes, my prisoner will to show us where it is located in the morning. I have previously searched the des Anges estate and the abbey without success.'

Georges was reassuring. 'There will be places you have missed. This gatehouse, the abbey, and the chateau are full of hidden passages and rooms. With my help, you will be able to search most of the abbey without being seen.'

'Georges, I was close to Henri for decades, but I was never made privy to the existence of a single hidden passage. How have you, in a few months, become aware of them?'

'Because I am a St. Michel. I am Emile St. Michel.' Luke could hear the gasp ofastonishment.

'God preserve us! Over the last two years, I failed to recognize you. We saw a lot of each other when you were a naïve teenager, making your feelings for your sister-in-law too obvious.'

Emile changed the subject and spoke in English as he turned towards Harman. 'Where is the treasure?'

'In the crypt of the chapel.'

'It can't be. I searched it thoroughly,' screamed Rousset.

Harman whispered, 'I am no fool. If I give you the exact location now, I am a dead man. But I assure you and swear on the blood of our Saviour that the treasure is in the crypt.'

Georges intervened, 'Gentlemen, we have all had a tiring day. The treasure is going nowhere. Let's sleep on it and, tomorrow, plan how we get this fortune out of a busy crypt. It is rarely uninhabited. The nuns are randomly set penances to spend the night there.'

Luke had heard enough and motioned to Andrew to return down the tunnel. When they reached the passageway between the chapel and the kitchen, Luke ordered him to leave through the forest tunnel and tell Mathieu what they had heard. Luke moved directly into the chapel full of nuns reciting Vespers. He hid behind a pillar until all them except Mary had left.

His sudden appearance frightened the prioress whose intuitive scream was only partly muted. 'Sorry, Mary, I did not mean to alarm you, but I came through one of the hidden passages to bring you bad news and to seek your urgent assistance.'

Luke repeated what he had heard without revealing Emile's true identity. He continued, 'I also searched the crypt—with Evangeliste. The two caskets left by Harman containing relics and ecclesiastical robes were opened, but there was nothing else except the coffins of countless nuns that, for religious reasons, the abbess refused to open. I have a hunch that the treasure is stored in the casket that purports to contain Lucy Harman's body. It was not identified to me during the original search. Do you know where that is?'

'Yes, Evangeliste told me only two days ago that Lady Lucinda Harman was on her way to collect her daughter's body, and I was to ensure that the casket was presentable. Come with me!' They made their way down into the crypt, and Mary pointed out a casket more ornate than the rest. She explained that Queen Henriette had had the casket constructed as the girl had died while under her care. Lord Harman left it temporarily at the abbey but promised to return as soon as possible to collect it.

Mary had done a good job. The woodwork gleamed. Luke looked around for a metal rod to help prize open the lid. Mary sensed his intention. 'No, colonel, I cannot permit the sacrilege.'

Luke turned to the nun, 'Mary, I, above all, will respect the body of my countrywoman, but I am sure that her remains are not in this coffin. Her father used it instead to hide the treasure.'

'But if Lucy is not in the coffin, why is her mother coming here as quickly as she can to retrieve the body?'

'She is coming to retrieve the treasure before her husband is forced to reveal its whereabouts to Rousset. She probably hopes she can use some of it to bargain his release.'

Mary fell on her knees and prayed. Luke opened the casket.

34

WHAT HE SAW SPURRED HIM into immediate action. He returned quickly to the chateau and, at once, informed Andrew and Mathieu that Lord Harman had to be rescued without delay and by way of the hidden passages. Mathieu was not convinced of the objective or the means. He argued that his men should attack the gatehouse with a superior force and that the arrest of Philippe and Emile should be the first priority.

Luke was dismissive, 'If your men were trained soldiers, it might be a reasonable proposal. And, although we have the edict declaring Philippe a traitor, we have nothing against Emile. An armed assault on his leased establishment might be illegal. Far more significant is that any attack on the gatehouse would lead to Harman's summary execution. As an Englishman, I feel responsible for his safety, but my priority as a servant of the Marquis des Anges remains to capture a French traitor. But, in the short-term, the rescue of Harman is a matter of life and death.'

Mathieu grudgingly acquiesced. He then offered to help. 'Will my men create a disturbance to cover your rescue of Harman?'

'No, anything out of norm will alert Emile and Philippe. They are able opponents. Don't underestimate them! At the moment, Emile does not know that we are aware of the secret passages. With luck, I will find Lord Harman and lead him away while the rest of the household sleeps. Do you have a plan of the abbey?'

'Yes, when we handed administration of the abbey to the lawyers in Rouen, we had copies made. I will get one.' Mathieu returned in a few minutes, and the three men perused the drawings.

Luke mumbled unhappily, 'I had hoped to appear through a wall panel, grab Harman, and disappear; but the plan shows all the bedchambers are on the upper level and well removed from the secret passage. I will have to cross most of the lower level, climb the stairs, and then find where Harman is being held.

Andrew, you will come with me, but stay hidden in the wall. If I am discovered, you will come to my rescue, making as much noise as you can. Our enemies must think there are several of us.'

'There will be,' said Mathieu. 'I am coming too.'

As they made their way to the abbey, Luke had a change of heart. 'We should not alert Emile and Philippe to our knowledge of the hidden passageways. When we rescue Harman, we will leave through an external door or a window. As soon as we exit the secret passage, while I search for Harman, both of you move straight to the nearest external exit and ensure that it is unlocked!'

The three men entered the secret passage and moved well into the gatehouse. Luke could hear some muffled conversation, but it was too far away for him to understand what was being said. All of a sudden, Luke and his companions visibly jumped. The ringing of a large bell, which was not far from their hidden location, deafened them. It was the entry bell of the gatehouse.

Luke heard Emile order a servant to open the door and ask Rousset and another servant to draw their swords in case this was a diversion for a robbery. Luke cursed himself. He had not allowed for servants. How many were there? And, clearly, at least one was armed.

He was further shocked when the door was opened and a voice asked in English for accommodation for his mistress Lady Lucinda Harman and her party. While a servant listened to this request, Rousset whispered to Emile, 'What luck! We can take the wife and use her to control the husband. We will be unstoppable with the two of them in our hands.'

Emile shook his head, 'Maybe later! At the moment, she has at least six men with her and a wagon which might contain more.'

He brushed his servant aside and moved to the door and replied, 'Unfortunately, these premises are now leased and cannot provide accommodation for travellers. Go to the convent itself. Just ring the bell at the entrance as you have done here.'

The door closed, and Emile, in a very buoyant mood, returned to Philippe. 'This is great news. The arrival of Lady Harman proves that Lord Harman has been honest with you. He has led you to the treasure. His wife has hurried here to redeem it before his lordship is forced to reveal it to us.

With Lady Harman in the abbey, we can use the secret passages to eavesdrop on the nuns—and on her ladyship. She may reveal the exact location of the treasure. Lord Harman must not know his wife is next door until it suits our purpose. Where is Harman by the way? The ringing of the bell should have woken everybody.'

'I put him in the room at the top of the stairs as you suggested,' replied Philippe.

'Good, the windows in that room are barred, and the stairs are old and in need of repair. They creak at the softest of feet. One of my heavily armed men will guard the room from the outside to ensure he cannot escape.'

Luke recognised that he would have to change his plan. Emile and his household were wide-awake following the intrusion of the bell-ringing entourage of Lady Harman. 'We must wait a couple of hours. Let's go back to the central passage where both tunnels intersect. I must ask Sister Mary to prevent Lady Harman opening her daughter's coffin until her husband arrives.'

Andrew was direct, 'How are you to rescue Harman if you have to climb up squeaky stairs and pass an armed servant?'

'He doesn't have to,' interrupted Mathieu. He pulled the plans of the gatehouse from inside his doublet. 'We all missed another set of stairs that lead directly to the upper level. It is a narrow, winding, towerlike stone structure attached to the forest end of the original building. The nuns used it to service the gatehouse with food and fresh linen. It has an outside entrance into the courtyard adjacent to the convent.'

Luke nodded enthusiastically, 'Andrew, see if you can find its external door! Mathieu, go to upper end of the passage and listen. Hopefully, you will hear something to our benefit. I will speak to Mary.' Luke took a few minutes to carefully reconsider his plan. He took a swig of brandy from his flask and moved to enter the chapel.

Before he closed the door, he was met by a panting Mathieu who had run back down the passageway. 'Quick, get out of here! Emile is copying your approach. He and Philippe will take it in turns eavesdropping on Lady Harman and the nuns hoping to hear the exact location of the treasure. Emile has already entered the passageway.' Mathieu and Luke escaped into the tunnel that led to the forest. Luckily, they intercepted a returning Andrew to whom Luke explained the situation.

Andrew smiled. 'Then follow me!' Andrew led them back to the edge of the gatehouse and the outside staircase. He had shattered the lock with a heavy jab from a large stone. Luke was excited, 'The time is right. We will strike now. There will be one man less in the gatehouse. We enter at the second floor quickly and quietly, follow the corridor to the centre staircase, remove the guard, grab Harman, and return the same way. With this approach, we avoid squeaky stairs, doorways, and windows.'

The men removed their boots and were soon on the appropriate level. Mathieu stayed at the door of the stone staircase while Luke and Andrew moved slowly along the narrow corridor that bisected the floor. The silence was suddenly broken by a series of loud creaks and a series of thuds as someone bounded down the stairs.

Luke could not believe his luck. The guard placed outside Harman's door had left his post. Given the smell of roasted chicken emanating from below, he was probably tempted to get some food. He may have been encouraged to leave his post knowing his master had left the building.

Luke opened the door to Harman's room and only partly avoided being hit by the leg of a broken stool. Luke grabbed the swinging arm and whispered, 'I am a friend. Follow me!' Luke released his grip and, within a few minutes, the four men were outside the gatehouse. They quickly moved into the cover of the forest.

Luke's adrenalin was flowing. He felt good. 'Andrew, take Lord Harman back to the hunting lodge! Mathieu return with at least four well-armed men to the abbey door as soon as possible! I will guard Lucy's casket until your men arrive. The abbey is also wide awake with the intrusion of Lady Lucinda Harman and her men.'

Andrew and Mathieu dispersed to their allotted tasks. Luke rang the bell at the abbey's entrance and was eventually met by Mary who was more than a little irritated. 'Not now, colonel, we are very busy.' Luke gained her undivided attention with his warning that an attempt might be made to steal Lady Lucy's casket at any time. He must be admitted to the crypt to guard it and that additional men would be arriving shortly to assist him. 'Sister, how many men did Lady Lucinda Harman bring with her?'

'She had six men, four are in the abbey, but two are sleeping with their horses in the stables. Why do you ask?'

'There are at least four men in the gatehouse ready to seize the casket as soon as they can identify it, and there are four men within the convent who are ready to abscond with it on behalf of Lady Lucinda.' Luke drew Mary into the middle of the room and whispered, 'Everything that is said between the kitchen and chapel can be heard. The casket will not be safe until Mathieu's men arrive. In the meantime, send seven or eight of your nuns to the crypt! Their presence might delay any premature attempt by either party—the Harmans or Rousset to seize the casket.'

Mary demurred to Luke's request but protested, 'Surely, Lady Harman has every right to take the casket. That is why she is here.'

'Of course, but does the casket contain what the Harmans claim? Inform Lady Harman that her husband has been rescued and will join her early tomorrow morning so that they might retrieve the casket together.'

Luke and seven nuns entered the crypt. The nuns encircled a casket with their heads bowed and prayed for the soul of the deceased. Luke hid behind one of the columns where he could see both Lucy's casket and the entrance to the crypt.

Mathieu and the gamekeepers joined him. Luke relaxed.

35

NEXT MORNING, LADY HARMAN AND her men came to the crypt. Luke introduced himself as the man who had rescued her husband and asked that she await his arrival before she took possession of the casket. Ten minutes later, Andrew arrived with James Harman. He embraced his wife who shed a few tears. He then turned to Luke and thanked him for the rescue and for guarding overnight the casket of their beloved daughter. He turned towards his men and ordered them to take up the coffin and carry it to the wagon that Lady Harman had brought with her. Luke held up his hand. 'Do not move the coffin! In assisting you, my lord, I acted for both the English government in London and the English Court in Paris. Neither is happy with your lies.'

Harman exploded, 'How dare you, sir. If you had not saved my life, yours would be forfeit for such calumny. Out of my way!' The irritated Harman motioned to his men to move the casket. Luke physically blocked their path with sword drawn and confronted Harman, 'My lord, stop lying! What is in that coffin is the worst kept secret I have known. The English Court, the English government, and a group of highly placed renegade Frenchmen know its real contents. Your daughter's remains were buried some time ago in your family vault at Harman Hall. You think this casket contains part of the fortune in coins, jewellery, and precious plate that the Catholic community of England entrusted to you for safe keeping, but part of which you wish to surrender to Oliver Cromwell to obtain a better deal for Catholics.'

'What the Catholic peers of England do with their possessions is no concern of yours. I have discussed our options for this treasure with them. Most agree with me that to make Cromwell a large donation to ease the restrictions on our worship in England is a reasonable use of the funds. Now, let me remove my property,' demanded Harman.

'It will not be your property for much longer,' boomed a familiar voice from the door of the crypt. It was Rousset who moved into the chamber and confronted Luke, 'You may be a competent interrogator, but you are a poor military tactician. All your men and those of Lord Harman are imprisoned in this crypt because it has a single narrow exit. One of my men can keep you confined here indefinitely. As it happens, I have with me twenty well-armed musketeers, drawn from my former colleagues in the Rouen garrison. I showed them the inventory that I found in Lord Harman's study of the goods contained in this casket. It was sufficient incentive for them to volunteer for this special mission. You are imprisoned, outnumbered, and in no position to deny my request.'

'Which is?' asked a frustrated Harman. 'I intend to open the casket to ascertain its contents and then have your men carry it to the door where my musketeers will relieve them of it. Do not attempt to attack or disarm me! At the slightest provocation, the musketeer with his weapon aimed through the broken window in the crypt's door will shoot Lady Harman and continue to execute others as the need may be. Now, let me open the casket to see exactly what we have!'

Philippe moved to the coffin. He ordered one of Harman's men to help him with the lid. With joyous expectation, he could hardly contain himself as the lid was slowly pushed aside. There was absolute silence. Philippe's strained face peered into the casket. As if in a trance, he began to scoop handfuls of sand from within the coffin. His face suddenly turned red and radiated absolute fury.

'You devious devil Tremayne! Where is it?' The Harmans pushed through their men and gazed into the coffin with utter disbelief. It contained only sand and rocks. They also turned on Luke. 'Is this some sort of trick? Return our property!'

Luke replied, 'I cannot. I have never seen the treasure. Yesterday, I opened this coffin in the presence of the prioress, Sister Mary, and discovered it was empty. That is why you Lord Harman had to be rescued immediately. If Philippe had brought you here this morning and discovered this empty box, you would have been slaughtered on the spot.'

'I still might slaughter you all. Who has been in the crypt alone in recent times?' asked an almost-demented Philippe. Another stranger pushed through the door of the crypt. He was a solidly built man with long hair, a large curly moustache, and a large uncontrolled beard. He announced himself simply as a business associate of Philippe. 'I know for certain that Colonel Tremayne has not been in a position to steal the treasure. But some of the nuns have been. Sister Mary could the nuns have removed the goods bucket load by bucket load?'

'It is possible, but the nuns are superstitious about this place. It is an area of punishment rather than relaxation. They are also naïve and chatty. Such goings on would be common gossip in no time.' The hirsute man whom Luke was certain was Emile St. Michel continued, 'Did anyone open the casket before you and Colonel Tremayne?' Mary hesitated, 'When we received the letter from Lady Harman indicating that she would come to retrieve the casket, Mother Evangeliste opened the coffin about three days before Colonel Tremayne and myself.'

Philippe began to rant and rave. 'The She-Devil has stolen the goods. How did she react when she opened the casket?' Mary calmly replied, 'I was not here at that precise moment. The Mother Superior acted entirely on her own.' 'How can that be?' asked Emile. 'It took two strong men to remove the lid. The Reverend Mother is a small fragile woman.'

Mary threw up her hands. It was beyond her comprehension. Luke played for time. 'Gentlemen, what now?' Philippe was direct. 'You all starve until someone tells me where to find the treasure.'

Emile openly disagreed, 'Don't be foolish! No one here knows where the treasure is. We have been tricked by a cleverer mind than that of an English peer, an English colonel, and a local steward. Mother Evangeliste, aided by a powerful mastermind, is behind this.'

Philippe was not convinced. 'No! It was more likely Cardinal Mazarin's top soldier who spent some time here. That would explain why the abbess has fled to Paris.' Emile shook his head in disagreement. 'If it was Mazarin's man, he would have had his troops invade the abbey and take the treasure openly in the name of France. I suspect the one man who could influence the righteous abbess is her patron, the local magnate and magistrate, the Marquis des Anges.'

It was Philippe's turn to disagree. 'I don't think Henri has it in him. He doesn't need the money, and he is too apathetic, but Evangeliste is a different proposition. What do we do now?' Emile was clear. 'I will disappear until Evangeliste returns and, during that period, follow-up on my suspicions regarding the role of the marquis in this theft. You too, Philippe, must vanish because as a declared traitor, anybody could take you dead or alive.'

Philippe was unhappy. The treasure still eluded him, and Emile had taken charge of its recovery. The latter moved towards the exit and announced, 'Ladies and gentlemen, Vicomte Rousset and I will now leave. His men will keep you here for two to three hours to give us ample time to make our escape—but you will hear from us again.'

Andrew breathed a sigh of relief, as did most of the other prisoners, and asked, 'Why did Emile let us go?' Luke answered, 'He knows that we did not steal the treasure nor are aware of its location. His interest is now on Evangeliste and Henri. Luckily, he is still unaware that we know about the hidden passageways. He will continue to use them to eavesdrop on the abbess when she returns.'

The single musket pointed through the small window in the door of the crypt sufficed to keep the growingly restless room of prisoners reasonably calm. After two hours, Luke moved towards the door. He grabbed the barrel of the musket. There was no one holding its butt. Philippe's band of mercenaries had long since gone.

Luke would have agreed with Emile and Philippe who, as they trotted away from the abbey, concluded that the treasure was still somewhere on the des Anges estate. Emile had conducted a careful surveillance of the area for his other project—to harass the des Anges—and had not seen any movement of large boxes or goods from the convent. His men had listened almost continually in the secret passageway monitoring the conversation of the nuns and their visitors.

Philippe momentarily lost his confidence. 'My god, was the treasure ever in that coffin?' He rode in silence for some time. Eventually, he slowly emerged from his bout of depression convinced by Emile that the Harmans were as shocked as he was to find the casket empty.

Luke had the same question for James Harman. 'My lord, was the treasure ever in this casket? Or was it a diversion to keep would-be thieves away from its real location?'

'Colonel, I suspect your motives and actions in this matter and therefore refuse to answer your questions. You and those dastardly Frenchmen can continue to speculate.' Without further ado, he and Lady Harman left the crypt.

Luke ordered Andrew to return to the English Court and inform Harry of developments and seek advice as to what he should do regarding the Harmans and Evangeliste's possible involvement in the treasure's disappearance. He and Mathieu sought an urgent audience with Henri and asked that Josette also attend. As was his want, it was two days before Henri made himself available.

He was terse. 'We have surely had enough meetings and revelations for the time being. I hope that your information warrants this diversion.' 'And why am I, a mere woman, present?' queried Josette jokingly. Luke recounted the developments at the abbey. 'My lord, could you offer hospitality to Lord and Lady Harman. I want to keep them nearby for the time being. They are currently staying within the abbey.' 'Do you have a reason for this request, Luke? asked Henri.

'My lord, I am not entirely sure that the treasure was ever in that casket. They may reveal something accidently as your honoured guests.'

'And what else have you got to tell me?'

'Sir, a person who I am sure is your brother Emile, is the man who attempted to kill Lady Charlotte. He has now got it into his head that you worked with the abbess to steal the treasure. I have sent Andrew to Paris to inform the English court and the French government of what has occurred. The cardinal may send troops here for your protection.'

Henri laughed. 'He is more inclined to place me in so-called protective custody.' He turned to Josette who had begun to sob. 'Dear sister, the return of your brother Emile and the role he is playing must be distressful, especially on top of the behaviour of your newly discovered half brother Philippe.'

Josette turned to Luke. 'Are you sure that this man is Emile St. Michel?'

'He told Rousset that he was. And his interest in Alain and the period of his sojourn in Canada make me pretty certain that he is Emile. As a child, did he have any distinguishing birth marks or scars that would make his identity certain?'

'No, he was a perfectly formed little boy who had no accidents that would have marred his body.'

Henri coughed. 'He did have one scar. On the discovery of his affair with Antoinette, my father, before exiling him to Canada, had him severely beaten. The man who wielded the whip went too far, and Emile's wounds became infected. He had to recuperate for several months before he sailed. The incident left a permanent scar across his back.'

36

EMILE'S BELIEF THAT HENRI WAS the mastermind behind the disappearance of the treasure worried Luke. He took immediate steps to protect the household. Twenty of the estate's most able-bodied servants were conscripted to a daily routine of military training. Henri provided the necessary weapons and ammunition from the family arsenal.

Luke hoped that Emile and Philippe would delay any action for some weeks. He assumed that they would gather more intelligence regarding the whereabouts of the treasure by using the secret tunnels to eavesdrop on the abbey before taking further action. Luke's greater fear was that the chateau might also be honeycombed with secret passages and rooms; out of which the enemy might emerge unexpectedly.

Luke and his enemies shared one common interest—Evangeliste. Emile believed that she knew the location of the treasure. He was determined to listen to conversations twenty-four hours a day in the dining hall, chapel, and other rooms adjacent to the secret passages to uncover as much information as he could. As what happened in the crypt could not be overheard from these hidden vantage points, Emile overcame this disadvantage by hiding one of his men in the ossuary. Emile was content to bide his time.

Philippe was not. He frantically searched the forest hoping to find a wandering abbess laden down with gold and silver. He posted men at the surrounding crossroads and sent others to Paris to try and find her. He would find this nun and the treasure.

Evangelique was well aware of her predicament and sought help from the highest quarters in the land. She was, at that moment, waiting to see Cardinal Mazarin in the company of her new found friend and protector, Marcel Guarin. Mazarin was eager to receive Guarin's report on the Marquis des Anges and was mildly annoyed that Marcel entered his apartment accompanied by a nun.

Marcel sensed the negative reaction and took the initiative, 'Your Eminence, forgive the intrusion of Mother Evangeliste, the superior of the Abbey des Anges. She has information that is relevant to my inquiry, and she seeks your spiritual direction as to how she should act on a matter that is central to it.'

Mazarin motioned for Evangeliste to speak, but it was Marcel who continued. 'When I finished my investigation at the Chateau des Anges, Tremayne suggested that I visit the Abbey as its superior had known the St. Michel family and Rousset for decades. Tremayne thought she might be able to fill in some of the gaps in my investigation. When I arrived at the abbey, in addition to answering my questions, she urgently sought my assistance.'

'Reverend Mother, why do you need Guarin's assistance?' asked Mazarin anxious to hear from the nun herself.

'Your Eminence, there was a casket left in my abbey allegedly containing the body of the murdered Lucy Harman. Rumours arose that the casket did not contain the girl's body but a considerable amount of treasure that had been put in the safekeeping of her father. Tremayne warned me that Rousset and probably the current tenant in the abbey's gatehouse would try to seize the hoard.

Then I received word that Lady Lucinda Harman was arriving with a large entourage to take the casket back to England. In the circumstances, I decided my earlier vow not to disturb the casket was now void. I opened the casket to ensure that it was in a fit state to be received by Lady Harman.'

'And what did you find?' asked the very interested Cardinal. 'I found the treasure,' replied a confident abbess. 'So why do you need Guarin's help?'

'I have concealed the treasure once more and I fear all parties including Lady Harman and her English servants and Vicomte Rousset with his band of ever-changing mercenaries will destroy the abbey in their frantic search for it. My sisters and I would be helpless to resist.'

'Could not the English colonel provide protection?'

'He is able, but he is only one soldier aided by a deputy and the civilian servants of the marquis. They would be no match for the greedy local troops bought by Rousset's tales of unfounded wealth for all who assist him.'

'Is the treasure still within the precincts of the abbey?' asked a persistent Mazarin. 'Wherever the treasure is, those looking for it will deduce that I could not have removed it unaided from the convent. The man in the gatehouse probably has had the abbey under surveillance for months.'

'What precisely do you want, Reverend Mother?'

'I need French troops to guard the Abbey until the treasure can be returned to its lawful owners.'

Mazarin remained pensive. He turned to Guarin. 'Is this important enough to deploy troops?'

'Yes, both to catch Rousset and to retrieve the treasure—but the soldiers should have been there yesterday. Our enemies could strike at any time, although hopefully they may await Mother Evangeliste's return.'

Mazarin was devious, but he was decisive when it mattered. 'It would take days for your men to reach Rouen. Send a message immediately to the naval headquarters at Le Havre! If the tides are right, they can have a company of marines at the abbey late tomorrow. Guarin, you will return there immediately to take charge of the operation. In the meantime, the marine commander will liaise with the English colonel employed by the Marquis des Anges and receive an initial briefing from him.'

'I must also return,' said Evangeliste.

'No, Reverend Mother, you will stay here for two reasons. First, the way you walked and your demeanour in the chair suggest that you have suffered physically from your journey here. There is no way you could make the return journey with Guarin.'

'It is true that my body aches. I had not ridden a horse, let alone for several days since I entered the church as a young girl.'

'There is a second reason why you must stay under the protection of my guards. As you know the location of the treasure, all parties will be after you. Rousset would torture you to death to obtain that information. He has already killed two women in this pursuit. Until Guarin and the marines are in place, you must stay here.'

'Thank you, Your Eminence. On the matter of the treasure, I need your spiritual guidance. How should I act? Who rightfully owns it? I understand that it has been collected for safe keeping from those of our faith in England to prevent it falling into the hands of the English Protestant republicans. Then I hear it rumoured that Lord Harman will use the treasure to buy support from the even more heretical and radical English army under General Cromwell. Would we, as Catholics, not have a duty to prevent this happening?'

'Reverend Mother, if only things were that simple. This is undoubtedly English treasure. France has no right to interfere.'

'Not even if Catholic treasure is to be handed over to Protestant heretics and regicides?' responded a passionate Evangeliste.

Mazarin placed his chin in his hands. Although he did not give a hint of his real thoughts to the animated nun, he could see the great diplomatic kudos for himself with Cromwell. He would recover the money and return it to the English Catholics, so that they could buy support from Cromwell. This would kill two birds with the one stone. His Byzantine mind began to weave several threads.

'Reverend Mother, let me worry about the problems associated with this. In the short-term, if you release the treasure, hand it over to Colonel Guarin. He will guarantee that it will be returned to its rightful owners, our brothers and sisters in England. I will use our king's aunt, the English Queen Mother, Henriette Marie, to facilitate its return.'

Three days later, Guarin and Evangeliste's report of the situation at the abbey was confirmed for the cardinal by a visit from Captain Lloyd and Sergeant Ford. Mazarin smiled and replied, 'I am ahead of you, captain. I have already taken action to assist. A company of marines should already be at the abbey under the command of Colonel Guarin. They have orders to liaise with Tremayne.'

Harry explained that the English king had freed him, Lord Stokey, and Ford with a small party of English soldiers to go to the abbey to help Colonel Tremayne. Mazarin was unhappy. This must remain a French affair—both the capture of Rousset and the recovery of the treasure. He was also very worried about Lord Stokey's presence. This English peer was dedicated to preventing Harman using the money to support Cromwell. He must get new instructions to Guarin immediately to forestall any misguided attempt by Stokey to obtain control of the treasure.

The cardinal revealed none of these thoughts to his audience. 'Captain Lloyd, Mother Evangeliste is currently here in Paris and desires to return to her abbey in its hour of need. Could you escort her? She would have returned with Guarin, but he had to hurry back to take command of the marines and protect the abbey. You may take a more leisurely trip knowing that there is a whole company of French marines ready to assist Tremayne.'

The Englishmen were annoyed. Escorting Evangeliste would slow them down. Harry was therefore pleasantly surprised when she appeared, not in clerical robes, but in a riding habit. He was astounded when against all protocol and ladylike behaviour, she, like Lady Mary Gresham, mounted astride her horse. Her only comment as she sensed the surprise of her male companions was that this was her last period of freedom before she faced the crisis at the abbey.

After the Englishmen had left, Mazarin read a report that had just come to hand. He had ordered his agents to investigate Georges Livet who had accused Henri of murder and treachery and who claimed to be Emile St. Michel, Henri's half brother and heir to the title and estates should Henri and his children die. The report greatly interested the cardinal. The relevant portions of it he had transcribed and sent on to Guarin.

Livet murdered his longtime partner, Emile St. Michel, and took complete control of the organization that St. Michel had created. He sold it and returned to France a very wealthy man. New evidence from several nomadic Indians, employed by the two men, confirms Livet as a murderer and a dealer in illicit arms to the rebellious Iroquois.

37

LUKE REMAINED PUZZLED BY EMILE'S alliance with Rousset. It was probably a profitable diversion from his mission to destroy Henri. Luke was now convinced that Emile attacked Charlotte to punish Henri for what he believed on the word of his nephew Alain was the marquis's murder of his first wife. Now, as he got to know Henri better, Luke doubted whether the death of Charlotte would be such a devastating blow. Henri would find a third wife and sire a coterie of additional heirs. Such was the world of dynasty.

Luke talked the matter over with Mathieu who gave his opinion as to Emile's machinations. 'Henri is one of the richest aristocrats in France. Emile wants to replace him and had two ways to achieve this end. The first was to blacken Henri's name to the authorities and have him convicted of treason. The government would deprive the St. Michels of their titles and seize all their properties. These it could reallocate to anybody it chose, possibly Emile—but it would be unlikely. Given Marcel's favourable report on Henri, this option is now dead. Emile is therefore forced to his other option—to kill Henri and the two children. If he could achieve this without being held responsible, he would then inherit the title uncontested.'

Luke winced and concluded, 'Yes, I have to assume that he is using the missing treasure and our concentration on the abbey as a diversion so that he can attack Henri, Charlotte, and the children at his leisure. I do not have the resources to watch the abbey and the family. Charlotte and the children must be sent away immediately.'

Pascal interrupted the conversation. 'The marquis wishes both of you at the riverbank. There is a naval frigate unloading a company of marines. Its commander, a Lieutenant Heritier, has paid his compliments to the marquis and sought permission to cross the estate to the abbey. Apparently, Evangeliste has obtained the help of the French government to protect it and the missing treasure. Heritier wishes to speak to you, Luke.'

Luke made his way to the small wharf where the young lieutenant was supervising the disembarkation of his men. Luke introduced himself, and the French officer saluted. 'Colonel Tremayne, I have orders to protect the abbey and to obtain a briefing from you as to the current situation. Colonel Guarin will arrive today or tomorrow to co-ordinate the mission which is to include your men as well as mine.'

'Who signed your orders, young man?' asked an intrigued Luke.

'Cardinal Mazarin and countersigned by an acquaintance of yours, Captain Sauvel, who sends his regards.' Both Harry and the marquis had referred to Sauvel previously, but the name did not awaken additional memories.

Luke suggested that the marines move immediately to the Abbey. He briefed the lieutenant as they marched. The two officers agreed that the marines would guard the abbey while Luke would concentrate on protecting the St. Michels.

Luke returned to the chateau and asked to see the marquis immediately. Henri was not pleased. As Luke entered his lordship's chamber, Henri said tersely, 'I do not appreciate demands from my servants.'

'My lord, forgive the impertinence, but recent developments have convinced me that the danger to you and your family is imminent—and very serious.' Luke outlined his fears. Henri was taken aback. 'Emile's desire to replace me does explain a lot. His knowledge of the chateau and the abbey would explain how he can move about without being seen, and his Canadian experience makes his ability to move through the woods undetected understandable.'

'I hope he does not know secrets of the chateau of which we are unaware. Are there any tunnels connecting the abbey to the chateau or even to the hunting lodge?'

'My father never told me of any secret passages in the chateau except the one from my reception room to a hidden vault. I did not know about the additional staircase in the tower. The power of our family has been such that there was never any need to have escape tunnels honeycombing the grounds. We have been secure in this chateau for hundreds of years. But I know that the abbey is riddled with hidden passages although I have no detailed knowledge of them. It is a secret handed down from abbess to abbess, although Evangeliste's predecessor was such a scatterbrain she probably neglected to pass on the information.'

Henri suddenly stopped as if overtaken by a dreadful thought, 'Luke, does Emile have help from members of the household or from within the abbey?'

Luke was taken aback. 'I have no evidence of such assistance. Do you have anybody in mind?'

'No, but I cannot see how Emile who has been absent for decades can suddenly appear and be so efficient in his activities without inside knowledge and assistance. Josette knew him well, as did Evangeliste. And Odette arrived here out of the blue, at about the same time as Emile moved to Rouen.' Luke was surprised that Henri doubted the women of his household but he promised to look into it. However, any further activity on the des Anges estate was put on hold.

Henri agreed that Charlotte and the children must leave at once for an unnamed estate on an island in the Bay of Biscay. He insisted that Luke accompany them to Le Havre. Pascal would stay with them on the island as tutor to the children. Luke was to return as soon as his charges were out to sea.

Henri persuaded the captain of the frigate who had transported the marines to take his family and senior servants back down the Seine. Even if Emile were watching from the forest, he would not be able to follow as the frigate with the advantage of tide and wind rapidly disappeared down river. Luke never knew the family's ultimate destination.

On reaching Le Havre, the frigate docked just long enough for the captain to have a new destination approved by the naval authorities. Luke was informed that he could return to des Anges on another frigate, which, at the turn of the tide, would sail back to the Chateau des Anges with further supplies of ammunition and food for the marines.

Luke was back in the chateau the following morning to welcome Guarin who wasted no time in drawing up plans. 'Luke, the report your man brought to Paris was thorough. The cardinal is convinced that Rousset will not give up until he has the treasure. His chances have increased with the assistance of Georges Livet. We have one advantage over them. Evangeliste has as good as told us that the treasure is still in the abbey.'

'She confessed to moving it?' asked Luke.

'Yes, but she refused to tell the cardinal exactly where it is, but she had a deep discussion with him as to the treasure's rightful owner.'

'Surely, there is no doubt about that. It belongs to the Catholic community in England and its temporary caretaker, James, Lord Harman.'

'Not according to your former colleague, Captain Lloyd! His friend at the English Court, Lord Stokey, refuses to accept that Harman's interests and those of the Catholic community any longer coincide. Consequently, the cardinal believes that if the treasure is found on French territory, it should be received by him. He will hand it over to Henriette Marie to decide what is in the best interests of English Catholics.'

Luke retained an open mind on Marcel's comments but he would discuss it further with Harry, Andrew, and Simon whom Marcel informed him were escorting Evangeliste back to des Anges. In the meantime, he would try once again to talk to Lord and Lady Harman who refused to leave the chateau until the treasure was recovered and in their possession.

Luke and Marcel walked through the forest on their way to the abbey. The former was surprised to find that the ship that had brought him back an hour or so earlier was still unloading. They were passed on the track by a small wagon dragged by two sailors. Its contents astonished Luke, and he turned to Marcel. 'The wagon is loaded with barrels of gunpowder?'

'Yes, Lieutenant Heritier, after assessing the situation, considered a supply of gunpowder would be useful in defending the abbey and defeating the enemy.'

'In what way? I can't see how gunpowder could be effectively used in this situation except in the muskets of the marines, and you do not need wagonloads of it for that purpose.'

'Apparently, one of the nuns told the lieutenant that there were secret passages that led into the abbey and that a bear had used it to get to food from the kitchen.'

Luke was furious. His major strategic advantage was that he did not want Emile or Philippe to know that he knew about the tunnels as he was using them to provide his opponents with false information.

The men had nearly reached the abbey when a sailor running at top speed overtook them. He recognized the distinctive red livery of Colonel Guarin. 'Sir, there is trouble ahead. My mate and I were hauling a wagonload of food when we came across a discarded dray and the bodies of two of our shipmates. They had been shot in the back by an avalanche of arrows. Their wagon is empty. Someone has stolen a dozen barrels of gunpowder.'

The two officers ran to the scene of the crime. Marcel was angry. 'These villains mean business. No one thought of arming sailors carting supplies through a friendly forest. It changes the nature of our whole enterprise. Gunpowder in the hands of our enemies could turn the odds against us.'

'Yes,' said Luke, 'and it changes the nature of my other responsibility in protecting the marquis from his ambitious half brother. Thank goodness, the marquise and her children are safe. Wait until Lloyd, Ford, Stokey, and Mother Evangeliste arrive, and, with the marine commander, we must rethink our approach to this changed situation.'

Guarin concurred. He would bring the expected arrivals straight to the hunting lodge and detach a troop of marines to guard it. He went on to the abbey to arrange the deployment.

Luke returned to the chateau, sought out Mathieu, and left a message for Henri. Mathieu agreed that, given the fresh information, all servants should be urgently employed searching every room, cellar, cupboard, and niche in the rambling chateau—any place where gunpowder could be stored. Emile was now in a position to demolish the building and to kill Henri.

While Luke took steps to protect him, the marquis put himself at risk. Tiring of the enforced company of the two armed servants that Luke had ordered to accompany him at all times, Henri slipped away while they were otherwise engaged and took a quiet stroll in the forest. Henri was deep in thought when he half heard a whirr and felt a sharp pain in his upper arm, and as he fell to the ground for cover, another sharp pain occurred in his back. Two arrows had struck him. He turned and, vaguely through clouding eyes, saw a man with a bear mask take another arrow from his quiver and advance towards him. Henri passed out.

38

As Marcel and the new arrivals—Harry, Simon, Andrew, and Evangeliste—turned a sharp corner in the path from the abbey to the hunting lodge, they saw only a few yards ahead of them a man standing over another. The attacker was about to loose an arrow into the prone figure. Marcel drew his sword and ran at the man who was wearing a bear mask and skin. Emile turned his bow towards the advancing soldier, but Simon who had nonchalantly been carrying a large stick threw it at the archer's arm with sufficient accuracy to slightly deflect the arrow.

Emile disappeared deeper into the forest followed by Marcel, Harry, and Simon. Evangeliste nursed an unconscious Henri in her lap while Andrew mounted guard to protect her from any further assailants.

The hunters quickly realised that the experienced woodsman had eluded them. They returned to his victim. Harry examined Henri's wounds and pronounced that the arrow had missed vital organs. Evangeliste sounded an alarm. 'These arrows are not like anything I have seen on the estate. They are similar to those that our Canadian missionaries showed us during their recent visit. Those American savages put a deadly poison on their arrow tips. We must remove the arrows immediately and clean Henri's wounds as quickly as possible.'

Andrew ran ahead to the hunting lodge to prepare a room for the now-conscious Henri. Just as he was being laid carefully on a bed, the windows in the hunting lodge shattered. A loud explosion had erupted in the nearest wing of the chateau. Harry, Marcel, and Luke left Andrew and Evangeliste to care for Henri and ran to the scene.

It was total devastation. A large section of the southern wing was a mass of rubble. As a large crowd of servants gathered, Luke organized them to sort through the remains looking for bodies. He turned to Harry and Marcel and soberly remarked, 'This could have been a disaster. The demolished section houses the living quarters of Lady Charlotte and the children and Pascal de Foix's schoolroom. It was only yesterday that I secretly escorted them to an unknown destination. Emile must have thought they were still here, and, because it was deserted, it was not one of the areas that my men thoroughly searched.'

Luke's relative joy quickly turned to concern. The mangled bodies of two persons of high status and six servants were found in the debris. Mathieu, who had heard the explosion from deep in the forest, arrived just as the dismembered bodies were being extracted from the fallen masonry. He threw up his hands in anguish, 'My god, given the departure of Lady Charlotte yesterday, I moved the Harmans and their entourage into her vacated apartment only this morning.'

Marcel was angry. He berated his companions, 'This is appalling. We have a company of marines, a dozen local men, six English soldiers attached to the Harmans, and an assorted group of experienced soldiers in our group, and, despite that, a single man appears to have wounded the marquis and killed two English aristocrats. Thank god, Luke, you had the foresight to remove the Marquise and her children! If Henri dies, then young Paul is the new Marquis. Does the boy and his mother have any armed protection?'

'No, their only companion is the elderly tutor de Foix. He is an old soldier but has not wielded a weapon in decades.'

'Where are they exactly?'

'I don't know. Her ladyship felt that it was safer that no one, except, I presume, Henri and the naval authorities should know.' Marcel continued his criticism, 'Not good enough! Henri may not be able to tell us. I will ask naval command the destination of its frigate.

Naval ships do not usually go around delivering the nobility to their island resorts. Henri must have more influence than I thought.'

Marcel sent to the abbey for experienced nuns to assist Evangeliste to care for the marquis and to the marine company for their surgeon. The surgeon carefully removed the arrows and endorsed Harry's original judgment that the wounds were not critical. Happily, he found no evidence of poisoning. With careful attention by the nuns and his own servants, Henri would fully recover. He was transferred from the hunting lodge to his apartment.

Mathieu spent the day supervising the retrieval of the English bodies and in cleaning up the bombsite. That evening, Evangeliste, Marcel, Harry, Simon, Mathieu, Andrew, and Luke gathered in the hunting lodge for the evening meal and to consider their strategy. Emile's next move, given that his attack on Henri and family had failed, had to be anticipated. Philippe and Emile would be in two minds concerning the unintentional death of the Harmans. One thing for certain, it would focus their attention on Evangeliste.

Marcel spoke, 'Reverend Mother, you know the location of the treasure. Rousset and Livet will stop at nothing to force that information from you. We will provide protection for you at all times, but you cannot return to the abbey until they are apprehended.' Marcel nodded to Luke to reveal their agreed plan.

He explained, 'We need to force our opponents out into the open. We will use the hidden tunnels and passages in the abbey to bring this about. I have already spread false information so that Emile and his men, who are listening from these places, will be misled. With your help, Mother Evangeliste, we can lead them into a trap.'

This provoked Simon. He angrily turned on Luke, 'You are not suggesting that we use Evangeliste as bait to snare our predatory opponents?'

'Not at all! We will encourage the nuns and troops to gossip that Evangeliste has hidden the treasure in a particular place and that it is about to be moved by the marines. That will force our enemies to act quickly—and we will be ready for them.'

Simon was still uneasy. 'Luke, I trust that the removal of the treasure by the French marines is a measure designed primarily to catch our enemies. With the death of the Harmans, I am now the rightful guardian of this hoard. Frankly, while I want Rousset punished for what he did to Harry and myself, his capture is not my first priority. The recovery of the treasure and its immediate return to a safe English Catholic environment is vital.'

Marcel and Luke gave each other a knowing look, and Harry wondered what the two colonels really had in mind. Harry was torn. He sympathized with Simon. He had received orders from Cromwell to regain the treasure for the Harmans who would use it to pay a special tax to the general to achieve greater toleration. He had no orders regarding what to do should another Catholic who was determined that it would not be used to assist the English army laid claim to the money. Harry was drawn between the noble ideals of his friend and his duty to retrieve the money for his commander-in-chief, Oliver Cromwell.

Luke brought him back to the task at hand. 'If we are to trap Emile and Philippe, it would help to know where the treasure is and remove it to safety before we spring the trap.' All eyes turned towards Evangeliste. She looked towards the heavens and finally spoke, 'When I opened the coffin in preparation for Lady Harman's visit, I was shocked to find it brimful with coins, jewellery, gold and silver bars, and precious plate. I had heard rumours that Lord Harman wished to use these Catholic funds as a sweetener to that Protestant heretic and regicide General Cromwell. I was determined that such a calamity would not happen.

I took steps to conceal the hoard. I had only just completed this task when I had an unexpected visit from Colonel Guarin. I asked him to escort me to Paris so I could discuss the situation with Cardinal Mazarin and also with the provincial of my order. I did not expect in my absence that Philippe and Emile would attempt to steal the treasure. It was fortuitous that it failed, and, now, we have heavy protection from the marines.'

Luke was direct, 'Are you ready to reveal where the treasure is and how a weak and fragile woman moved a casket laden with precious stones and metal? It would take six grown men to move it.'

Evangeliste smiled. 'Gentlemen you are not as clever as you think. A poor ignorant nun has tricked and confused not only the enemy but all of you as well. However, I will not reveal its whereabouts until you all swear on Mary, Mother of God, or, for you Protestants, on the Holy Scripture, that you will, in addition to capturing Emile and Philippe, restore the treasure to the English Catholics now represented here by Simon.'

The four soldiers flinched. For different reasons, Harry, Andrew, Marcel, and Luke could not swear to Evangeliste's proposition. Marcel spoke for them all, 'Reverend Mother, we understand your position, but as soldiers, we have orders that may not conform with your suggestion.'

Simon was appalled. He glared at the four recalcitrant men. 'I thought that some of you were my personal friends and others, friends of Mother Church. How you can refuse to swear to Evangeliste's just request amazes me. What higher authority is there than God?'

Harry, stung by Simon's rebuke replied, 'Unfortunately, we are servants of man. As soldiers, we have taken a solemn oath to serve our masters, whether it is one of the conflicting English administrations or the government of France.'

Simon, who completely misunderstood Harry, asked, 'Surely, King Charles is not after this money?' Marcel saw an opportunity to increase the friction within the English camp. 'The English king is desperate for money, and to deprive his republican opponents of this treasure would be a financial and diplomatic coup.'

Luke felt impelled to respond, 'Just as Cardinal Mazarin might see it in his interests to use the possession of the treasure to play the English Court and the government in London off against each other.'

Evangeliste and Simon were disgusted. The nun finally spoke, 'Stop your selfish bickering. Is there no decency and honour left in these troubled times? In such circumstances, I will certainly not reveal the location of the treasure—but I am willing to help you entrap our enemies. My nuns may jubilantly shout all over the abbey that Mother Evangeliste has found the treasure and has hidden it wherever you think appropriate.'

Luke thanked Evangeliste and asked, 'Where would be a plausible place to pretend to hide the casket?' Evangeliste suggested a number of places and the soldiers considered the tactical advantages and disadvantages of each location. Marcel argued for a locale in which their numerical superiority could be brought into play. He did not want to repeat Luke's earlier mistake of having his men in the crypt, which had been blocked off by one or two of the enemy.

Harry queried the more open scenarios that Marcel suggested. 'Emile and Philippe are not fools. If we choose a place too far removed from the crypt, they will ask the same question that puzzles us—how could a slight woman move the treasure such a distance.'

39

SIMON WAS DECIDEDLY UNHAPPY. 'WHY link the capture of Emile and Philippe with the treasure? We have superior numbers. Surely, we can hunt down the two fugitives? They must be hiding in the forest or in one of the hidden tunnels to which you refer. Forget about the treasure. It is safe, wherever it is. Concentrate on the capture of the renegades and negotiate later with Evangeliste regarding the gold and silver!'

Harry secretly agreed with his friend but acquiesced in the clear intention of the colonels, Marcel and Luke, to use the treasure as bait to tempt the villains to strike. Marcel answered Simon, 'Emile is a brilliant woodsman. He could successfully hide from a regiment of soldiers, let alone a small company of marines. He can afford to wait until the time is right and, in the meanwhile, make further attacks on Henri and his household.'

Simon had had enough. With great passion he angrily exclaimed, 'But Rousset cannot. He needs money quickly to escape the country and begin a new life in the affluence to which he is accustomed.'

Andrew interrupted the dialogue. 'News that the treasure is to be moved will force Rousset and Livet to act. Don't only talk about the move but do it! Dozens of marines can protect the casket, which could be taken through the woods to the Seine and shipped down river to safety. Our enemies will have no option but to strike during the journey across the woods or lose any chance of obtaining the treasure. It will be out in the open, and we have superiority of numbers.'

Simon was a little happier. 'Let's further confuse them. Send three or four wagons, each loaded with a casket from the abbey, to the river! Emile will not know which one to attack. Surprise is his prime asset. If he makes a mistake and attacks the wrong wagon, we will be more than ready for his subsequent attacks—and the treasure need not be on any of the wagons.' The group agreed.

Marcel responded, 'An excellent idea, my lord. Give me two days to arrange for a naval ship to be in position. As an added precaution, I will ask for the marines on that ship to fan out from it into the forest to shepherd the incoming wagons. Otherwise, Livet may consider that the loading of the casket onto the ship is the moment to strike.'

Luke added, 'Have the marines within the Abbey discuss amongst themselves which wagon has the treasure. Let them gamble on which it is! Just before they leave, we will have one of them mention confidently to another to put his money on a specific wagon—and hope Emile's men hear it.'

Two days later, the household, now reduced to Luke, Mathieu, Josette, and Odette met for the midday meal with their guests Marcel, Harry, Andrew, and Evangeliste. Henri remained in his bedchamber as a continuing loss of blood had delayed his recovery. There was a renewed fear that the arrows had affected Henri's blood as it was slow to clot. A servant was reluctantly sent to Rouen to obtain a physician.

Josette was delighted that Evangeliste had moved from the spartan conditions in the hunting lodge to her well-guarded apartments. 'For years, my friend, you denied me this pleasure by declaring that your vows prevented you leaving the abbey. Recent events have forced you to suspend that vow?'

Luke gently intervened, 'The most basic and overriding reason of all—saving Evangelique's life. Josette, your apartment will now be protected by the marines.' 'But why should I be protected?' asked Josette, either naively or provocatively. Mathieu was incredulous. 'Josette, your brother has been shot and the area of the chateau, which normally contains your sister-in-law and her children, has been blown up. This is a concerted attack to destroy the St. Michel family.'

'And you suspect my full brother Emile. Why would Emile wish to harm me? My death, unlike that of Henri and young Paul, will give him no advantage. And I do not accept that this bomb-planting terrorist is Emile. He was always a gentle sensitive lad.'

After the meal was completed, Simon escorted Josette and Evangeliste to the former's apartment, and Andrew, with several marines, patrolled the perimeter of the chateau buildings while others were stationed inside the building and close to the women. Marcel, Luke, and Harry returned to the hunting lodge where Marcel announced, 'Tomorrow is the day. I have confirmation that a naval frigate with an additional half company of marines will berth at the small des Anges wharf, and the marines will be deployed in a fan formation by dawn. Mathieu has provided three wagons and drivers from the estate. Are there enough spare caskets?'

Luke answered, 'Yes, there are more than we need at the far end of the crypt. The casket makers use it as a workshop. There were at least three completed coffins standing on their end.' The soldiers drew up their detailed plans for the next morning.

Later that day, an anxious Andrew returned to the lodge and alerted Luke to an alarming turn of events. 'After the midday meal, Simon escorted Josette and the abbess back to Josette's apartment. When, after an hour and a half, I completed my circuit of the chateau, I saw Simon only then leaving the apartment. It seemed a long time for a social chat. After some time, Evangeliste reappeared and headed into the woods.'

'The stupid woman!' exclaimed Luke.

Andrew continued, 'I was delighted to see that one of the marines allotted to her protection followed her; as did I. Some distance along the path, Simon met her. They walked together with their heads almost touching discussing some matter they considered highly confidential. Just before the forest ended and the verge of the abbey grounds replaced it, the nun stopped and appeared to give Simon further directions. He then disappeared in the direction of the abbey entrance where I heard him identify himself to one of the marines, and he entered the convent.

As soon as Evangeliste was left alone, the marine shadowing her made himself known. They argued in French, but it was clear that the young marine was not impressed. He led her back towards the chateau. I let them pass. I waited for some time to see if Simon reappeared. He did not, so I thought I should report to you.'

Luke shook his head in disbelief. 'What is that devious nun and conniving Catholic peer up to? You cannot trust a Papist!'

'Don't refer to Simon like that in front of Harry. They are very close friends,' riposted Andrew.

Luke thought aloud, 'Evangeliste has told Simon where the treasure is hidden. To be honest, with the death of Harman, it probably does belong to him. And my immediate priority now is to bring Rousset and Emile St. Michel to justice before they kill Henri.

The treasure, and the machinations enveloping it, is of secondary interest. Whatever Simon and Evangeliste are up to does not concern me provided it does not interfere in our operations against the treasure hunters. Don't mention this to Marcel whom I suspect has orders to confiscate the hoard for France!'

That night, the soldiers and Lord Stokey met again to finalize the arrangements. Marcel reported that three caskets had been filled with sand and rocks and were ready to be taken to the wagons at first light. Heritier's men were instructed to make as much noise as possible throughout the abbey as the caskets were loaded to confuse Emile as to their origins. The wagons were already assembled in the courtyard, between the gatehouse and the abbey. Gillot had promised his three drivers would arrive at first light.

The soldiers agreed that one of them would sit beside the driver and another would ride beside the wagon. Harry and Simon would take the first wagon, Marcel and Heritier the second, and Luke and Andrew the third. Luke suggested another ruse. 'Emile will have realised by the number of marines that this is a French operation. Place twice as many marines in the vicinity of the second wagon. If he thinks like I do, he will then assume that all talk of the treasure being in the third wagon, which is the misinformation I have spread, is designed to mislead him. The heavier concentration of marines, with the two French officers around the second, indicates its real location.'

They agreed to assemble at first light and leave the abbey at dawn.

They were not the only ones planning diversions. As Marcel, Harry, Simon, Andrew, and Luke left the hunting lodge just before first light and trotted towards the abbey, there was a massive explosion, which lit the sky with burning debris. They galloped towards the convent. It was intact, except for a few shattered windows. The gatehouse however was a pile of smoking rubble. Marines were running everywhere, trying to extract the bodies of their dead comrades and rescue any who were still alive. A third of the marine detachment slept in the gatehouse, a third were on duty, and a third slept in tents on the edge of the forest.

Also, totally destroyed were the gatehouse stables, which accounted for most of the noise and fireworks. The marines had stored their ammunition, and extra weapons there, which happily for a cavalry officer such as Luke, was empty of horses.

Heritier was distraught. He was lucky to be alive. Concerned about the activities of the following day, he was unable to sleep and had left his luxurious room in the gatehouse. He joined his men in the abbey protecting the caskets in the crypt from any preemptive strike by Emile and Philippe.

As he stood surveying the massacre before him, a young ensign joined him. The young officer had run from the woods with his men. As he viewed the horror in front of him, he revealed additional misfortunes. 'My god, we were lucky. I came to report that, while we slept, our muskets and ammunition belts were stolen. The men have no weapons, other than their daggers, and I have only my sword.'

'Well, as you can see, we cannot replace them,' replied Heritier. He turned to Marcel, 'Sir, only a third of our men have weapons, and some of those will be light on for ammunition. If Rousset recruits many men from his old command at the garrison of Rouen, we will be outnumbered.'

As the officers discussed the changed situation, the wagon drivers arrived leading their horses. Their leader was agog. 'Thank god we did not leave the horses here overnight. By sheer chance, we left the wagons in the courtyard near the abbey, rather than next to the stables.'

Sister Mary directed the marines to the caskets that were to be loaded onto the wagons. As instructed, other marines invaded the convent and wandered all through it making as much noise as possible. When the cavalcade left the abbey, it was protected by only a third of the marines that had originally been designated for the job, and only a small proportion of them had muskets.

Marcel, nevertheless, deployed his weaponless troops, 'Let the unarmed men walk parallel to the path on either side of it. They can act as an early warning system of trouble. They will call out a number at regular intervals. If we don't hear their number we will be alerted.'

Luke was alert. He was in his element.

40

THE WAGONS WOUND THEIR WAY slowly along the forest path as the flanking marines shouted out numbers to indicate their wellbeing. The first wagon moved more quickly than the others and was soon out of sight. Marcel was not happy. His disquiet grew as one of the out runners left his designated position and ran onto the main path. He signaled for Marcel, who was riding beside the wagon to move away from it.

'Well, man, what is it?'

'Sir, we have just found three dead men with arrows in their backs. They are still warm. I think they are the real wagon drivers.'

'Good god! Can you ride lad?'

'Yes sir.'

'Take my horse and ride full speed ahead and inform Captain Lloyd of your news.' Marcel signaled Lieutenant Heritier to leave his seat beside the driver, and walk with him. Marcel informed Heritier of the news, who signaled for one of his unarmed men to take his horse, which had been tied to the tailgate of the wagon, and tell Colonel Tremayne who was with the last dray.

Just as Luke received the disturbing news, there was another explosion. Through the trees, he saw that several outbuildings of the chateau were ablaze. Simultaneously, he became aware that his outrunners were silent. He acted quickly. He jumped onto the wagon and, without warning anybody, slit the throat of the driver. He then explained to Andrew, 'He was one of Emile's men.'

Luke faced a dilemma. The wagons were about to be attacked, but he believed his first duty was to protect the marquis. Could he abandon the wagon to Andrew's capable protection and run to the chateau to assist?

The decision was made for him. A hail of gunfire began from both sides of the path. Marcel, some distance ahead of Luke, heard the explosion and then the musket fire. He returned with half of his marines to aid Luke. Nevertheless, he was worried that the gunfire was a diversion to tempt him into that very action. Luke had earlier adopted a precaution of having a platoon of marines walking some hundred yards behind him to protect his rear. Even with these reinforcements from Marcel and the rear guard, the enemy quickly revealed superior firepower.

The outnumbered armed marines fell back around the wagon and returned fire at a well-concealed enemy. Luke was alarmed at his casualties and distracted by the blazing building nearby and his concern for its inhabitants.

The gun battle lasted for a quarter hour when the enemy ceased firing and a disembodied voice rang out from behind the trees. 'Colonel Tremayne, your friend Philippe and I had no desire to harm you. You are completely surrounded and seriously outgunned. Withdraw your men from the wagon and retreat to the chateau where your help is needed!'

Luke, who had been joined by Marcel and Heritier, considered the demands. Marcel pragmatically advised, 'The treasure is not in the casket. Do not sacrifice your life and, in your case, Heritier, those of your men for nothing. Accept the terms and beat a rapid retreat! Once Emile finds the casket is empty, our lives will be forfeit.'

Luke was just about to accept when Emile changed his mind. 'Philippe suggests that you English are so devious that the treasure may not be in this wagon at all and that the double guards around wagon two was genuine rather than a diversion. My men will by now be inspecting that lightly defended dray as you, Colonel Guarin, withdrew most of the armed men to assist Tremayne. I want all of you to walk three paces away from the wagon while I inspect the casket.'

'God, there will be all hell to pay any minute,' whispered Luke. He indicated to his men to prime their muskets for one last volley. Emile and Philippe emerged from behind a large tree. As soon as they were in the open, the firing resumed at twice the intensity as before.

Luke was taken by surprise and dived to the forest floor. At first, he assumed that the talk had simply been a diversion and Emile intended to massacre all those present. Then he realised that the shots were not aimed at him. He saw Emile stagger as if hit, and Philippe fell to the ground. After ten minutes of concentrated fire, marines led by Harry Lloyd and an unknown marine officer emerged from both sides of the path. They were dragging behind them a wounded Philippe who had difficulty walking and whose face had been badly disfigured.

The firing ceased and the marines rounded up those of Rousset's men who had not fled. Harry explained, 'I had just arrived at the river when I was told of the true identity of the wagoner. He was summarily shot in the head by one of the marines. When we heard the gunfire and explosion, and knowing that the armed marines were grossly outnumbered, the young ensign rescinded the order for the fanned reception, and, instead, we outflanked the attackers on both sides of the path. Fortunately, the ship had brought another full company of marines, rather than a few platoons promised to Marcel.'

'Enough chatter, Harry, where is Emile?' asked Luke.

'Somewhere close, surrounded by marines! He was with Rousset one minute and disappeared the next.'

Marcel and Luke followed Harry's directions and were soon with a group of marines. Their leader reported, 'The hairy man must be somewhere within our circle. We have him completely surrounded. He has either climbed a tree or gone underground.'

Marcel turned to Luke, 'He has gone underground. Evangeliste told me that this central stretch of the woods is covered with old mining shafts and natural caves.'

He called for more marines and reorganized the search. Some troops concentrated on the trees; others, including Luke and Marcel, looked for any openings that might lead underground. Their task suddenly became easy. Luke picked up a trail of blood that led to the bottom of a sharp incline and into a bramble bush. He pulled the bush aside revealing a fairly large entrance to a cave whose interior was lit by a number of tapers.

Just inside the entrance to the cave were several barrels of gunpowder. Even more alarming were rows of small pots, many with fuses already inserted and with gunpowder spilling over the edges, all resting on a straw strewn floor. Deeper within the cave was Emile. He was stripped to the waist and attempting to staunch a serious wound. He had his back to the cave opening and did not initially hear the soldiers enter.

Luke looked astonished and then smiled. The back of this man was not scarred. It was not Emile St. Michel. Josette would be delighted with his news. Marcel's voice echoed around the cave, 'Georges Livet, raise your hands and move slowly to the exit, or we will open fire.'

The big shaggy man surprisingly obliged and moved slowly to the exit. Suddenly, he moved as lightning, grabbed the taper that lit the entrance, and made to throw it into the rows of grenades. Marcel fired and Georges fell to the floor.

The burning taper flew from his hand falling towards the straw on the floor. Luke threw himself at full length and managed to catch the fiery brand inches from its destination. Unfortunately, a spark flicked onto the floor, which immediately burst into flame and burned rapidly towards the grenades and the barrels.

A desperate Luke and Marcel ran for their lives. A series of small explosions was quickly followed by a massive blast that obliterated the cave and created a crater twenty yards in diameter. Both men were hit by flying debris and bled from several superficial wounds.

The marines assisted the colonels back to the main path where Lieutenant Heritier gave orders for half of the new marines to march to the abbey to help with their wounded comrades and the other half to assist at the chateau. Another small detachment led by Marcel dragged Philippe to the frigate. Luke, Harry, and Andrew moved immediately to the grounds of the chateau. Mathieu had firefighters battling the blaze, which was confined mainly to outbuildings. It had been designed as a diversion, rather than to destroy the building.

After all, Georges, the would-be marquis did not want to inherit rubble.

At that moment, an agitated Josette appeared. To calm her, Luke announced his good news, 'Dear Josette, the murderous bomber, who wiped out half a marine company and twice bombed the chateau and attacked Charlotte, is not your brother. The man purporting to be Emile St. Michel had no scar on his back.'

'Where is he now?' 'Dead, shot by Marcel and then blown to pieces by the gunpowder he stole from the marines.'

'What about Philippe?'

'He is a prisoner aboard the French frigate anchored at the wharf. But what troubles you?'

An agitated Josette announced, 'Evangeliste is missing. I saw her walk across the courtyard towards the out buildings well before the explosion. I have not been able to get closer because of the intense heat.'

Luke turned to Mathieu, 'Have your men found any bodies?'

'Yes, two store men were found. The smoke must have killed them. Their bodies were not damaged in any way.'

Luke clambered on to the smoldering rubble and pushed aside half charred beams and large blocks of stone. He was so intent on moving a stone, which seemed to have someone pinned down that he did not hear the warning from Andrew. The column beside Luke began to topple. As the base crashed to ground, the top stone slid off, delivering Luke a glancing blow on the side of the head.

Harry and Andrew raced to his side. He was unconscious but breathing normally. They carried him back to the hunting lodge. Josette and Odette offered to nurse him.

Marcel returned from the frigate and was brought up to date by the others on Luke's misadventure. He, in turn, informed them that the frigate had already left and that Rousset would soon be in the naval prison at Le Havre and tried within days. His murder of so many marines would provide certain and quick judicial retribution. Captain Sauvel had been recalled from duty off the Garonne to preside over the tribunal as Mazarin had ordered an immediate and expeditious trial.

Harry, with a trace of bitterness, commented, 'I trust he will be treated well at Le Havre. I hope the naval prison is as congenial as the Bishop's. By the way, where is Simon, and where is Evangeliste?'

It was Marcel with a cheeky smile who surprisingly answered, 'They are with each other.' There was a gasp of astonishment from his audience and then absolute silence. He continued, 'The captain of the frigate last saw them together, driving the first wagon—with a casket still aboard. They persuaded the captain that their wagon contained the body of a nun who wished to be buried in a distant convent where she had spent her childhood. Evangeliste claimed it was imperative to inter the corpse as soon as possible. They were last seen driving through the forest in the direction of Rouen.'

'I knew they were up to something,' said Andrew who revealed his surveillance of the two. Harry asked, 'Is the treasure in that casket?' 'Simon's presence suggests that it is,' concluded Marcel. 'Where are they headed?' questioned Andrew. Harry guessed, 'The English Court! Simon is a high ranking and respected peer. He will see that the money is in safekeeping and not squandered on tawdry political ends.' Harry could not believe he was uttering such words.

Andrew remained puzzled, 'How did she do it? How did Evangeliste move the treasure? She could not relocate the casket by herself. She would need the help of six men. How did the treasure disappear from the casket in which Lord Harman swore he had placed it? Before we return to Paris, let us have another talk with the prioress, Sister Mary.'

The next day, Marcel, Harry, and Andrew were in Evangeliste's chamber now occupied by Mary. Marcel joked,' You must know something we don't! You are occupying the abbess's room,' Sister Mary smiled. 'Two days ago, Lord Stokey came with verbal and written instructions from Evangeliste.'

Mary fished around in a half-open drawer and passed a letter to Marcel who summarized it for the benefit of the other two. 'Evangeliste has appointed Mary as acting abbess and retreated to the motherhouse of the order to recover her serenity.'

41

IT WAS HARRY WHO ASKED the key question, 'Mother Evangeliste helped Lord Stokey obtain the treasure to which, with the death of Lord Harman, he is entitled, but we are amazed at how she could remove it from the casket which allegedly contained Lucy Harman's body.'

Mary smiled. 'Lord Stokey told me that if asked this question by any of you confused gentlemen, I was at liberty to reveal what Evangeliste had done.' 'Tell us!' pleaded an almost boyish Marcel. Mary asked the men to be seated and, simultaneously, Sisters Claire and Anne entered the room carrying trays of refreshments. Mary was enjoying the situation.

'When Lord Harman brought the one casket here on his third visit, containing, as we thought, Lucy Harman's body, Evangeliste had it placed at the opposite end of the crypt to the two caskets containing the holy relics and ecclesiastical robes that he had left here earlier. These, Colonel Tremayne and she opened together.

When Evangeliste heard that Lady Lucinda Harman was coming to retrieve her daughter, she opened the relevant casket to make sure it was in a fit state for collection. She found no corpse. The casket was full of gold and silver plate, coins, and jewellery. She recognised at once that she could not move the heavy box by herself.'

'But she must have,' commented Harry. Mary contradicted him, 'No, she did not!' 'Evangelique left the treasure where it was?' suggested an alert Marcel.

'Yes, the treasure never moved. Evangeliste had the carpenters make an exact copy of the ornate casket holding the treasure—the one commissioned by Queen Henriette. Evangeliste and I moved the empty new casket and placed it besides the two coffins, which Luke and Evangeliste had previously opened at the other end of the crypt. We filled it with sand and rocks. We never moved the original. We relied on Colonel Tremayne assuming the three Harman coffins were adjacent to each other.'

'But, surely, Harman himself would have realised that the coffin was in the wrong place?' queried Harry.

'He would have, but I, acting on Evangeliste's instructions, informed Lady Lucinda, as soon as she arrived, that the carpenters and others had moved the coffin next to the original two, should they wished to retrieve all three.

Yesterday, when the marines moved the caskets to the wagons, I substituted for the one we had filled with sand and stones the original containing the treasure and had it placed on the first wagon.'

'Didn't the marines notice the difference in weight?' Andrew asked.

'No, for two reasons, different marines moved each casket, and I had persuaded Lieutenant Heritier that a little sand would fool nobody. He should include some heavy stones. In the end, each of the three coffins—the sand and stone filled caskets and the one containing the treasure weighed about the same. Each was topped with sand so that on opening, all three looked identical.'

'What about the other two Harman coffins?'

'Lady Harman visited me just before her frightful death and indicated that the relics and robes should been relocated back into the other two boxes, and her men would collect them. They are still here. Evangeliste said that Lord Stokey would retrieve them in due course.'

Andrew was full of admiration. 'So Rousset and Livet, when they had the Harmans and Colonel Tremayne bailed up in the crypt, found no treasure in a coffin that Evangeliste successfully passed off as the one purporting to contain Lucy's body. The treasure was at that very moment only yards away at the opposite end of room still in the coffin in which Harman had originally placed it?'

Mary nodded. She had enjoyed her discussion, but it was time to change the subject. 'Enough of this sordid affair! I understand that Colonel Tremayne is not well. I will send a couple of nuns to assist the ladies of the household with his nursing and recovery.' Sisters Claire and Anne who were clearing away the refreshments looked innocently at the prioress offering their services to the English Colonel who had done so much to vindicate them.

When the soldiers returned to the hunting lodge with the two nuns, they found Luke awake but very confused. Harry and Andrew went to his bedside and were delighted to hear his opening words, 'Thank goodness, there is someone here that I know. Harry, where am I? And why is Andrew here. He is not involved in this mission. Is this the English Court?'

Harry looked at Andrew with a mixture of delight and exasperation. Luke had recovered his memory of the events before he was pushed into the Seine but, now, remembered nothing of his life between then and the blow from the falling masonry. Over two days, Harry and Mathieu brought him up to date on his life at Chateau des Anges and the general developments involving Rousset, Livet, the Catholic treasure, and the English Court.

Josette and Odette and Sisters Claire and Anne who wished to help were at a disadvantage because Luke's hard earned grasp of the French language had been completely forgotten.

The return of Luke's memory had him full of energy and with a desire to fulfill his mission. Henri who increasingly recognized Luke's value tried to retain his services but was politely rebuffed. Luke wanted to complete his assignment for General Cromwell.

Three weeks later, Luke was farewelled in style by a fully recovered marquis. The evening before Luke's departure, a banquet was held in his honour with the household, Marcel, Harry, and Andrew in attendance. The marquis thanked Luke for his services to the family and in successfully completing the tasks he had been allotted. He thanked the visitors for capturing those that sought to destroy him and, looking at Marcel, hoped that Rousset would receive the ultimate punishment and that the cardinal would cease his investigation into the St. Michels.

Marcel took the opportunity to make a statement. 'Viscount Rousset was executed yesterday morning for the murder of forty marines. Rather than give him the satisfaction of death by firing squad or by the sword, Captain Sauvel, the commandant of the naval base and president of the judicial tribunal at Le Havre, ordered that he be hanged and quartered as a common criminal.' The men applauded. Josette shed a tear.

The Englishmen set out for Paris. On their arrival at the English Court, a very anxious Cate Beaumont met Harry. 'Where have you been? I have received several messages from the general.'

Harry introduced Luke and explained what had happened. 'Now, Cate, what are our orders?'

'The first order I received was that you, Harry, and Andrew should return to England immediately and bring Colonel Tremayne with you, even if it had to be done by force. The general has dismissed the parliament and has ratified a new constitution with a big slice of kingship in it.'

'Charles is being invited back?' asked the incredulous republican Andrew.

'No, Sergeant! Oliver Cromwell will be proclaimed as Lord Protector of the realm—a king in all but name. He orders that you leave the Royal Court immediately before a furious Charles expels or even imprisons you. The only reason for your presence here was to hold out hope to the king that the English army would recall him to the throne.'

Harry reacted, 'As a matter of honour, I will personally inform Lord Ashcroft and, if possible, the king. We must then leave before some Royalist fanatic takes a shot at us.'

Cate had not finished. 'Colonel Tremayne and the sergeant must leave as soon as possible, but a second message has changed your orders, Harry. You are to move to the French Court, and, on arrival there, Cardinal Mazarin will meet you. You will be the Lord Protector's personal envoy to the cardinal—an arrangement suggested by him.' Harry grinned, gave Cate a big hug, and kissed her passionately.

Luke smiled. 'So your time at the English Court was not wasted?' Harry explained, 'In order to maintain Cate's cover, we pretended to be lovers. It gave me access to her code and instructions from the general. Over the months, our relationship became closer and closer. I am delighted it can continue as I will not now be leaving Paris for some time. When I do leave, I hope the widowed Lady Catherine Beaumont will become Mistress Catherine Lloyd.'

They had hardly finished enjoying Harry's personal news when an orderly entered the room informing Harry that Lord Ashcroft wanted to see him immediately. The three Englishmen followed the orderly. Lord Ashcroft welcomed Luke and praised Harry for the effective role he had played and the genuine assistance he had given the king.

He explained that the king had just heard the news from London and realised that Cromwell had been playing him for a fool. He had no option but to immediately expel his clandestine agent from the Court. Harry accepted the news and informed Lord Ashcroft that he would not be leaving Paris but would take up a similar role at the French Court. He hoped to be a visitor to the English Court, if Charles should allow it, as he was courting Lady Beaumont.

At that moment, the door opened, and Charles Stuart entered the room. He went straight to Luke. Harry intervened, 'Sire, the colonel has recovered his memory.'

Charles smiled. 'I am so glad and am sorry we could not renew the friendship forged in the highlands of Scotland. Your deputy did an excellent job in duping me for almost a year into believing that your general would recall me to my rightful throne. I choose to believe that you could not have been part of this duplicity and that neither of you were aware of the general's ultimate intentions. But there is now no reason for you to stay. I have no choice but expel you from the court.'

Harry waited until the king had shaken Luke's hand and the colonel had given Charles a formal salute to ask, 'Sire, I seek permission after my expulsion to return to your court to pursue my courtship of the Lady Catherine Beaumont.'

The King smiled, 'And Ashcroft and I thought she was a fellow Cromwellian agent, and the relationship was just a cover, although the most exhaustive enquires by Lady Gresham could find no real evidence against her. How can I create an obstacle to true love? But report your presence to Nicholas whenever you visit!'

Lord Ashcroft intervened, 'Perhaps, as his last duty for you, sire, Captain Lloyd can update us on the developments regarding Rousset and the English Catholic treasure.' Harry recounted the events at the chateau and Abbey des Anges. Charles interrupted, 'Yes, I have heard most of that from Simon, although he left des Anges before the death and capture of the villains and Luke's happy accident.'

Harry asked, 'Did Simon get the treasure safely to court?'

'I do not know. He did not trust this impoverished monarch to keep his royal hands off the silver and gold. He sought permission to return to England with the treasure. He will collect other caskets on his way to Le Havre—two containing relics and robes that are part of the Catholic treasure and two containing the bodies of Lord and Lady Harman. He has already left.' The young King turned towards Luke, 'Colonel, for old times' sake, dine with me tonight!'

Luke and Charles dined alone. Most of the conversation centered on their mutual adventures in Scotland where Luke had saved the king's life. Luke regretted that his chance to work at the English Court had been taken from him, and, of all his missions, there was nothing he could report to General Cromwell.

Charles replied, 'From what Simon told me, you have brought great credit to yourself in assisting the Marquis des Anges maintain his credibility and the life of his family. One day, you and I will meet in better circumstances. The frown of fortune cannot forever be directed at me.'

Next day Luke and Andrew set out for England.

Epilogue

OVER THE NEXT MONTH, THE new Lord Protector created a personal bodyguard that was headed by the now full colonel, Luke Tremayne, whose higher rank was confirmed by protectoral decree. The guard was composed of key units of Luke's old cavalry regiment that had been divided for several years between London and Dublin. The reorganized regiment was settled at Whitehall, and its companies took turn weekly to protect the person of Oliver Cromwell and the fabric of the buildings in which the new Lord Protector lived and worked.

Mazarin found an apartment for Harry in the Louvre. Nine months later, when relations between England and France were placed on a conventional footing, Harry returned to England and was married to Lady Catherine on his family estate. His uncle who had settled in Maryland but had recently moved to Massachusetts attended the wedding. At the wedding banquet, to Luke's surprise, Harry Lloyd declared that he had resigned from the army and that he and his new bride would accompany his uncle to the Americas.

On their return to Whitehall, Luke offered Andrew a commission as captain and as his official deputy in the Protector's bodyguard. Andrew refused, preferring to remain as the senior sergeant of the regiment, but, in reality, Luke's right hand man.

During Harry's last months in Paris, Simon, Lord Stokey returned to the English Court. Harry, in the presence and with the permission of Lord Ashcroft, confessed to him his real role at the court. After the initial surprise and with the assurance from Ashcroft that the king had endorsed the clandestine role, Simon shook Harry's hand and wished him well. He was a surprise guest at Harry's wedding.

He never revealed where he had relocated the treasure. He did reveal that Evangeliste, anxious to expunge from her soul the tainted events at the Abbey des Anges, had volunteered to set up a new house for her order—in Canada.

Oliver Cromwell ruled England as Lord Protector from 1654 until his death in 1658. In 1654, after secret negotiations, Cromwell signed a treaty with France, which recognized the Protectorate. The next year, England went to war against France's enemy, Spain.

Mazarin continued to rule France until 1660 when, on his death, Louis XIV began his long personal rule that did not end until 1715. During which period, France became the dominant power in Europe. Also, in 1660, the English army in Scotland led by Major General George Monk finally fulfilled Charles's forlorn wish of 1653. It recalled the king to the English throne.

Printed in the United States
By Bookmasters